JUSTICE FOR ERIN

BADGE OF HONOR: TEXAS HEROES, BOOK 9

SUSAN STOKER

AUTHOR NOTE

Many of you know by now that I tend to write heroines who are struggling with something in their lives...thus making them more like you and me than perfect, fictional cookie-cutter women.

In this story, Erin has struggled with food and her weight her entire life. This is a fictional story, but what has happened to her, happens to thousands, maybe millions of women all over the world. Being overweight (or underweight, or any other kind of "different") is no excuse to treat someone like crap.

There's a reason someone is overweight. A reason you probably have no idea about. Molestation when they were young, verbal abuse, anxiety, a cry for attention...I could name a hundred different reasons...all of them perfectly understandable why someone would turn to food for comfort. The bottom line is that it is *never* okay to belittle, make fun of, take pictures of, mock, laugh at, or otherwise treat someone in a way you wouldn't want your own mother/sister/brother/husband/friend treated.

Think about it. You're at the gym and you see someone who is overweight. Instead of making fun of them or taking pictures to show your bestie later so you can laugh, why don't you *encourage* them? They're *there*! Trying to do what's best for themselves. I'll never understand how people can make fun of others when they're working out.

Take the time to watch a show like *My 600-lb Life*. Every single person on that show talks about how they want to die. How painful it is to get out of bed every day. How terrible it feels to go out in public because they're *always* made fun of. How they would do anything to lose the weight. And every single person has reasons for how/why they turned to food for comfort. And those reasons might have broken you and me, but they're still here. Trying to live their lives in this awful world that looks down on them because they're overweight.

Before you roll your eyes at someone using an electric cart in Walmart or the grocery store, think about their feelings. Help them get something off the top shelf if they need it. And for goodness sake, if they happen to stumble and fall, be a decent human being and *help them*.

There's too much hate in this world. Maybe if we all stopped making fun of others, and holding everyone up to the advertising standards of "beauty" that are forced down our throats, we could look around and see beauty in our differences.

I hate to sound preachy, but I'm afraid I have. And you know what? I don't care. This is important. You have no idea what someone is going through simply by looking at them. None. So be nice. That's all. *Just be nice.*

1

ERIN SMILED AT CONOR PAXTON, the Texas Parks and Wildlife game warden she'd invited along on the annual Thanksgiving trip she chaperoned, as she tried to stop freaking out. She'd spent the entire day telling herself that Conor wouldn't actually show up, that he was just being polite when he'd agreed to come. But when she'd pulled into the parking lot of the rec center at the University of Texas-San Antonio, he was waiting for her.

And what a sight he was.

Standing next to his beat-up old Chevy pickup with his arms and legs crossed, looking as if he hadn't a care in the world. Erin knew he was good looking, it was hard to miss, but when he smiled, it completely transformed him. He went from a solid eight on a scale of one to ten, to a twenty.

He was tall, a bit taller than she was. He had brown hair, and brown eyes that twinkled when he was teasing her. His shoulders were broad and the muscles in his arms made it clear he wasn't a man who sat around eating doughnuts with his law enforcement buddies. He moved with an athletic grace that seemed effortless. Erin had seen him step in and control a drunk man twice his weight at the bar without breaking a sweat.

In other words, he was so out of her league, it wasn't even funny...but that didn't mean she didn't fantasize about him.

Erin had thought her heart would stop when he'd aimed that happy welcoming look her way, but she'd managed not to wreck the fifteen-passenger van she'd been driving and calmly parked.

She'd known Conor for a few months. Every now and then he came into The Sloppy Cow, the establishment where she worked nights as a bartender, with his friends. More often than not, he made a point to stop and talk to her at some time during the night. She lived for those talks.

She wasn't a very social person. Didn't have a lot of friends. She was too busy, and too wary, to cultivate true friendships. Between her day job of being a professor at UTSA in the kinesiology department and working nights at The Sloppy Cow, not to mention her background, friends had been hard to come by.

But when Conor started paying attention to her, it felt good. Really good. It had been a long time, if ever, since Erin had felt good about herself. Somehow Conor had broken through all the walls she'd built up. Then one night at the bar, she'd spontaneously invited him to join her on a UTSA-sponsored canoe trip to Big Bend State Park and the Guadalupe River.

She'd been kinda shocked when he'd immediately said yes.

Since then, they'd exchange emails and a few texts. She'd seen him at The Sloppy Cow and, if she wasn't mistaken, he'd flirted with her. *Her*. Eat-more Erin. She would've thought it was a cruel prank if she wasn't thirty-five and well past the age where people played mean jokes on her.

She'd tried to ignore the flutter of her heart and had greeted him in what she'd hoped was a normal tone. They'd met at eleven forty-five at night on Thanksgiving Day. The plan was to drive through the night, arrive at Big Bend State Park when the ranger office opened and pick up their backcountry permit, which would allow them to canoe and camp over the next three days.

Erin was responsible for everyone on the trip, including Conor, although she had a feeling the game warden could easily take care of himself. She had the required personal floatation devices for the group, along with extras. She'd inspected the canoes and paddles before she'd loaded them on the trailer. She'd given Conor and the college guys strict instructions on what they could and couldn't bring, including weight limits. This was the third time she'd done this exact trip, and she knew the river almost as well as the back of her hand.

The drive typically only took six hours, but she could extend it if needed by making pit stops for gas and to stretch their legs, making them arrive just as the ranger office was opening. They'd be on the river by noon and on their way. They'd have two nights to spend in the backcountry, and on Sunday, if there were no issues, they would head back to San Antonio by noon and home by seven that night.

Not too long after she'd arrived at the rec center parking lot, the four college kids who were also going on the trip had joined them. Erin didn't know them very well, but she'd had two meetings with them in the last month, and was satisfied they weren't going to give her a hard time. After they'd arrived, she'd searched everyone's bags for contraband. Not her favorite thing to do, but the last thing she wanted was to have someone bring an unauthorized weapon into Mexico or have to deal with drunk kids because they'd snuck some tequila or other alcohol on the trip.

Happily, she didn't find anything she shouldn't have and they were soon on their way. The guys—Alex, Chad, Matthew, and Jose—seemed like good kids. They were juniors at UTSA, except for Alex, who was a senior. They were in the same fraternity, which made Erin a little nervous, as she didn't have a good history with men and women involved in the Greek life, but so far, they'd been nothing but polite.

The guys were sitting in the last two rows of the van, their bags stacked in the two seats between them, and her and Conor, giving the adults a sense of privacy, although Erin knew if she spoke too loud, the boys would easily be able to hear her.

"I'm really excited about this trip," Conor told her with a smile.

They'd just turned onto I-10 and had at least five hours to go before they headed south on State Road 385.

Erin smiled back at Conor. "I'm glad. I'd hate to think you were dreading it."

He chuckled. "Are you kidding? I not only get to spend three days outside enjoying nature, but I get to do it with a pretty woman by my side."

Erin knew she was blushing, but tried to blow off his words. He didn't mean them, he was just being polite. She knew exactly what she was and what she wasn't. "You spend a lot of time outside, huh?"

As though he knew his words had made her uncomfortable, Conor went on as if he hadn't paid her the best compliment she'd had in a really long time. "Yup. Perks of being a game warden. I put a good amount of miles on my work truck, but I wouldn't change it for anything in the world."

"What do you do? I mean, I know you're a game warden, but I'm not exactly sure what that entails."

Conor slouched down in his seat and crossed his legs at the ankles. He settled in, getting comfortable, then said, "Basically, I enforce all Texas Parks and Wildlife rules. I'm also a state peace officer as well. I provide testimony in court when needed and can arrest someone for breaking the law just like any other police officer can. I help with emergency management operations in regards to natural disasters, conduct investigations of hunting licenses...making sure people hold the correct licenses to be fishing and hunting."

"Wow," Erin breathed. "I had no idea. I guess I thought you just worked with animals."

"Well, I do, but it's a lot more than that. I can't tell you how many times I've arrested people who were camping or fishing for DUI or marijuana possession. They think that just because I'm a game warden, I'm not a *real* police officer."

"You like it." It wasn't a question. Erin could hear the pride and excitement in Conor's voice when he was explaining what his job entailed.

"Yeah, it's amazing. Some days I can be tromping through the woods looking for a poacher. Other days I'll be sitting in court, and still other days I'll be chasing down leads on who shot and killed a bald eagle. I admit that I decided to apply to the academy after I graduated from college simply because I couldn't imagine sitting behind a desk all day, but now that I've been doing this for almost fifteen years, I have a newfound respect and affinity for wildlife."

"Fifteen years? You don't look old enough."

"I'm thirty-five," Conor told her. "And if you wanted to know how old I was, you only had to ask."

"Oh, I wasn't trying to pry," Erin told him, horrified he might think she was digging for information.

"I know you weren't. It was my awkward way of wanting you to know." He shrugged. "And I figured if you knew how old I was, you wouldn't mind reciprocating."

Erin glanced at Conor out of the corner of her eye. Was he flirting with her? She saw his eyes glued to her and a smile on his face. Yup. He definitely was. Feeling out of her depth, but for once liking the feeling, she said, "I'm also thirty-five."

"How long have you been working for UTSA?" Conor asked.

Erin tried not to stiffen. She wasn't used to talking

about herself. Taking a deep breath, she told him the basics. "I graduated with my undergraduate degree with a double major of kinesiology and education. I worked as a middle school gym teacher for a while, then took some time off, went back to school, got my master's degree, and was hired by UTSA. I've been there about four years now."

"And you love it."

"I do."

"Is the pay really so bad that you had to take the second job at The Sloppy Cow?"

Erin shrugged and tried to play off the question. "Not really. But I like to be busy." It wasn't exactly a lie. She didn't need the money. The salary from her teaching job at the university was plenty for her to live on, but she didn't like to be by herself in her apartment. She knew it was weird. For someone who didn't have any close friends, she sure spent a lot of time away from home. But she had her reasons.

"I get that," Conor said easily. "There are days where I'm around people from the time I start work to the time I get off shift. I want nothing more than to go home to some peace and quiet. But then I get home and sit down to watch TV and realize how bored I am."

"What do you do when you get bored?" Erin asked, genuinely curious.

He shrugged, and she thought he seemed a little self-conscious. "Usually go for a run."

"You run?" Erin asked, surprised, even though she shouldn't have been with how in shape he was.

"Yup. Love it."

"Me too."

"We should go together sometime."

Erin's breath caught in her throat. Did Conor just ask her out? She decided to play it cool. He was probably just being polite, and working out together wasn't exactly a date. Was it? "Cool."

"You do any races?"

She nodded. "Yeah, usually just 5 and 10Ks. I'm not really into the marathon thing."

"Me either. I figure there won't be a time when I need to run for twenty-six miles to get away from any kind of animal. Being able to run fast for one or two miles is more likely," he said, grinning.

"Do you have to run from animals a lot?" Erin asked with a tilt of her head.

He chuckled. "Nope. I've learned to read them way before that happens. Besides, there's no way I could outrun most of them. Although it *has* come in handy when I have to get away from a mama skunk protecting her babies."

Erin laughed quietly, ever aware of the guys in the back of the van. She could hear them snoring from all the way in the front seat. It was dark outside and it felt like she and Conor were in an intimate bubble in the front of the van. "You ever do triathlons?"

"Yeah. I prefer the straight runs, but I've done one or two. I can't stand being wet from the swim and having to jump on a bike. I tend to get chafed, if you know what I mean."

She did. She *so* did. After the last triathlon she'd competed in, her inner thighs were rubbed raw after the bike portion and hurt for a week. "Yeah, it sucks." She smiled over at him once more.

They talked about nothing in particular for the next couple of hours. Erin had never felt so comfortable with a man before. Some of it was the darkness of the night, but she knew most of it was simply Conor.

She'd felt the same way when they'd spoken at The Sloppy Cow. He was polite, funny, and seemed genuinely interested in what she had to say. She didn't have a lot of experience with men, but she was pretty sure her interest in him was returned. It was a heady feeling for a woman with her background.

She remembered one incident at the bar when they were talking and a gorgeous woman in a tight miniskirt and a blouse that showed off her...assets, had walked right up to Conor and leaned into his side. She'd pressed her tits against him and put her hand on his arm.

She'd asked, "Buy me a drink?"

He'd stared at her with a look of disgust so plain to see on his face, *Erin* took a step back. "Are you kidding me?" he'd asked acerbically.

"You looked lonely. I thought you might like some company," the gorgeous, but apparently clueless woman had responded.

Conor had pried her hand off his arm and taken a step away from her even as he said, "First of all, I'm not lonely. I'm talking to Erin. Secondly, if I wanted your company, I would've asked for it. And thirdly, if I was going to buy anyone a drink, it'd also be Erin, but I know she doesn't drink while she's working. So why don't you run along and find someone who's remotely interested in what you're offering."

"*You* aren't interested?" the woman had asked with raised eyebrows.

Instead of being mean, which Conor totally could've been, he'd simply said, "No."

"Your loss," the woman had said, shrugging.

Erin had frowned at Conor when he'd turned back to her, and blurted, "Why did you turn her down? She seemed like a sure thing."

He'd stared right into her eyes as he'd leaned his elbows on the bar, getting closer to her, and said, "In case you missed it, I was talking to *you*. I'm not looking for a one-night stand. And the only sure thing I'm interested in, is you."

She'd been so flustered that he'd apparently chosen her over the incredibly beautiful woman, Erin hadn't said a word. She'd merely turned away and started to make drinks as if he hadn't just blown her mind.

Her being flustered hadn't seemed to faze him though. He'd continued to talk to her when she wasn't busy and by the end of the night, she'd almost forgotten the incident. Almost.

Shaking her head and forcing herself back to the present, she said, "I'm going to stop and get gas in about five miles."

"You want me to drive for a while so you can get some sleep?"

"Nah, I'm okay," she told him. "I took a long nap earlier today, so I'm good."

"You sure?" he asked.

Erin nodded. "I'm sure. But you should get some sleep. You look tired."

"I am. Worked seven days in a row to be able to take this weekend off."

Erin's eyes widened. "Really?"

"Yup. Thanksgiving is generally a busy time for us. We're at the tail end of duck season, and deer season started this month. When people have time off work, they tend to get outside if the weather is nice."

"Yeah, we've had an unusually mild fall this year," Erin agreed.

"And I spent today with my family," Conor continued. "My mom outdid herself with the spread this year."

Erin nodded, even though she wasn't exactly sure what he meant. She couldn't remember the last Thanksgiving meal she'd had. Okay, that was a lie. She'd been eight. The last holiday she'd spent with her dad before he'd left. She cleared her throat and made small talk. "You're close with your mom?"

"Yup. My parents are the best. They've been married for forty years and act like newlyweds."

A pang of jealousy swamped Erin, but she beat it down and asked, "You have any brothers or sisters?"

"Two sisters," he replied. "Younger. They're busybodies, but they mean well."

Erin swallowed hard. "You sound like you're close."

"They're everything to me," Conor said easily. "They were pains in my butt growing up, but at two and four years younger than me, I did my best to look after them."

"And they were there today?"

"Of course. It's Thanksgiving. Karen is the youngest at

thirty-one, and she's not married yet, although if the way her boyfriend was acting is any indication, it's gonna happen sooner rather than later. And Mary, my other sister, was there with her husband and two kids. They're hellions, but they make holidays fun."

Holidays were miserable for her, so Erin couldn't compare what he was talking about to anything. "Hmmm."

"You spend the day with family before or after your nap?" Conor asked.

Just the thought of her mother made Erin's chest tighten, and a feeling of being inadequate swamped through her. Every time she thought about her mom, she felt that way. She shrugged. "Nope. I don't have any family. I spent the day preparing for the trip, making sure I had all the forms required by the university, and getting the van and canoes ready to go."

Erin felt a warmth on her arm. She looked down in surprise and saw Conor's hand lying atop the long-sleeve T-shirt on her forearm. "I'm sorry. If I'd known, I would've invited you over. My mom would've loved to meet you."

"I don't really do holidays," Erin blurted, then winced. It sounded bad when she said it out loud. "I mean, since it's only me, it's just silly to get all wrapped up in them. I usually work or do trips like this. It lets the other faculty members spend time with their loved ones."

Conor's hand tightened and he said softly, "I'm officially inviting you over to my parents' house for Christmas then. No one should be alone at Christmas."

The long-ago Christmas when she was eight flitted

through Erin's head, and she gave Conor what she knew was a pathetic smile. "There's the exit. You want to try to wake up the guys?"

He stared at her for a long moment before squeezing her forearm in the sweetest gesture, then nodded. "Sure. I can do that."

"Thanks."

As if he knew she was thanking him for dropping the subject of Christmas, Conor slowly brought his hand up to the side of her head and brushed a lock of hair behind her ear. "You're welcome."

Then he turned and roused the boys in the back of the van.

Erin took a deep breath and tried to concentrate on the road. She could still feel Conor's light touch. It had been so long since she'd been touched with such gentleness.

He's just being himself. He's so far out of your league it's not even funny. He wouldn't want to be anywhere near you if he knew how you used to look. That you can't sit down and eat with his family. That you're a thirty-five-year-old virgin. Don't read anything into his actions, Erin. You'll just set yourself up for heartbreak.

Her mini pep talk done, Erin eased the van and trailer into the gas station. Once they got to Big Bend, she could concentrate on getting the group ready to go rather than how Conor made her feel. Asking him to come along on the trip was the worst idea ever.

2

AGREEING to go on the canoe trip was the best idea ever. Conor happily stood by the gas pumps and filled the van while Erin went inside to use the restroom.

She was such an enigma. There were times she seemed so strong and with it, then he'd get a glimpse of the unsure and vulnerable woman lurking underneath the surface. It was *that* woman he wanted to get to know. Oh, he liked the take-charge bartender and professor, but Conor could tell there was so much more to Erin. She had such expressive eyes, and when she'd looked at him and admitted that she didn't "do" holidays, he wanted to take her in his arms and tell her everything would be all right, that she could lean on him and he wouldn't let her down.

He'd been attracted to her from the first moment he'd seen her. But the more he got to know her, the more he realized it wasn't her physical features that turned him on, it was who she was as a person.

Oh, she was good looking, there was no doubt. She

was tall—he'd always liked tall women. Her light brown hair was medium length, long enough to leave down and frame her face, but she usually had it up in some sort of ponytail. Her unique green eyes shone with laughter when she joked around with Sophie or some of the other women in his group of friends. She was slender, especially for her height, but she went out of her way to hide her assets.

Conor knew it was insane, but he wanted Erin Gardner more than he'd ever wanted anything in his entire life. He'd watched her at The Sloppy Cow for months now. She was generous and intuitive. She knew how to diffuse situations that had the potential to get out of control. She could handle bullies, handsy men, patrons who had drunk too much, and still had the compassion to bring a plate of food to the homeless man who occasionally hung around the back of the bar.

But when he tried to flirt with her, tried to let her know he wanted to get to know her better, she acted as if no one had ever told her how pretty she was before. Like she had no idea how to respond. It had taken him a month or so to realize she wasn't rebuffing him, but honestly had no clue how to flirt. The more he paid attention, the more he realized when it came to male-female interaction, she was as innocent as a teenager just entering the dating fray.

And that made him feel protective toward her. No, more than that. It made him want to beat the shit out of anyone who said or did anything out of line when it came to her. Erin was a breath of fresh air. Innocent. She was a rarity in his world, and he wanted to cherish her, show her that he could be the kind of man who would treat her like a queen.

He had no idea what her story was, but it was more than obvious she had one.

So when she'd taken a deep breath and invited him to go on the canoe trip with her one night at the bar, he'd immediately agreed, knowing he'd do whatever it took to get the time off work to go. It had taken a bit of wrangling, but he didn't regret it. The three hours they'd been together so far had been enlightening, and he'd learned more about her than he'd found out in months of talking to her at the bar.

"If you want to go inside, I can finish that," she said from beside him.

Conor turned to see Erin standing next to him. She was shorter than he was, but not by a lot. He figured she was probably around five-nine or so. A perfect complement to his six-one. Her hair was lying down around her shoulders for once. It was slightly curly, and his fingers itched to reach up and let one of her curls wrap around his hand. Her unique jade-green eyes looked at him with sincerity.

She had a runner's body. Even if she hadn't told him she liked to run, he would've guessed it. She had a pair of expensive shoes on her feet that screamed "runner" rather than "I sometimes jog on the weekends." He had the same brand back home in his closet.

In all the time he'd known her, he hadn't seen much of her body. She always wore long-sleeve shirts and slacks. Even though they lived in Texas, and even in the summer, she'd worn the long-sleeve shirts. Some were Vnecked, giving a hint of her curves, and others were boat or regular scoop neck. They were light, not heavy, and hugged her trim body, but Conor longed to see more skin than just her hands, neck, and face.

"Conor?"

"Sorry," he told her, mentally shaking his head. "I got this. What kind of man would I be if I let a lady pump gas?"

"One who wants to use the restroom and get something to eat?" she immediately retorted.

"That was a rhetorical question, bright eyes. Hear me now. You will never pump gas when I'm with you."

She stood next to the van looking perplexed and irritated at the same time. It made him want to pull her into his arms, but he refrained, barely.

"I'm perfectly able to do it myself. *Have* been doing it my entire life, in fact."

"I have no doubt you're a champion gas pumper, but the fact remains that it's not gentlemanly to let a woman fill up the gas tank."

"I don't think it has anything to do with being a gentleman," she continued to argue.

Conor leaned into her, and was rewarded when her beautiful eyes opened wide at his action. "It has everything to do with the fact that I want to do this for you. All the crap jobs you've had to do by yourself your entire life are now mine to take care of for you...at least when I'm around. You don't feel like doing something, all you got to do is call me. Changing tires, washing your car, hanging pictures on your walls, mowing the grass, raking, even changing lightbulbs. I want to take care of that for you."

Conor didn't think Erin was even breathing. He brought a hand up to her face and ran his pinky finger down her slightly upturned nose. "Breathe before you pass out, bright eyes," he whispered.

"Why are you calling me that?" she asked.

"Because you have the most amazing eyes I've ever seen. They're bright green."

"Oh, well, I've always thought they were weird. Conor, I don't mind changing light bulbs...but there isn't any grass to mow at my apartment. The ground crew does that kind of thing. But believe it or not, I hate getting my car washed. It just seems like a waste. I mean, I'll clean it, but then drive through a mud puddle and it'll get dirty again. It just doesn't seem like there's a point. But if you really want, you can do that for me."

He chuckled. "Done."

"Uh...why are we talking about this?"

"Because you asked why I wouldn't let you pump gas."

"You're confusing," Erin informed him.

Conor smiled and leaned away from her and reached for the pump, which had clicked done while they'd talked. "It's okay. You'll get used to me."

"Whatever," Erin mumbled under her breath and reached for the door handle.

"You didn't get anything from inside?" Conor asked. "I'm going to grab a coffee. You want anything to snack on?"

"No."

There was so much more to her answer than that one word. It was the flat and final way she'd said it that alerted him to the fact he'd inadvertently brought up a touchy subject, so Conor let it go. He had all weekend to learn more about her. He didn't need to know everything right this second, even if he wanted to. But he filed her answer away in the back of his mind.

He was observant, crazily so. All the other game wardens had commented on it at one point or another. He could read things in interrogations and out in the field that other officers missed. He could almost always tell when someone was lying. He'd even been asked by some of his law enforcement friends to unofficially sit in on interviews to give his thoughts on them.

"I'll be right back. I'll corral the guys while I'm in there."

"They were ransacking the chip section last I saw them," Erin told him.

Conor grinned. Funny. The glimpses of her sense of humor that came through now and then were like precious gold to him.

"I'll do my best to keep them from buying them out."

"And keep them away from the candy aisle too, would ya? I'd hate to have to postpone our trip because of a sugar coma."

He knew his smile was goofy, but couldn't help it. "Sure thing, bright eyes." Then he turned and strode toward the convenience store.

He grabbed some snacks he knew the other guys would eat and that they could take with them on the river and headed back to the van. Erin was sitting in her seat going over the map on her phone.

"All set?" he asked.

"Yup. We're good."

They sat in comfortable silence as she pulled onto the interstate again. Conor thought about their earlier conversation and had so many questions he wanted to ask. But he also wanted to keep her relaxed, as she was now. He rested his head on the back of his seat and found he was perfectly happy just watching her. The faint glow from the dashboard and oncoming cars gave him enough light to see her with. And he liked what he saw.

Two hours later, Conor woke up from his nap when the van hit a pothole.

Erin's guilty eyes met his and she said, "Sorry," in a low voice, obviously hoping not to wake the sleeping men in the back.

"It's okay. I was having a weird dream, it was time for me to wake up anyway."

"You get those too?"

It was a telling question, and Conor wanted to demand she share her dreams with him, but he refrained, barely. "Occasionally. Where are we?"

"Just pulled onto 385. We've got about another hour to go."

"We're making good time."

Erin shrugged. "I've got this route memorized by now. Although obviously not where all the potholes are."

He chuckled softly. "Obviously."

They grinned at each other.

"Have you been to Big Bend a lot?" Erin asked him.

He rejoiced in every question because it meant she wanted to know more about him. At least he hoped that's what it meant. "A couple of times. It's obviously pretty far out here, so I don't get to this neck of the woods as much as I'd like. But I love it out here. It's so different from San Antonio. It's what I would think life on a different planet would look like. Dry, weird scrub bushes, and beautiful in its own way."

"I think so too," Erin agreed softly. "I know some people hate it, but there's something so...untainted about the entire area that I love."

"Untainted...interesting word. But I like it," Conor told her. "You like camping?"

"Love it," she replied immediately. "My dad used to take me all the time."

"Did he pass away?"

"What?"

"Your dad, did he pass away?" Conor repeated. "You said that you didn't have any family, so I just assumed... I'm sorry if I overstepped." He didn't like the pained look on her face at his question. He mentally kicked himself for pushing too fast for information. But he was like a sponge, wanting to soak up every scrap of information he could about her.

"No...it's okay. I just don't talk about him much. He disappeared when I was eight."

"Disappeared?"

"Yeah. I woke up one morning and my mom said he'd left us. I never saw him again."

She said the words without much emotion, but she was gripping the steering wheel so hard, Conor could see her white knuckles in the dim early-morning light. He made a mental note to find out more later, when she was more comfortable with him.

"You been camping lately?"

She visibly relaxed when she realized he wasn't going to push for more information about her dad. "I went a couple of weeks ago. I don't like the heat in the summer, but I do try to get out as much as possible this time of year."

"Where?"

Conor saw her relax even more, now that they weren't talking about her family. "Well, Fredericksburg is a favorite, but it's kinda far away for a weekend jaunt. I've been to Government Canyon State Natural Area several times."

"Who do you go with?" Conor asked, almost not wanting to know the answer. If she said a guy, he wasn't going to be happy.

"No one. Just myself," Erin told him lightly.

"Wait, what? You camp by yourself?"

She shrugged. "Why not?"

"Because it's not safe," Conor said harshly.

"Sure it is. I haven't ever had any issues. Campers are some of the nicest people I've ever met."

"Jesus," Conor said under his breath. He glanced at Erin, who seemed perturbed now. He wanted to smile at the cute expression on her face, but refrained. He ran a hand through his dark brown hair and tried to explain. "Look, I'm thrilled that you haven't had any issues, but it's honestly *not* safe. I know more about what happens in campgrounds than the average person...and trust me when I say, it's probably not a good idea to go by yourself."

"Like what? You can't tell me not to go camping and not say why. I mean, if you tell me women are raped out there every night, that's one thing. But if it's because people get stuff stolen when they leave it unattended, that's not going to sway me. I normally get to my campsite in the evening and spend the night, then pack up my stuff and usually take a hike and come home. I don't leave anything unattended. I'm not stupid."

"I never said you were." Conor tried to backpedal a bit. "And no, there haven't been any rapes in the local campgrounds lately, as far as I know, but Erin, you're a beautiful woman alone. There's no telling what some asshole who sees you will do."

"What?"

He tried to explain. "It makes me feel a little better that you usually aren't out there for an entire weekend, but all it will take is one man drinking a little too much and deciding he wants some, for you to be in trouble."

"I'm not going to be in trouble, Conor. Guys don't look at me that way."

Conor stared at Erin in disbelief. "Uh...yeah, they do, bright eyes."

"You don't have to flatter me to try to scare me," she said in an even tone that somehow still oozed hurt. "I know what I am and what I'm not."

"What you are and what you're not," Conor repeated, his eyes squinched as he stared through the morning light at her.

"Yeah." Her arm waved in the air as she tried to explain. "I'm not like that beautiful blonde who came on to you at The Sloppy Cow that one time. She had confidence and beauty and every man's eyes in the room were on her. Me? I'm plain and introverted. My hair is a dull brown. No man who looks at me would ever think I'd be worth risking his freedom to rape."

"You have *got* to be shitting me." Conor didn't like the flinch his words caused on her pretty face, but he seriously couldn't believe what he was hearing. "Erin, you're wrong. Dead wrong."

"Conor, I'm not. I—"

"The first time I saw you at the bar, I wanted you. I wanted to know what your lips tasted like. I wanted to feel your body against mine. Under mine. I got a hard-on just from seeing you smile at Sophie when you spoke with her. And keep in mind, I hadn't even said one word to you. I didn't know how funny and awesome you were then, I only knew how you looked."

"Conor," she whispered, obviously flustered.

He lowered his voice, just loud enough that only she could hear him. He didn't want the guys in the back to overhear his words, but they had to be said. She had to understand how she affected him. How she affected men. "I wanted you naked in my bed, Erin. I wanted to spread your legs and feast on your pussy. Then I wanted to pound into you so hard, you'd feel me for days. I imagined how you'd look when you came. Your head thrown back, fingernails digging into my biceps, hair mussed around your head and your eyes shooting emerald sparks as you went over the edge. So if you think for one second other men don't look at you and think the same thing, you're delusional."

She didn't say anything, but Conor saw her hands clench the steering wheel once again as if her life depended on it.

He closed his eyes and sighed. "Shit, I'm sorry," he apologized. "I know I'm way out of line, and I don't want things between us to be weird, but every word was true. And you should know, I don't have sexual feelings like that for women I see in my daily life. You were an exception, and it surprised me as much as I obviously just shocked you. There's just something about you that caught my attention. But if I felt that with just a look, I know other men probably do too. The thought of you trying to fight off a guy, or two, or three, makes me crazy. I just want you safe, bright eyes. That's all."

"I don't have anyone to go camping with," Erin said after a long moment. "Sometimes I just need to get out of my apartment. Need to get away from everything."

Conor understood that. Understood the lure of nature. But he couldn't understand how she didn't have any friends. Hell, his friends' women loved her. Mackenzie and Mickie had gone on and on about how awesome she was. Even Hayden had said she was all right, and that was a huge compliment coming from the sheriff's deputy. "I can't believe that."

"It's true. I don't have many friends. Not the kind that I'd want to go camping with."

"Next time you need to get away, call me. I'll go with you," Conor said without thinking.

He'd been staring at her, and saw the quick shocked glance she shot his way.

He hurried to continue so she wouldn't immediately turn him down. "Get to know me this weekend. See that I'm a good guy. I can control myself. What I said earlier notwithstanding. I'm attracted to you, Erin. I don't think that's a big secret. I certainly haven't tried to hide it in the last couple of months. You can absolutely trust me. I'm thirty-five, not eighteen. I can control myself. But I hate the thought of you lying in a tent by yourself and being ambushed."

"The biggest danger I've faced is stepping in a fire ant mound," Erin informed him. "I'm allergic. I can handle a bite or two, but I swell up really bad. Any more than that and I blow up like a balloon."

"All the more reason to camp with someone else. You have an EpiPen?" Conor asked.

"Of course."

"Good."

"What I'm saying is that...I think you're an exception, Conor. Honestly. Men don't see me the same way you seem to."

"I'm not an exception, but I'm okay with you thinking I am, bright eyes."

He relaxed when he heard her chuckle. He'd been afraid his blunt words would make her uncomfortable around him. And that was the last thing he wanted.

"You'd really go camping with me?" she asked.

"Yeah. I absolutely would. In case I haven't made it obvious enough, I like you, Erin. A lot. I was thrilled you asked me to come on this trip with you. I know nothing can happen between us this weekend and I'm not expecting it to. You're responsible for all of us, and I can respect that. But you should know that I'm going to do everything in my power to try to get you to like me back. And so you're forewarned, I'm going to ask you out on Sunday when we get back to our cars. I hope spending time with me over the next three days will influence you to say yes when I do."

She was silent for five full minutes. Conor wanted to reassure her. To explain more. Tell her again that he'd never hurt her. That he had a good feeling about the two of them. That he'd fight whatever demons she had swirling in her beautiful eyes if she gave him the chance. But he kept quiet, letting his words sink in.

Finally, when he thought she was going to ignore his declaration altogether, she said, "No one has ever said anything like what you did to me before. And no, I wasn't offended. I'm confused and not sure you're really seeing what you think you are, but the first time I saw you, I thought about what it would be like to have someone like you making love to me. You don't have to try too hard to make me like you though. I asked you to come on the trip because I already liked and trusted you and wanted to get to know you better."

"Thank God," he breathed. Then asked, "Someone like me?"

She nodded. "Gorgeous. Respected. Popular."

"Erin," he said sternly, "I don't want you to imagine someone *like* me. I want you to imagine *me* making love with you."

She bit her lip, and if he could see better in the morning light, Conor knew he'd see her blushing, but he was thrilled when all she did was nod.

"Glad we got that out of the way," he said quietly. "Now...talk to me about the logistics of the trip. Where are we parking, where are we putting in, how far do you think we'll get each day...things like that."

"You really want to know?" she asked.

"I really want to know," he confirmed. "I studied a few maps of the river and state park this week. I have a fairly good idea of where we'll be, but I don't know what you're planning. You've done this before, so I know you're the expert here."

They spent the rest of the way to Big Bend talking about the upcoming trip. Now that his intentions were clear, and he knew Erin was interested in him, Conor relaxed. He was honest with her, he wouldn't push her for anything in the next couple of days. He didn't want to interfere with her job.

But the second she parked the van back at the university Sunday night, his self-imposed restraint would be done. He was going to ask her out and he hoped like hell she was going to say yes. He wanted Erin Gardner to be his, in every sense of the word. He'd warned her, given her a glimpse of the kind of man he was, and she'd admitted she'd imagined him in her bed as well.

He felt his dick stir, but ignored it. He had a feeling he'd be sporting a hard-on for the woman next to him a lot in the upcoming weeks and months. Because he had no doubt Erin wasn't going to jump into bed with him just because he wanted her there. He'd need to woo her. Help her gain confidence in her self-worth.

Making Erin his, and having her in his bed and life for good, was the end goal. It was the most important challenge of his life. One he was determined to win.

3

ERIN PULLED the van into the dirt parking lot at the Rancherias River access point. They were going to canoe the Colorado Canyon section of the river, then continue on to Santa Elena Canyon. They wouldn't make it all the way through the second canyon, but Erin knew a good take-out spot to camp for the night. The plan on Sunday was for her to hitchhike back to where the van and trailer were parked. She'd done it each time she'd taken this trip. Almost all the traffic on the roads was either the companies who managed river trips or individuals who were rafting or canoeing down the Rio Grande.

She got to work loosening the straps holding the canoes to the trailer when Conor came up beside her.

"Is it safe to leave the van here?"

Erin shrugged, but didn't look up from what she was doing. "Safe enough. One year someone broke in, but since we didn't leave anything inside, they didn't mess with anything. The broken window was a pain on the way home, but the kids I had with me were awesome and didn't complain about the wind, noise, or temperature at all."

"I don't want to overstep my place, but I talked to Thomas, one of the game wardens stationed here in Big Bend, while you were getting the permits. He said it would be okay to park the van and trailer in the lot behind the station."

Erin stopped what she was doing and turned her head to stare at Conor.

He continued. "I'm sure whatever you've done in the past will work too. I just wanted to make sure no one messed with the university's property. It had to be a pain to deal with the damage report and all when you got back when it was broken into, right?"

She nodded.

"Right. Thomas said we could leave the van there, then he'd drive whoever dropped it off back here. We can leave the keys with him so we don't accidentally dump them on the bottom of the Rio Grande." He chuckled and shoved his hands in his pockets in what Erin would've sworn was a nervous gesture. "But you might already have something like that planned."

She slowly shook her head. "I was going to leave the van here, and put one set of keys in my pack and give the other set to one of the students to keep in his pack. Just in case. But leaving the van at the warden station is so much better than leaving it here. Thank you, Conor. That was thoughtful."

He smiled then and pantomimed wiping his brow in relief.

Erin stared at him for a beat before saying softly, "I

might be in charge of this trip, but that doesn't mean I can't take suggestions and have to do everything my own way, or the way I've done it in the past. Your input is important to me. I've done this trip before, but you're no slouch when it comes to outdoor stuff. Please don't think I'm going to jump down your throat if you suggest something."

"Even when it might be something that means you aren't putting yourself in danger?"

Erin tilted her head in confusion and asked, "Like what?"

"Like hitchhiking back to the warden station to get the van."

"It's not dangerous, Conor. The rafters tend to all look out for each other."

"Right, but there's always the possibility that whoever picks you up *isn't* a rafter, and when he sees a good-looking woman standing on the side of the road, he gets nasty ideas in his head about what he wants to do to that good-looking woman."

Erin wanted to be upset at him, but she couldn't be. Not when he was complimenting her. "So, what do you suggest?"

"I'd like to say that I'll go with you, but that would leave the guys by themselves, and I don't think you'd agree to that."

Erin shook her head in agreement.

"Right. So ideally, I'd go instead. I can go and get the van and trailer while you and the others pack up. By the time you get the canoes out of the water and the packs ready to go, I'll be back with the van."

Erin thought about it for a second, then nodded. "That sounds good."

"Just like that?" Conor asked with a small smile.

"Yup."

"Good."

"Good. Now, you want to help me with these canoes?" Erin asked, reaching for the one on the top of the trailer.

He didn't immediately answer, but instead turned and whistled. Erin jumped at the sound and spun to face him. He was gesturing to the guys. "Come on, help Erin get the canoes down. Where do you want them?"

Erin knew she should be upset at the way Conor had taken over, but she wasn't. She'd take all the help she could get. She pointed to a patch of grass off to the side and close to the river. They wouldn't be ready to put in for at least an hour or so. She needed to figure out what should go where in the canoes. She couldn't overload any one craft, and with only three, it would be trickier to get all the supplies safely strapped down.

They had extra water, a chemical toilet, tents, extra floatation devices and paddles, a couple of coolers with enough food for the entire trip, as well as their personal bags and a first-aid kit. It was a lot, but it wasn't like they could leave anything behind.

Without fuss, the guys made quick work of moving the canoes off the trailer to where she'd pointed. They helped empty the van of all their stuff as well.

"You want me to take the van to the warden station?" Conor asked.

Erin nodded. "If you don't mind?"

"I don't mind," he said with a warm glint in his brown eyes.

It looked like he wanted to say something else, but after a moment, turned toward the college students and asked, "Who wants to go with me to drop off the van?"

Chad volunteered, and soon the pair was pulling out of the parking lot, leaving nothing but a cloud of dust in their wake.

When they returned forty minutes later, Erin was just about done packing the canoes.

"Looks like you got a lot done while we were gone," Chad commented as he came up to the group.

"Yup. I've just about got it all set. I want to go over the commands one more time before we start off. The river is calm for at least three miles downstream. That'll give everyone a chance to get comfortable with the commands and maneuvering. The first rapid won't be major with the water depth right now. We'll get out and scope out each set of rapids to determine the best way to get through it without capsizing. Conor and I will go first each time, with you guys spotting us. Then you'll go one at a time until we're all through. Rancherias Rapid is first and it's a good one to get your feet wet...figuratively." Erin smiled at the group.

She loved this. The excitement and enthusiasm was always at an all-time high right before the trip started. This area wasn't known for its white water, but there were a number of fun rapids that were fairly easily navigated. But that didn't mean people didn't tip over. They did. All the time.

"And for some incentive...I've got the chemical toilet

in my canoe to start out, but whoever tips over today will be carrying it tomorrow."

At the groans from the guys and the good-natured teasing that immediately started, Erin laughed. It never failed. No one wanted to carry the toilet, even though it was airtight, watertight, and smell-tight.

"Listen up!" she called out, getting everyone's attention once more. "All right, just to review, the person sitting in the back of the canoe is in charge of steering. They will call out the strokes the person in front is to take. Listen to them. This isn't a matter of thinking you know better. If the person in front starts doing their own thing, you'll end up paddling in circles and generally annoying me, because you'll be bickering and fighting all the way down the river. Got it?"

Everyone nodded their assent and she continued with the refresher lesson. "Good. Okay, the easiest command is forward. Lean forward, put your paddle in, straight up and down, not at an angle, and pull backward. Then do it again. That's all there is to it. The person in the back will steer the canoe down the river. Reverse is exactly what it sounds like. You'll immediately start paddling backwards. Right draw and left draw are next. It's important that you do this stroke on the correct side of the boat. This stroke is used to change direction. It's vital when you're going through a rapid because if a rock pops up in front of your craft, you want to avoid hitting it."

Everyone chuckled, as Erin intended them to.

"Right, so the draw is a deep stroke. Lean out over the water and pull the paddle toward the canoe. The person in back can then use the sweep stroke at the same time to quickly turn the canoe. Everyone remember the sweep stroke?"

Again, there were nods all around.

"Great. Any questions?"

Everyone shook their heads.

"Ready to go, or do you want me to stand here jabbering with you some more?"

Choruses of "We're ready" rang out from the guys.

Erin smiled. "All right then. Grab your kneepads... and yes, I know they don't look cool, but you'll be thanking me before twenty minutes goes by, so don't give me any lip about wearing them. And before you ask, yes, you have to wear the life jacket. Trust me, if you tip, you'll want it. Besides, it's the law. And since we have our very own game warden with us, we don't want to do anything illegal." She nudged Conor with her elbow good-naturedly.

As everyone got busy getting ready to shove off, Conor walked with her over to their canoe. "You're really good with them," he said. "You know how to give them just enough information so they're prepared, but not enough that they get bored and stop listening."

"They weren't really listening to me," Erin countered. "They all think they know exactly how this is gonna go. Trust me, I've seen it time and time again. We'll all shove off and the first thing that'll happen is that they'll go in big circles as they figure it out." She smiled. "But that's why I purposely like running this section of the river. The first part takes a couple of hours and by the time we get to the Rancherias Rapid, they'll be ready."

"I'm in front, aren't I?" Conor asked with a smile.

Erin knew she surprised him by the look on his face when she said, "That's up to you."

"Really? You'd let me steer?"

"If you want to tip the canoe right off the bat and have to carry the toilet for the rest of the trip, yes."

His brows shot up in mock affront. "What? You don't think I can do it?"

"Oh, I'm sure you're probably an expert with your experience as a game warden," she said with a smirk. "But I already packed the heavy stuff toward the rear of the canoe. If you sit back there, you'll swamp it with your weight added. When we go over those first rapids, we'd fill with water so fast it'd make your head spin. Besides, I've never tipped on any trip yet, and I don't intend to this time. I'm driving."

Conor smirked and pulled his life jacket on. "Far be it from me to get in the way of a professional."

"That's right. And don't forget it."

Erin loved bantering with Conor. She was half-afraid he'd turn out to be uber controlling. He was, after all, used to being in the outdoors, and she hadn't lied, he probably *was* an expert canoer. But she liked being in charge on the river. Liked controlling where and how the canoe moved. She always felt so out of control in her everyday life, she took every chance she got to feel in charge for once.

"Your chariot awaits, ma'am," Conor said, bowing and throwing his arm out in a sweeping movement.

She giggled. "Thanks, but you need to get in first. I need to shove us off."

He growled. "So much for my chivalry."

She patted him on the arm. "It's appreciated."

The look he gave her was so intense, Erin wanted to take a step away from him, but held her ground. She was rewarded when he brought a hand up to her face and tucked a wisp of hair behind her ear that stubbornly refused to stay confined in her ponytail. "I can't deny that I like to be in charge. I'm overprotective and tend to err on the side of caution, especially when it comes to those I care about. But I also can't deny I'm looking forward to being able to relax and simply enjoy spending time with you and letting you take over dealing with logistics. I can't remember the last time I've been able to do that."

"Conor," Erin whispered, flustered.

"But that doesn't mean I won't be looking out for you while you're looking out for the rest of us. I'll always put your well-being first, bright eyes. So when I do or say something that seems out of line, keep that in mind. Yeah?"

"As long as you don't undermine my authority, I'm okay with that."

"I'd never do that. This is your show, Erin. I'm just along for the ride. But I've got your back."

"I appreciate it."

Conor nodded and brushed his index finger down her nose. "Right. Then it looks like we're out of here." And with that, he stepped into the river and waded to the front of the canoe. He settled into the seat as if he'd been doing it all his life.

Erin had a feeling this definitely wasn't his first canoe trip, but she didn't say a word, merely watched Alex,

Chad, Matthew, and Jose get settled into their own canoes and push off from the riverbank.

She waded into the river, pushing the canoe until it easily floated, and scrambled into her seat in the back. Smiling, feeling free from the pressures of her everyday life, Erin said loudly, "Let's get with it, men!"

Everyone responded in kind and they were off.

Hours later, and after the guys had paddled in circles, then argued and finally gotten the hang of steering the canoes, they arrived at the Rancherias Rapid.

Erin gestured for everyone to follow her to the side of the river. They all pulled their canoes out of the water far enough that they wouldn't float backward and out into the current, and tied them up. Then they walked to a slight ridge to scope out the rapid.

She walked the group through how to approach the rapid and they discussed everyone's thoughts on the easiest way to maneuver through the water. Since the water was at a medium level, it made maneuvering easier than if it was low (too many rocks) or high (faster water and more dangerous if the canoe tipped).

There weren't any tree branches they could see and there was only one large boulder visible in the path. Unfortunately, the rock was smack dab in the middle of the river, right where the canoe would naturally be pushed if it wasn't steered correctly.

She pointed at the rock. "See the big boulder in the middle?" She waited until everyone nodded. "It forms what's known as an upstream V. The point of the V is the rock, and the water flowing around it forms the lines of the V. See it?" She used her hands to help explain and give the guys a visual.

Again, everyone nodded their assent.

"Look to the right of the rock, what do you see?"

Jose tentatively said, "Lots of foamy water."

"Correct, and what does that mean?" Erin asked the group.

"Rocks?" Chad asked.

"Exactly. But on the other side of the big boulder is what's known as a downstream V. It's easier to see from here, that's why we're scouting out the rapid before blindly heading into it. The downstream V is what you want to aim for. The point is facing downstream and there's dark green water in the middle of it. That's what you want to aim for. It's usually the best entrance to any rapid. Current that is dark means there aren't any obstacles in your way. Which is a good thing. So as you approach this rapid, try to stay to the left of the rock. You can go right, but it'll be bumpier because of the rocks under the water...and not as safe or fun. Whatever you do, don't hit the boulder. Got it?"

"What if we do?" Matthew asked. "Hit the rock?"

"Don't," Erin returned immediately with a smile.

"But—"

"If you hit the boulder head on, or if the canoe turns and you hit it sideways, you'll most likely tip. And if you do, this is a good reminder for everyone, don't panic. I'll be on the side with a throw line. If you really get in trouble, I'll toss it to you and you can grab on and we'll tow you to the edge. You should put your feet downstream and ride it out. The water's cold. It'll take your breath away, but it's not freezing. You'll be fine. Once you're out of the rapids, look for your canoe. It might be swamped and we'll have to rescue it, but it may be floating by you."

She could see the panic in the young men's eyes. She tried to reassure them. "You'll be fine. This is supposed to be fun, remember?"

When they didn't look reassured, Erin said, "If you really want to, you can portage your canoe. Carry it around the rapids."

No one said anything.

"Come here," she ordered, gesturing for the four guys, and Conor, to gather round her. When she had their attention, she said, "The first time I did this, I was scared out of my mind. But I did it. And it was fun. You just have to get past this first rapid and you'll get the hang of it. Even if you do tip, who cares? This isn't the Colorado River. It's not the Grand Canyon. You'll be fine. We'll all laugh and make fun of you...good-naturedly, of course. You got this. Okay?"

One by one, the frat brothers all nodded.

"Good. Alex, you and Jose go stand on the side just below the rapid with the throw line. Matthew and Chad, you stay here and watch me and Conor run this. Listen to the commands I give, see how we run it. You're up next. Alex and Jose, after we make it through, you come up here and watch Matthew and Chad go through, and me and Conor will man the safety line. Got it?"

They all nodded. Alex and Jose took the throw line from Erin and began to pick their way through the scrub bushes to stand at the end of the rapid.

Conor and Erin headed back toward the canoes.

"You were great with them," Conor murmured.

"Thanks. The first rapid is the hardest. It's scary, no matter how tough someone thinks they are. And that rock in the middle seems like a huge obstacle from here. When they're in the river headed right for it, it can be intimidating."

They pushed their canoe into the river and Conor insisted that Erin climb in first. She did, and he shoved them away from the bank and climbed in. Before they headed downstream, he turned around and smiled at her. "I know I've already said it, but I'll say it again. Thank you for inviting me. This is awesome."

She couldn't help but smile back at him, his enthusiasm contagious. "I take it you're having fun."

"Yeah, bright eyes, I'm having fun. I get to watch you kick this river's ass and show a bunch of guys how running rapids is done. I could spend the rest of my days doing this with you."

She didn't know how to respond, but he didn't seem to expect a response. Conor turned around and faced front. He dug his paddle into the river and Erin automatically put her own in to steer them in the right direction.

After a moment, she smiled. She knew she probably looked like a loon, but couldn't help it. Conor was right. This *was* fun. And part of the fun she was having was because he was there with her.

She turned her concentration to the river around them. The last thing she wanted to do was show the others what *not* to do. The water was flowing quickly but not out of control, and she easily steered them to the left of the big boulder in the middle of the river. She called out only two commands when the water wanted to pull them the other direction. Right sweep and forward.

They shot past the boulder like a bullet out of a gun and into the downstream V. Their canoe bumped over the rapid and Erin heard Conor whoop in delight as they streamed past Jose and Alex, and heard them yelp back in response. She called out another right sweep command and, even through his excitement, Conor obeyed. She turned the canoe toward the shore and Jose and Alex helped them pull the craft up onto the rocky shoreline.

"That was awesome!" Jose exclaimed.

"You made it look so easy," Alex commented.

"It *is* easy," Erin told him as she stepped out of the canoe and reached for the throw line. "You can do this. Just steer to the left of the boulder and you'll shoot right through the downstream V. Exactly like we did."

The guys nodded and headed for where Chad and Matthew were still standing.

When their backs were turned, Conor put his arm around Erin's shoulders and pulled her into his side. "That was cool," he said simply.

"Yeah." Erin tried to tell herself the increase in her heart rate was because of the adrenaline still coursing through her body from the run through the rapid, but knew she was lying to herself. She could feel Conor's body heat. They were both wearing knee-length shorts, and she couldn't feel any of his skin against hers, as she was wearing her trademark long-sleeve T-shirt, but the heat of his body seeped through their clothes. It seemed to wrap itself around her heart and warm her from the inside out.

Seeking some self-preservation, she stepped out of his embrace and concentrated on making sure the safety line was ready to throw.

Conor stepped up behind her and stood at her back. *Right* at her back. He rested the fingertips of one hand on her hip. It was barely a touch, but it felt like a brand to Erin.

He leaned down and said in her ear, "Don't be nervous around me, bright eyes. I'm a toucher. I like to touch and be touched. I'll respect your authority around the others, but don't ask me to keep my hands to myself. I can't do it. I don't want to. I'm drawn to you like a moth to a flame. But the last thing I want is to make you uneasy around me. That's *not* my intention."

Erin licked her lips and swallowed hard before saying quietly, "I like it, but...I'm not used to it. I'm so *not* a toucher."

The fingers at her hip pressed harder, and Erin forced herself to stand still. He wasn't hurting her, wasn't really even crowding her. He was just standing behind her. Very close behind her. "Good. My goal for the weekend isn't to turn *you* into a toucher, but to help you not flinch every time *I* touch you. That okay?"

She bit her lip this time and nodded. She glanced over her shoulder and caught his eye. "I'm not good at this."

"This?"

"Flirting. Boy-girl stuff. Dating. Whatever you want to call it."

"You're doing fine."

"But I'm not doing anything," Erin protested. "I don't know what *to* do."

"You don't have to *do* anything, bright eyes. Just be yourself. Smile. Tease me. Be the kick-ass woman you've always been since the day I met you. I was attracted to that woman and I'm still attracted to her. What did you tell the guys? Relax and have fun?"

Her eyebrows went up, letting him know she was skeptical.

Conor chuckled. He brought his hand up from her hip to lightly brush against her biceps. "Trust me. You standing here letting me touch you, when I know you're not used to it, affects me more than the most experienced flirt."

She opened her mouth to protest when he said quietly, "Here they come."

Erin turned to look at the river. Matthew and Chad were heading toward the rapid. Absently, she felt Conor step away from her, giving her room to work if needed. She appreciated it. He respected her boundaries while at the same time pushed at them. But when it came down to it, he understood that she had responsibilities to the university and to the four young men who had been entrusted to her care.

She was in way over her head with Conor, but for the first time in her life, she was hopeful that maybe, just maybe, she'd met a man who saw her. Not her outer shell, but *her*.

4

HOURS LATER, and after navigating Closed Canyon, Quarter Mile, and Panther rapids, they'd pulled to the side of the river to camp for the night. Thanks to Erin's expertise, the guys had no problems making it through each rapid.

Jose and Alex had tipped over in Quarter Mile, and Matthew and Chad had fallen out in the notorious Panther Rapid. It was Conor's belief the second duo had gotten too cocky, had enjoyed making fun of their friends for being dunked, and had made stupid mistakes on their run through it. But everyone was safe and there were obviously no hard feelings amongst the group, which made the trip more fun.

Conor watched as Erin directed the guys where to put their tents. He grabbed the chemical toilet and walked in the direction Erin pointed to set it up. She'd obviously camped here before because she was like a well-oiled machine, organizing their kitchen area, where the fire would go, and generally making sure everything was where it needed to be before the sun set.

When he asked if he could help with dinner, she merely shook her head and reassured him that she had it under control.

"I did pack a present for the guys, if you want to give it to them."

"A present?"

"Yeah, for a first day on the river well done," she told him with a small smile. "It's in the bottom of the blue cooler."

He dug into the cooler she'd indicated and raised his eyebrows when he saw what she'd hidden away. "Seriously?"

"Yup. I know it's not exactly university approved, but what guy doesn't like a nice beer at the end of a long, hard day?"

Conor shook his head. Nothing Erin had done turned him off. Not one thing. Even when she'd been skittish with his touch at the first rapid, she'd admitted that she liked him touching her. She had more bravery than a lot of men he'd met over his career.

He strolled over to her slowly, holding her gaze as he did. When he was standing in front of her, blocking her from the other men's prying eyes, he leaned close and said quietly, "For the record, what *I* like at the end of a long, hard day is my woman in my arms, sated and relaxed after making love."

"Conor," Erin protested, blushing, but she didn't say anything else, simply stared up at him with wide eyes. Her hair was mussed and she'd put on a pair of sweats and a jacket, as the evening had cooled down. She wasn't trying to seduce him, but she was nevertheless.

"I'll just go give your present to the guys."

She nodded at him but didn't take her eyes from his face.

"You look at me like that much longer and I'm not going to care who sees me kiss you."

That broke her out of the trance she'd been in. She blinked and bit her lip as she took a small step away from him.

Conor smiled. He brought his hand up to her face and tucked the stubborn lock of hair back over her ear. He'd been doing that all day, and every time it made him want more. Want to ease his hand to her nape and pull her into him. Touch her lips with his. But he was being patient. With every touch, she was getting more and more used to him.

He heard her sigh as he turned and headed for the college students. He smiled as he held up the six-pack Erin had so thoughtfully packed and the guys cheered.

Hours later, when the frat brothers were all sleeping in their tents and darkness had descended on their little corner of the world, Conor was sitting next to Erin, their backs to the campfire, as they gazed out at the river happily bubbling along.

"How are your bites?" he asked.

"They're okay. They'll itch for the next couple of days, but it's nothing I haven't suffered through before," Erin told him.

"You'd think with how allergic you are, you'd've noticed that fire ant hill next to the dishwashing station you set up," Conor teased. He wasn't happy she'd been bitten, especially when he saw firsthand how badly her body reacted. Within fifteen minutes of the little critters biting her ankle, it had swelled up to twice its size. But she'd calmly taken a couple of antihistamine tablets and told him she'd be fine.

"Right?" she laughed. "I guess I was concentrating too much on other stuff. It's bad, but I've kinda gotten so used to seeing their mounds around, I just don't notice them anymore."

"You need to be more careful," Conor warned. "Especially out here. In case you haven't noticed, we're not exactly within driving distance to an emergency room." His voice lowered. "You could've died, bright eyes. I've got a satellite phone, but even with your EpiPen, there's not much I could've done for you. There's a lot I want to experience with you. So be more careful, yeah?"

She didn't respond for so long, Conor didn't think she was going to acknowledge what he'd said at all. But when she did, her words literally hurt his heart.

"I don't really get what you're doing here. But you have to understand, every day of my life since my dad walked out, I've known that I'm on my own. My mom is a bitch who never cared about anyone but herself. She only noticed me when she yelled at me. I have coworkers, but no one who I think would be overly upset if I never showed up at the university again. You're the only person in my entire life who has said they would care if something happened to me."

She folded her knees up and wrapped her arms around them. She looked vulnerable and unsure about herself. Conor moved without thought. He scooted behind her and enfolded her into his embrace, wrapping his own arms around her so her back was against his chest. He covered her hands with his and simply held her.

She continued, softer now. "I don't have a death wish, but I never thought much about watching out for fire ant mounds or making sure I had an EpiPen handy at all times simply because it didn't matter. If I died, I died." She shrugged. "It's not like anyone would be upset over my death."

"Erin—" Conor began in a tender tone.

"I'm not done," she interrupted.

"Sorry." He grinned, but was glad she couldn't see it. He didn't want her to misunderstand his humor. He didn't like what she was saying, but loved that she was comfortable enough to be a bit snarky with him.

"But then you sauntered up to my bar with a look in your eyes I couldn't read. I thought you were drunk at first. I had no idea you were thinking...what you said you were thinking when we were driving down here. But as the weeks went by and you kept coming back to The Sloppy Cow and making a point to talk to me as much as you did, I thought maybe you might like me. But then I'd change my mind and decide that maybe you were just being polite and agreed to come on the trip because you simply enjoyed being outdoors."

She craned her neck and looked over her shoulder at him. "It never crossed my mind that you might worry if something happened to me because I've never mattered to anyone before."

"You matter to me," Conor said immediately.

Erin turned back around to face the river. "You matter to me too. I'll be more careful."

There was so much Conor wanted to say, but he instinctively knew what Erin had just shared with him was a huge step for her. He didn't want to freak her out by telling her she was fast becoming the most important person in his life. That if she died, he'd never be the same man again. No, that was a bit much for a fun little canoe trip.

Deciding a change in subject was in order, he said, "Your shoelaces are unique."

He felt her shift against him, giving him more of her weight as she relaxed. She held up one of the hiking boots she'd put on when they got off the river earlier. "My dad gave me this flint. It was during one of our last camping trips. He said that no true outdoorswoman would be caught dead without a way to start a fire. The laces themselves are made out of paracord and the ends are actually steel striker tools. The ferro rod looks like a decoration, but when used with the striker knives, can produce enough sparks to start a fire pretty easily."

Conor was impressed. "How come I didn't know about these magic laces?"

She chuckled. "I have no idea, you're obviously a slacker."

"So, you've had these laces for what...almost thirty years?"

"Well, not these exact ones. The originals my dad gave me disintegrated years ago. But I keep replacing them. The flint, however, *is* the same one he gave me."

"It makes you feel closer to your dad," Conor surmised.

Erin shrugged. "It's stupid. He left me...us."

"Tell me about it?"

He didn't think she was going to, but after a moment or so, she finally sighed. "I was eight. We'd been camping the week before, on the trip I just told you about, where he gave me the shoelaces. I was in bed, and he and my mom were arguing, as usual. Frankly, I'd pretty much stopped worrying about it. They were always bitching to each other about something. When I woke up the next morning, my mom told me he'd left. He'd packed up some of his stuff and walked out on us both. He didn't leave me a note or anything."

"And you never heard from him again?"

"Nope."

Conor thought about it for a long moment. Then asked, "What did your mom do?"

"Mom? She went on with her life. Made me miserable."

"I mean, did she report him missing?"

Erin shook her head. "No. She said he told her he was done with us and that he wasn't ever going to come back. Said he was going to send divorce papers."

"And did he?"

Erin shrugged. "No clue. Figured it didn't make much difference one way or another."

Conor shifted Erin in his arms until she was sitting sideways in his lap. She put one arm around his shoulders to keep her balance and looked at him in surprise.

"Erin, it makes all the difference in the world. Did your mom ever get remarried?"

She shook her head.

"And you don't know if *he* did. The government cares about that sort of thing. If he was married, taxes filed by both your mom and dad would need to reflect that. Have you ever thought about looking for him?"

Erin sighed and turned her head to look at the water again. "No. If he didn't want anything to do with me anymore, why would I bother?"

"Tell me more about your mom," Conor asked, his law enforcement brain working overtime.

"Mom? Why?"

"I want to know everything about you," Conor told her honestly.

"I already said she was a bitch. I wasn't lying."

"In what way?" Conor ran his hand up and down her thigh in a slow, steady rhythm. He wanted Erin to relax against him again. He held her securely with an arm at her back.

"Every way," Erin said flatly. "She wasn't ever a happy person, but after Dad left, she was even less happy. She yelled at me all the time. She drank...a lot. She told me that I was the reason Dad left and when I..." She paused then.

Conor leaned in and nuzzled the sensitive skin by her ear. He wasn't trying to get fresh, but instead wanted to console her because it was obvious she was struggling with telling him about her childhood. But she *was* telling him. And that made Conor feel that much closer to her.

Making their situation seem even more intimate, Erin

turned her head away from the river and rested it on his shoulder, tucking herself into him even more. One arm was already around his shoulders and she rested the other on the middle of his chest. "When I gained weight because I wasn't happy, my mom got even worse. Instead of trying to make me feel better, she made me feel like crap. The second I graduated from high school, I was out of there and never looked back."

"You haven't seen your mom since then?" Conor asked, tucking her even closer to his chest.

"I didn't say that. She knows where I work, and every now and then she'll pop up in my life just to try to make me miserable."

"Where does she live? In San Antonio?"

"No. Over in the Houston area."

Conor didn't like that her mom still tried to make her daughter's life hell. He *really* didn't like that. "I'm sorry you had to go through all that, bright eyes. From where I'm sitting, it sounds as if you're better off without her. You're an amazing person. You got your degree, you have a great job, and you're kind. Not everyone is. You're sensitive, caring, and empathetic to others around you. More importantly, you're outdoorsy, like me, and I like being around you."

She didn't say anything for a long moment but Conor felt her take a deep breath, as if his words affected her deeply. Finally, she whispered, "And in shape. Don't you mean that too?"

Conor didn't understand her tone, but he immediately said, "No. Am I attracted to you? Yes, I think that's obvious." He shifted his hips under her, making sure she felt his erection under her ass. "But that's absolutely not why I like being around you. I've met lots of beautiful women, bright eyes. But I'd like to think I'm not that shallow. I like you because of who you are in here." He tapped her forehead lightly. "I'm happy you're in shape because it allows you to more easily do things like this canoeing trip, camping, and running. Things you obviously love. But in no way is your being slender a deal breaker for me."

Erin's only response was to tighten her arm around his back for a moment.

They sat together for at least another half hour. Conor tried to keep their conversation light and nonthreatening. He knew he'd brought up the difficult subject of her parents, and her seemingly out-of-the-blue accusation that he was with her because of her weight was obviously a touchy subject as well.

But as they spoke about what the weather would be the next day and about the final exam she'd be giving her classes when she returned to work, Conor couldn't put the disappearance of her father from his mind.

It sounded fishy. If the man had enjoyed spending time with his daughter as much as it seemed he did, he couldn't imagine him just leaving as abruptly as Erin described. If *he* had a daughter, there was no way he'd just up and leave.

His cop senses were screaming at him that there was more to the story. He didn't want to overstep with Erin, but he couldn't let it go. When he got back to San Antonio, he'd speak to some of his friends. Maybe Cruz or Dax. The FBI agent and/or the Texas Ranger might be able to do some discreet searching through their databases for any information about Erin's father. He'd need more information from her, like his name, where in Houston she'd grown up, how old her dad was, things like that, but he had time to learn those details.

"It's getting late," he said during a lull in their conversation. "We should probably get some rest."

"Hmmmm," Erin murmured against his chest.

Conor had felt her relax and give him her weight about twenty minutes ago. Her trust felt awesome, but his butt was numb and they did have another full day on the river the next day. They both needed to get some sleep.

"Come on, bright eyes. Up you go," he urged, helping her sit up straight.

She yawned and stretched in his lap before climbing to her feet. He stood up next to her and reached for her hand. It felt natural and easy to hold her hand as they walked toward their tents. They'd set them up near the others.

Conor stood in front of her tent and took Erin's head in his hands. "I've never had a date as good as this one," he told her honestly.

"A date? Is that what this was?" she asked, a smirk on her face.

"Yup. Our first."

"Oh. Well, all right then."

"And because it was a date, I can't let you go without a kiss." Without giving her a chance to refuse, Conor leaned down.

But she didn't refuse. She went up on her tiptoes and met his lips with hers.

Her eagerness was evident in the way she wrapped her arms around his neck and pressed herself against him. But it was her hesitation and insecurity in the kiss itself that made Conor's heart skip a beat.

If he wasn't mistaken, she hadn't done this very often. Her nose knocked against his and it took several passes of his tongue over her lips for her to open to him. Then when she did, she froze in his arms as he surged inside her mouth. She let him take the lead in their kiss, mimicking each and every one of his movements. It was as if she was learning what to do from him.

That brought Conor up short. He pulled his lips from hers and hugged her to him. She lay her head against his shoulder as they stood embracing each other.

Conor's thoughts spun. Was it possible she hadn't done this before? How? He almost couldn't believe it. But then the implications hit him.

Virgin. Or at the very least, extremely inexperienced.

If he thought he'd felt protective of her before, it was nothing compared to how he felt now. He wanted to be the one to show her passion. What making love was all about.

He might be completely off base, but he didn't think so. And it simply made him more determined than ever to make her his own.

He pulled back and cleared his throat, swallowing against the lump there. "I had a good time today, bright eyes. I can't wait to see what tomorrow brings. I'll make sure the fire's out. Sleep well and I'll see you in the morning."

"Thanks for being a good canoe partner," Erin said softly. "See you tomorrow."

Conor nodded and shoved his hands in his pockets as he watched her step into her small tent and zip it up behind her. Only then did he move. He went to the campfire and poured the bucket of water on it they'd put nearby for safety, raked the coals to make sure the flames were completely out, then headed to his own tent for some shut-eye.

The day had been exhilarating, peaceful, fun, and educational. The more time he spent with Erin, the more he learned about her and the more he liked her. He couldn't wait for tomorrow.

5

THE NEXT DAY on the river was much the same as the previous one. An hour or so of lazy paddling followed by scoping out the next set of rapids, then running them. Jose and Alex tipped over once again, but for the most part the rapids were good to them.

They made camp on the US side of the river around four. Chad asked why they didn't camp on the Mexican side and Erin informed them that it was illegal. They could stop for breaks and emergencies, but laws prevented them from actually camping on that side.

Erin got their dinner going; they were having a simple meal of spaghetti. It was easy to cook the noodles once the water was boiling and the sauce wasn't hard to heat up. Lunch had consisted of sandwiches, chips, and fresh fruit.

The meals were chosen for ease of transport, as well as being high in calories and satisfaction. It was important to be able to carry all the food for the multi-day trip, but also to have meals that would fill everyone up.

Food was an issue for Erin. It always had been and it always would be. Every single thing she put into her mouth stressed her out. Shaking her head, she carefully toasted the garlic bread as she looked up at Conor. He was standing off to the side with the boys, showing them animal tracks in the dirt and explaining what each was.

She couldn't believe she'd told him as much as she had the night before about her past. She didn't talk about herself to anyone, but Conor made it so easy. And sitting in his lap while she'd done so had made her feel safe and comforted as she'd talked about her horror of a mother and childhood.

What she didn't tell him was exactly how much weight she'd gained after her dad had left. How she'd sneak food into her room and eat it under the covers, away from the accusing eyes of her mother. She didn't tell him how her mom would call her names like fatty, and tell her how disgusting she was. She didn't admit that feeling full comforted her, made her feel satisfied and happy when nothing else did. That when she was eating, she could block out the mean things her mother said about her dad and how inadequate she felt.

She didn't tell him that even though she'd hated herself, she couldn't stop eating.

Erin closed her eyes for a moment. Food had always been a crutch for her. It was the one thing that hadn't ever let her down. So even now, after several surgeries, years of hard work, and too many visits to therapists to count, she still craved losing herself in food. She wanted that full feeling. That feeling of satisfaction.

But food also scared her. She never wanted to go back

to the way she was, but every day she felt the lure of eating. It was why she spent so much time away from her apartment. If she was exercising, she couldn't eat.

She could consume just about anything now, but was very careful about what she put in her mouth. Everything she ate could be the one thing that tipped the scales and put her back on a path of destruction. So she ate small portions, and quit way before she reached the overfull sensation she used to crave.

She'd eat the pasta with the men tonight, but only a small portion. No bread and only a little bit of the sauce. The cookies she'd brought for dessert would also go uneaten by her. She'd have an apple later to help satisfy her sweet tooth.

She'd seen Conor watching her and could tell he wanted to insist she eat more. But he got points for holding back his thoughts. She was an adult, she knew what she needed to eat and what she didn't. Erin would be the first to admit that hadn't always been the case, but she'd learned a lot about her body over the last eight years or so, and knew exactly how many calories she needed to function properly.

Throughout the day, she'd opened up to Conor more and more. He'd talked about his parents and sisters, and she'd reciprocated by telling him more about her dad. He'd been about the same age as she was now when he'd left, thirty-five. She had no idea where he might've gone. He had been an only child and his parents had been tragically killed in a car accident when he was in college. He'd had no family other than her and his wife, but apparently, that hadn't been enough to keep him with them. She even admitted to Conor that her middle name, Dallas, was the same as his first, and how he'd been so proud to introduce her to people as Erin Dallas Gardner.

She called out to let everyone know dinner would be ready in five minutes and was sad this was the last night she'd have with Conor out here on the river. It was almost shocking to realize how much she was going to miss this. He'd said he was going to ask her out, but there was something so peaceful about sitting by the river and getting to know him. She generally wasn't one to enjoy spending time around people. It made her nervous and she always worried over what they thought about her. But there was none of that with him.

With his little touches and smiles, not to mention the nickname he'd given her, he'd made it more than clear he liked being around her. And the feeling was definitely mutual. She wasn't an expert on men by any stretch, but for the first time ever, she wanted to take a chance with one.

They all settled on the folding camp chairs Erin had brought, each with a heaping plate of pasta.

"I can't believe how awesome the food has been," Alex said through a mouthful of food.

"Yeah, I can't cook like this when I'm at home with a full kitchen available," Jose agreed.

"How you don't weigh four hundred pounds is beyond me," Matthew murmured.

"Right?" Chad agreed. "If I ate like this all the time, I'd totally be a blimp!"

"You already are, asshole," Matthew joked.

Chad reached over and smacked his friend on the back of the head.

"If I had a chick who cooked like this for me, I wouldn't care how fat she was. I'd just make her wear a bag over her head in bed," Jose said.

"I don't think it'd be worth it," Alex threw in. "I don't think I'd be able to get it up if I had to figure out what was tit and what was a fat roll."

All the boys laughed.

Erin stiffened in her chair and looked down at the food on her plate. Any hunger she'd felt earlier was now gone. She knew the boys weren't talking about her, but their comments still struck a little too close to home.

The insults and taunts she'd endured throughout high school, and even in college and beyond, echoed in her head. "Eat-more Erin. Why do you eat so much? Your face is so pretty, if you'd just lose some weight you might be able to get a boyfriend. You have a great smile, the rest of you, not so much. Don't sit next to Eat-more Erin, she'll snarf down your lunch before you can."

"Don't be rude," Conor said harshly, surprising Erin and bringing her out of her miserable inner thoughts and memories.

"Dude, I wasn't being rude," Matthew said. "I was paying her a compliment."

"No, you weren't," Conor returned. "You were disparaging everyone who you think doesn't meet society's definition of beautiful. You think people who are overweight don't have feelings?"

"No, that wasn't—"

"It was," Conor interrupted Matthew. "Look, I get it.

You guys are young. You're in a fraternity. You have the world ahead of you. But I'll tell you right now, if you choose a woman who's thin and good looking over someone you think has a few too many pounds on her frame, instead of concentrating on who she is on the inside, you'll regret it for the rest of your life."

The boys were silent as Conor continued to berate them.

"I'm not an idiot, I know what a woman looks like is important. You have to be physically attracted to someone in order for a relationship to work. But guys, ignore what society says is beautiful. Forget what your buddies say you should like. If you like tall women, go for it. If you prefer for your woman to be short, no problem. Maybe you're an ass man...so find a woman who has an ass that you can grab hold of. You like tits? There's nothing wrong with being attracted to a woman with more meat on her bones because she'll most likely have boobs you can play with."

His voice lowered as he made his final point. "But whatever you do, never make fun of someone because of how they look. Ever. You don't know what's going on inside his or her head. Most people are struggling with stuff you have no idea about. None. And you making fun of someone only shows how ignorant *you* are, it has nothing to do with them.

"Some of the most successful people in the world were bullied growing up. Chris Rock, Jessica Alba, Jennifer Lawrence, Taylor Swift, Madonna, Steven Spielberg, Michael Phelps, and Barack frickin' Obama, for Christ's sake. Be a man, and stop that shit right now. Even if you weren't targeting someone specific a moment ago, words have power. Think before you speak and treat people with respect. You never know when someone you make fun of today might become the President of the United States tomorrow."

Erin kept her head down, but raised her eyes to see what the boys' reaction was to Conor's impassioned speech. She half expected them to be rolling their eyes, but surprisingly, it seemed as if they'd actually heard what Conor had said. Had taken his message to heart.

"Sorry."

"We didn't mean anything by it."

"You're right."

"Yeah, we were wrong."

Their responses were surprising as much for the words, as for the emotions behind them. They seemed genuinely upset about what they'd said.

The rest of dinner was quiet as the men quickly finished the food on their plates.

"We're gonna do the dishes," Matthew declared, standing and heading for the makeshift kitchen Erin had set up earlier. One pan with soapy water, another with plain water for rinsing, and a third with bleach for disinfecting.

"Are you done, Ms. Gardner?" Jose asked.

Erin looked up at the young man. He was standing next to her, and when he saw he had her attention, he gestured toward her still half-full plate with his head. "You can take your time. We'll take care of your dish whenever you're done."

"I'm done," she told him, holding her plate up to him.

She couldn't eat another bite with the way her stomach was roiling.

Conor held up his empty plate and Chad took it as he walked over to Matthew.

"Don't forget the pots," Conor told the other men.

Alex went to the fire and managed to grab both pots Erin had used to make their supper and keep hold of his own plate and silverware.

Erin brought her feet up to the seat of her chair and hugged her knees as the guys began to clean up from dinner.

"Walk with me?"

Conor's question startled Erin and her feet slipped off the edge of the chair. She would've fallen out if Conor hadn't grabbed her arm.

"Sorry! I'm clumsy. Sure, I'll walk."

"Guys!" Conor called over to the others. "We're headed a ways down the river. We won't be far. Don't go anywhere."

"Where would we go?" Alex called back, laughing as he indicated the deserted Texas countryside with his hand.

Conor chuckled and tucked Erin under his arm and turned them to walk along the edge of the river.

The moon was full, giving them enough light to see where they were walking without needing a flashlight.

Erin hated the feelings of inadequacy and insecurity that coursed through her body. She was thirty-five. Way too old to let the words of boys almost half her age affect her as much as they were. They were just saying what anyone would. In today's society, being fat was the worst thing that someone could be.

Any other kind of disability could garner sympathy and maybe even respect, but being fat was apparently open season for inviting mean comments and harsh judgment.

Conor walked them downstream until he came to a large flat rock that overlooked the water. He gestured to it and Erin sat. He stepped behind her then lowered himself down. His legs stretched out on either side of her and she inhaled sharply when his arms wrapped around her, much as he'd done the night before.

Erin could sense his body heat along her back and shivered a bit at the feeling. It was chilly out. Not cold, but tonight was supposed to be one of the coolest nights of the weekend. Conor propped his chin on her shoulder as he held her.

She could smell hints of the soap he'd used to clean up, and when he tucked his chin into the space between her neck and shoulder, his scratchy beard reminded her that he hadn't shaved that morning.

It should've been awkward. But it wasn't. Erin wasn't thinking about what her body looked like or how she smelled after cooking over the fire and paddling on the river all day. She simply soaked in the contentment she felt at being held in Conor's arms.

"I hate when people make fun of others," Conor said in a low voice, puffs of air from his words wafting over her neck. "It sucks, and I know they're young, but I firmly believe that parents should teach their children that being a bully isn't okay."

Erin laid her hand on Conor's forearm. "They didn't mean anything by it. They were just shooting the shit with their buddies."

"But that's just it," Conor countered. "It's so ingrained in them that they don't realize how offensive they're being even when others are around. If people thought more about the words that came out of their mouths, we'd have fewer bullying incidents. Fewer suicides. Fewer people would have to rely on antidepressants to get them through their day."

Erin had been so stuck in her own head, hearing the boys' words and thinking they were aimed at her, that she hadn't realized Conor wasn't just preaching to them because he thought it was the right thing to do. He had a deeper reason. Now that she was paying attention, she could feel the tension in his body. He hadn't walked off with her to make *her* feel better, he'd done it to make *himself* feel better.

"You want to talk about it?" Erin felt hypocritical asking the question when she wasn't ready to open up to him, but she couldn't help herself.

She wasn't sure he was going to respond, and vowed not to push. She wouldn't like to be pushed so she wasn't going to do that to him.

After taking a deep breath, he began to talk.

"You have no idea how many kids I've had to cut down after they've hung themselves in some remote pocket of the forest. Or how many people I've seen with bullets blown through their brains because they couldn't handle how society told them they should look. Or act. Or be. And it all starts with words. Maybe it's kids in elementary school making fun of the way they look. Or sound. Or how smart they are. Then it continues through their school years. Some make it through high school, and others don't. But it doesn't stop. They're judged by so many people in their lives and they can't take it. So they end up taking their own lives because they can't live up to what society thinks they should be. I hate it. I love my job, but I dread the calls about missing persons. I'm always afraid what I'll find when we track them down."

Erin squeezed his arm and turned. He kept his arms around her, but now her side was pressed against his chest. She wound her arms around him and clutched her hands together, holding him tightly. She rested her head on his shoulder and simply held him as he spoke.

"The thing that amazes me the most is when people make fun of overweight people at the gym. I seriously don't get that. I mean, they're at the *gym*...working out. Trying to lose weight. Why in the world would you make fun of them for that?"

Erin agreed one hundred percent. She remembered after her surgery she'd gotten up the courage to go to the local YMCA and use the gym there. She was trying to walk to burn calories. She saw a group of women, grown women, laughing at her and taking pictures of her with their cell phones. They weren't even trying to be subtle about it. It had been humiliating, and the last time she'd gone to work out there.

"I just wish kids could stay as innocent as they are when they're young. I've watched so-called normal four-year-olds play with kids with Down Syndrome and have the time of their lives. Then a mere three years later, those same children are making fun of that kid because it's how they've seen others treat them. And it never stops. I hate it."

His words tilted Erin's world on its axis. She'd never thought about others like her. Oh, she knew all about bullying and how hurtful words could be, but hadn't *really* thought about how other people dealt with it. She only knew how she did…by eating. But suddenly her eyes had been opened. She'd been lucky. Very lucky. She might not have close friends or a loving family, but she had the inner strength to keep pushing through. Many didn't. And that was sad, so sad.

"Someone you're close to was bullied," Erin stated softly. It wasn't really a question. She knew to the marrow of her bones it was where Conor's angst was coming from.

"Yeah." He didn't elaborate.

"He or she is lucky to have you supporting them."

"I've done my best."

Erin lifted her head. She twisted and brought a hand up to Conor's face and placed it on his cheek. Her thumb brushed against it softly. His five o'clock shadow was scratchy against her skin. She'd never been this up close and personal with a man's beard before, but she liked it.

Without a word, she stretched up to him and touched his lips with hers. It was a brief caress. A mere brush of lips, but the electricity that went through her body was immediate and surprising.

Conor's arms tightened and he stared down at her with an intense gaze that Erin didn't have the experience to interpret.

"What was that for?" he whispered.

"You looked like you needed it," Erin told him honestly.

His lips quirked up in a small smile. "I did. Thank you."

"You're welcome."

His head tilted to the side and he pressed the weight of it into her hand, still resting on his face. "I just hope some of what I told them tonight sinks in. I can't control what they say and do after this trip, but I just pray they reach down inside themselves and find some compassion for their fellow human beings."

"I think it will," Erin said. "They honestly seemed to be thinking about what you said."

Conor sat up straight then. He scooted around so he was sitting next to her and brought his hands up to either side of her neck and held her gaze. She grabbed onto both his wrists. They sat like that for a long moment, staring at each other, the attraction thick between them.

Then, without a word, Conor leaned forward. He moved slowly, giving Erin a chance to pull back, to stop him, but she didn't. She held her breath then closed her eyes as he got close.

Then his lips were on hers. But he didn't simply brush them against hers, he lingered. He nipped and stroked until she opened for him.

As soon as she did, his tongue surged inside her mouth. Erin's stomach clenched and she dug her fingernails into his wrists. The small spike of electricity she felt earlier was now a full-blown electrical storm.

He tilted her head to the right as he turned his own to

the left and pressed deeper into her. How long they sat like that, their mouths fused together, their tongues dueling and learning the feel and taste of each other, Erin had no idea.

Conor slowly pulled back with a groan. She kept her eyes closed, not wanting the moment to end.

"Thank you," Conor said.

Erin's eyes popped open. "For what?"

"For pulling my head out of my ass. For making me appreciate what's in front of me."

"Uh...you're welcome." It wasn't exactly what she wanted to hear from him, but she'd rather eat an entire chocolate cake by herself than admit she was disappointed.

"And thank you for inviting me. For kissing me. For giving me the best kiss I've ever had in my life."

Okay, that was better. Much better. "You're welcome," she whispered again, with more feeling this time.

Conor moved his hand and brushed his thumb over her lower lip. Erin could feel the wetness from his kiss on her skin. Involuntarily, her tongue came out and licked her lips, brushing against his thumb as she did.

"Fuck, you're sexy, bright eyes," Conor murmured, then leaned down and captured her lips with his own again in a short, intense caress.

Then he pulled back and said, "We should probably head back and make sure the guys are all right."

"Yeah," Erin said with zero enthusiasm.

"I already told you this, but I'm serious, when we get back, I want to see you again," Conor blurted. "And not just at The Sloppy Cow. I want to take you out. Get to know you better. Let you get to know me. Have you meet my family. They're gonna love everything about you. I just...I don't want this to be a vacation fling."

Erin wasn't sure about meeting his family, but she *was* sure about wanting to see him again. "I'd like that."

He sighed in relief. As if he hadn't been sure she'd agree. "Good." Then he shifted and carefully stood. He helped her stand and wrapped an arm around her waist as he turned them back toward camp.

They walked in silence, but it was comfortable, not awkward.

Erin mentally shook her head, wondering how the heck this had happened. She had a date. Oh, it wasn't set in stone yet, was still kind of vague, but she had hopes that Conor had been serious. That he really did want to see her again.

She didn't remember the rest of the night. Didn't remember what she said to the guys as she and Conor came back into camp. Didn't remember saying goodnight to anyone. When she was lying in her sleeping bag in her tent, all she could remember was the feel of Conor's lips pressed to her own. How he'd held her against him as he'd kissed her. She'd never forget it, not ever.

6

THE NEXT DAY passed in a flash. They packed up camp, had a leisurely canoe about two miles downriver to the take-out point. Then, while she and the others worked on getting everything situated for the trip home, Conor hitchhiked back to the ranger station. When he arrived back, the trash had been thrown away and their bags were lined up, ready to be put back into the van.

Loading the canoes was easy with all five men helping, and Erin tied them securely down for the trip home. Before she knew it, they were on their way.

Erin couldn't remember ever laughing as much as she did on the six-hour drive back to San Antonio. Alex, Matthew, Jose, and Chad were hilarious, joking and laughing with each other, and even including Erin in their good-natured teasing. But it was Conor who made the drive memorable. Every time she glanced his way, he was looking at her. He'd smile in a secret way that made her remember every second of the time they'd spent together over the last couple of days. Especially their intimate kiss last night.

When they stopped to get gas, he once again refused to allow her to man the pump, but this time she noticed the other men observing them. Thinking that Conor was a hell of a role model, she gave in graciously. She used the restroom and gathered some snacks for the guys, and a bottle of water for herself.

They got back to the UTSA rec center around six. The college kids waved goodbye and disappeared into the night. Then it was only her and Conor left.

"I had a good time," he said as soon as they were alone.

"Me too."

"Thank you for inviting me."

"You're welcome. I'm glad it worked out."

"You owe me," he said, his lips quirking up.

"For what?" Erin asked.

"For making you look good in front of the guys. I did everything you told me to and we didn't tip once."

Erin grinned at him now. "Is that right?"

"Yup."

"So what do I owe you?"

Conor took a step toward her, getting into her space. Erin's smile died. She'd been teasing him, but the look on his face was anything but teasing now. The evening light was dying, and the darkness, combined with the fact they'd spent the last three days together twenty-four/seven, made the moment very intimate.

"I'll start with a kiss."

Erin glanced around them. They were truly alone for

the first time since they'd left three days ago. She wanted to be sophisticated, mysterious, and all the other traits she assumed people who had more experience than she did embodied, but the only thing she could squeak out was, "Please."

One of Conor's hands went under her chin and lifted her head to his. The other snaked around and landed on her lower back. He pulled her into him at the same time his head lowered to hers.

Before she could freak out about where her own hands should go or how she should kiss him, his lips were on hers and she couldn't think at all.

The kiss was just as explosive as it had been the night before, but this time they were touching from hips to chest. She could feel the warmth of Conor's body against her own in the chilly evening air. She tilted her head automatically this time, not needing his direction.

They made out in the middle of the parking lot for several moments. Each lost in the feelings coursing through their bodies and enjoying the connection.

Conor finally pulled back and ran his hand over her hair reverently. "Go out with me."

"Okay." Erin almost didn't recognize her voice.

"What's your schedule like?"

Erin tried to get her brain to work. "Um...I'm working Monday, Wednesday, and Friday nights at The Sloppy Cow this week. Also, since I took this weekend off, I've got Saturday night too."

"Damn. I've got Monday and Tuesday day shifts, but then I start nights on Wednesday for a week."

Erin tried to keep the disappointment from her face,

but obviously failed, because Conor leaned forward and rested his forehead against her own and said, "Just because our schedules don't mesh doesn't mean we aren't going to see each other."

"How?"

"Where there's a will, there's a way," Conor replied calmly. "We both need to eat, so maybe we can meet up at lunch or dinner somewhere in there."

Erin pulled back and looked up at him solemnly. "I don't do meal get-togethers."

Conor blinked down at her, startled for a beat, then said, "Then we don't need to eat. We can just meet and talk."

Erin closed her eyes. Shit, she was a moron. She was embarrassed and tried to explain. "It's just—"

Conor's finger landed on her lips, silencing her explanation. "It's fine. If you think I haven't noticed that eating around others makes you uncomfortable, you're wrong. I don't care what we do, bright eyes, I just want to spend time with you. I *like* spending time with you. I just don't want to leave here today without at least one time and place scheduled where I can see you again. I fully plan on calling you, and texting and probably emailing too, but it's not the same as getting to see you in person. Seeing your smile and hearing your laugh. I'm addicted to you, Erin, so no matter what I need to do to see your beautiful eyes in person, I'm willing to do it."

"Oh." It wasn't the most eloquent response, but it was all Erin could manage at the moment.

Conor dropped his finger from her mouth and clasped his hands together at the small of her back. He held her to him and didn't seem at all nervous or insecure about the fact they were plastered together in a public parking lot.

"I teach in the mornings, but I'm done after my office hours at two." She looked up at him and bit her lip before suggesting, "Maybe we can do something in the afternoon on Wednesday before you go to work and I have to be at the bar?"

"Yes," was his immediate response. "And Thursday and Friday too."

Erin's lips twitched. "You're assuming I'll want to see you again after Wednesday."

"Yes, I am. Because I can't be the only one feeling the connection between us."

Erin slowly shook her head as she held his eyes.

"Right. I've never felt this with anyone else, Erin. We just spent three days together and I'm dreading saying goodbye to you. I'm greedy. I want more. I want to spend all my days with you, laughing and just talking. But I also want to take you to bed. Spend my nights with you plastered to my side. I want to know what turns you on and what makes you moan in pleasure. I want it all. No, I *need* it all."

"Conor," Erin protested, blushing in embarrassment, and at the same time shifting where she stood in desire.

"Tell me I'm not alone in feeling that way," Conor demanded.

Erin looked up at him. "You're not alone," she obediently repeated. "But...I have to tell you something." She stopped, not at all sure she was doing the right thing.

"What is it, bright eyes?" Conor asked tenderly. "You

can tell me anything. It's not going to change the way I feel."

She decided the best way to deal with the issue was just to say it outright. "I haven't done this before."

"What?"

She brought a hand up, gesturing between them. "This. Dated."

His body went hard and he narrowed his eyes at her. "But you've been out with a guy." It wasn't a question, but it still was.

Erin shook her head and tried to explain without really explaining. "Not really. I wasn't popular in high school and when I was in college, all I was interested in was graduating. I didn't have time for parties or looking for a guy. Then I started working and had some medical issues. I just..." Her voice trailed off. The more she tried to explain, the more pathetic she sounded.

Conor moved then. He took her head in both of his hands and tilted it up so she had no choice but to look at him. "I want to know more about everything you just said...I want to know everything about you. But I can be patient. You can tell me what you want, when you want. But, bright eyes, what are you saying? That you haven't been with a man before? That you're a virgin?"

Relieved that he'd guessed and she didn't have to actually say it, Erin simply nodded.

When Conor didn't respond, just looked at her with his chest heaving with increased breaths and his nostrils flaring, she got defensive and felt the need to clarify. "I just wanted to tell you in case you...you know...weren't interested anymore."

"Not interested?" he said, his eyebrows drawing down in confusion.

"I don't know the rules," Erin admitted. "To dating. You know, what's appropriate and what's not. Am I supposed to let you touch me after two dates, three? And texting...how much is too much? Can I use emojis, or do I have to wait until we've been seeing each other for several weeks?"

"What the fuck is an emoji?"

Erin didn't think, if his tone was anything to go by, that this was going well. "Uh...it's the little pictures that you can include in emails and texts. You know, smiley faces, hearts, animals...stuff like that."

Conor didn't respond verbally, but tilted his head up and looked at the night sky as if searching for Divine intervention.

Erin tried to take a step back, but Conor didn't let go of her face. At her movement, he looked down at her again. "What else?"

"What else what?" Erin asked in confusion.

"What else don't you know about dating?"

"Oh, uh...well, everything. I don't know when it's appropriate to meet your family. How often we're supposed to see each other during the week. If you want me to touch you when we're in public. And I know I'm not that good at kissing, but I think I'll be a fast learner. I mean, even from last night to today, I think I've gotten better..." Her voice trailed off. She was nervous, and didn't understand the intense look on Conor's face.

"God. You're killing me, bright eyes. First of all, I can't

believe you haven't been on a date. You're gorgeous. What the fuck is wrong with the men you've been around?"

"I haven't always looked like this," Erin admitted immediately.

"I don't give a shit," was Conor's response. "You're an amazing person. Funny, smart, generous, giving...any man would be honored to have you by his side. I know *I* sure as hell am. But more than that, you shine with an inner light that's impossible to miss."

"Conor—" Erin protested, knowing she was blushing.

He didn't let her continue. "And as far as rules to dating go? There aren't any. Not between us. You do whatever you want. If you want to send me a text with a thousand fucking emojis, go for it. I'll think it's cute as fuck. You want to call me five minutes after I drop you off? Do it. Because I know I'll already be missing you. There's no rulebook when it comes to us, Erin. I'll teach you everything you need to know about dating. And since we're talking about it..." Conor moved his hands then. He wrapped one around her waist and pressed on her lower back, bringing her into full contact along his body. The other snaked under her hair and landed on her nape. His thumb brushed back and forth against the sensitive skin there, making goosebumps race down Erin's arms.

He brushed his lips against hers in a barely there caress and continued. "I'm fucking ecstatic that no one has touched you. I've never been the kind of person to care about a woman's sexual background. If she'd been with a thousand men or just one, it didn't matter to me. She was with *me* at the moment and that was all that mattered. But I find, knowing that you haven't been with anyone else, that it's sexy as hell."

"It doesn't turn you off?" Erin asked softly.

"Fuck no! Does this feel like I'm turned off?" he asked, pressing his hips into her.

She could feel his erection against her and shook her head.

"Right. I'm turned the fuck on. Just the thought of introducing you to the pleasures that can be had in my bed has me on edge."

"I know what it's all about," Erin told him. "I mean, I've seen videos, and I've been going to my gynecologist for years. I don't think I even have a hymen anymore."

"Oh, bright eyes, you might know the mechanics, but you have no idea how amazing I'm going to make you feel."

She paused for a moment, wanting to make sure he completely understood. "I've had an orgasm, Conor. I might be a thirty-five-year-old virgin, but I have a vibrator. Technically, I suppose I shouldn't even say I'm a virgin."

"Honey, the thought of you using a sex toy on yourself makes me crazy. I want to watch you get off that way— but you're wrong. If you haven't been penetrated by a real-live cock, you're still a virgin."

Erin tried to hold back her giggle, but she couldn't.

"What's funny?"

"A real-live cock?" she asked between giggles.

"Yup," he told her, smiling. "*My* real-live cock is gonna be the first to breach your virgin pussy. You'll come for the first time on my dick and you'll realize just how pathetic a vibrator can be in comparison."

Erin froze, turned on by his words. She supposed she should've been offended by his frank speaking, but she wasn't. She shifted in his hold and felt the wetness between her legs. "Are you allowed to say that this early in our relationship?"

"No rules, bright eyes," Conor said. "We can both say whatever we want, whenever we want. Societal rules be damned. It's just us. If I want to tell you how proud and excited I am that I get to be your first, then I will. If you want to tell me that you got off while using that vibrator of yours, you can. No holds barred between us. Okay?"

"Okay," Erin immediately agreed. "But, you'll tell me if I do something crazy?"

"Like?"

She bit her lip. "Well...I don't know. That's why you'll need to tell me."

"I'll let you know," Conor said. "But you should be aware that I love your enthusiasm. I don't think there's anything you could do that would chase me away."

"I'm not ready to have sex with you yet," Erin blurted.

Conor didn't even tense. "I know. And now that I know you haven't done this before, I'm not inclined to rush our physical relationship, bright eyes. I want to get to know you better, ease you into that part of dating."

"But..." Erin looked away from Conor's intense eyes for a moment, then took a deep breath and looked back at him. "That doesn't mean I'm not willing to explore. I like kissing you. I like the way you feel against me."

"Good. And for the record, I like kissing you too." And

with that said, Conor leaned forward and kissed her. His hands held her tightly against him as he devoured her mouth. After several long moments of deep kisses, Erin pulled back.

"So...Wednesday afternoon?"

"Yeah. That sounds amazing."

"I thought of something."

"What's that, bright eyes?"

"Do you run in the mornings?"

Conor pulled back then and looked her in the eye. He reached out and grabbed her fidgeting hands in his own. "Yeah, usually, except when I'm working the night shift, obviously."

"Me too. Do you think...you want to go together?"

"Yeah. Are you any good?"

Erin smiled. "I'm good."

Conor returned the grin. "We'll see then, won't we?"

"It's on," Erin said in a stronger tone, feeling less off-kilter now that they weren't talking about her virginity and they weren't kissing.

"Tomorrow?"

"Sure. Want to meet here? UTSA has a track, but there's a five-mile route that I do most mornings."

"What time?"

"Six? My first class is at eight, and that gives me time to shower after working out."

"Perfect. My shift starts at nine. It'll give me time to get home after our run and still get to work on time."

They smiled at each other for a long moment before Conor broke it. "I like you, Erin Gardner. I'm incredibly excited to get to know you better."

"Am I allowed to say I like you too, Conor Paxton?"

"Yeah, you're absolutely allowed to say that," he said, then cleared his throat. "And with that, I need to get going. Are you returning the canoes tonight?"

Erin shook her head. "No, the outdoor rec place is closed. I'll leave them here and take care of it tomorrow after my first class."

"You need any help?"

Erin appreciated him asking, but quickly reassured him. "No, I'm good. Thanks though."

"Any time, bright eyes. Thank you for inviting me."

"Thanks for accepting."

They stared at each other for a minute. Finally, Conor grinned ruefully and said, "I'd stand here all night looking at you, but I really do need to get going."

"I know."

Conor dropped her hands and took a step back, reaching in his pocket for his keys. "I'll see you in the morning."

Erin nodded and watched as he backed away from her, then eventually turned and walked toward his truck. She kept watching as he threw his bag in the back, climbed inside, started it up, and put it in gear. She waved as he turned his head to look at her one more time, thrilled when he lifted his chin in a very manly goodbye and drove out of the lot.

Pulling out her phone, Erin used her thumb to unlock it and clicked on Conor's name in her contacts. Her thumbs raced over the screen as she typed out a quick text. She hoped he'd been serious when he'd said there were no dating rules between them because even though she hadn't ever been on a real date or been in any kind of relationship, she had a feeling what she was doing wasn't normal and would probably scare off any man who wasn't Conor.

ERIN: You just left and I already miss you.

AT THE END of her sentence, just for fun, she added several emojis...a crying smiley face, a snowman, a cactus, a goat, a flashlight, a campfire, a police car, and some sort of Asian symbol. Then she put her phone back in her pocket, made sure everything on the trailer was secured, the van was locked, and went to her blue Jeep. She smiled the entire time.

7

A WEEK LATER, on a Tuesday night, Conor sat in The Sloppy Cow with Daxton, Cruz, Quint, TJ, and Calder. They were having a guys' night out at the bar. Of course, the "night" would most likely only last until around eight-thirty, when those who had women at home would wrap things up. TJ and Calder would probably hang around for another hour or so, then they'd probably leave too.

But Conor planned on staying for as long as he could get away with it. Erin was working tonight and, even if he couldn't talk to her, he enjoyed sitting at the bar watching her do her thing.

She looked especially good tonight. She was wearing one of her ever-present long-sleeve shirts, but it hugged her slender body and highlighted her tits, even without showing an inch of skin. The jeans she was wearing were molded to her body and Conor knew after his friends left and he shifted to a stool at the bar, he'd be able to ogle her ass every time she bent over.

"You got something to tell us?" Dax asked dryly from his right.

Conor turned his head away from the object of his fascination and smiled at his friend. He knew exactly what he was asking, but decided to fuck with him for a while. "So you heard huh? Yeah, I'm up for promotion."

"That's not what I was talking about," Dax said grumpily. But then added in a more upbeat tone, "But congrats, that's awesome."

Not having the patience Dax did, Cruz asked, "What's the deal, Conor? Two weeks ago, you and the pretty bartender were dancing around each other like eighth graders at your first boy-girl dance. Now you're both making googly eyes at each other. If I wasn't so in love with Mickie, I'd be disgusted. Now spill."

"I take it the canoe trip went well," TJ added.

Conor knew he had a goofy grin on his face, but couldn't help it. "The canoe trip went well. Really well."

"And?" Quint asked when Conor didn't elaborate.

"That's it. We're dating now. Taking things one day at a time. She's busy, and so am I. But I'll tell you...she's special, and I like her. A lot."

Calder clapped him on the back. "That's awesome. She seems great."

"She is," Conor agreed immediately. "And she's perfect for me. She loves camping and we've gone running together a handful of times."

"She can keep up with you?" Dax asked, knowing how serious Conor was about his running.

"If she wanted, I have a feeling she could run circles around me."

"No shit?" Quint asked, his eyebrows rising in disbelief.

"No shit," Conor confirmed. "We went last Monday for the first time and I was all ready to go slow for her sake, but within the first half mile, I knew we were a perfect running match. She didn't try to race to impress me, but she also wasn't humoring me by slowing her own pace."

"She seems,"—TJ paused, obviously trying to think of the right word—"less jaded than someone I thought you'd end up with."

"That's because she is," Conor immediately agreed. "She might be a bartender and have to deal with drunk pigs on a regular basis, but she has no clue when it comes to society's rules or dating."

"What do you mean?" Calder asked.

"For instance, last Sunday, after spending three days together on the canoe trip and having an intense conversation in the parking lot where she worked, I left. And not two minutes later she texted me. She wanted to let me know that she already missed me."

The men around the table were quiet for a moment, then Cruz whistled low. "Hang on to her, Conor," he said. "I can tell you from experience, a woman who doesn't play games and who isn't afraid to tell you that she had a good time is someone you want to hold on to. Mickie's that way with me, and I count my lucky stars I pulled my head out of my ass and she's now mine."

"I have every intention of keeping Erin," Conor informed Cruz and the others. "I love that she calls me just because she had a five-minute break and was thinking of me. I love that she doesn't hesitate to tell me what she's thinking when she's thinking it. We haven't been able to see each other in person very much, at least not when we're both off work, but it doesn't matter. Texting her, hearing her voice over the phone, or simply watching her while she's doing her thing," he gestured to the bar with his head, "it's enough...for now."

"She's got demons," TJ said softly. His words weren't harsh or accusatory, they just were.

"I know," Conor said.

"You need to tread lightly," TJ insisted.

Conor was irritated now. "I *know*," he repeated. "If you think I spent three days with her last weekend and didn't notice that, you're insane."

"All I'm saying is that she might seem untouched and innocent, but she's been through something big. Something that made her retreat from the world. Hide. She has some of the most expressive eyes I've ever seen. She seems okay on the outside, but inside she's dealing with something heavy," TJ said without any doubt in his tone.

The men were all quiet for a long moment. They all knew TJ had been through his own kind of hell. He'd been a member of a top-secret Delta Force team for quite a few years before quitting the Army altogether and joining the highway patrol. He'd seen his share of death and destruction, and if he said Erin had PTSD of some sort, then she most likely did.

"I know. That's why I'm not pressuring her for anything," Conor said.

"There might come a time when you *need* to pressure her," TJ countered. "Sometimes in order to deal with the shit eating you alive, it has to be brought to light and banished once and for all."

Conor ground his teeth together. He didn't mind his friend giving him advice, but he didn't like thinking about Erin having to deal with whatever it was that was eating at her. But now that TJ had brought it up, he remembered what he wanted to ask his friends.

"Ten-four," he told TJ, then turned to Cruz and Dax. "Need a favor."

"Name it."

"Sure."

Conor loved his friends. They didn't even know what the favor was, but agreed without hesitation anyway. "I'm hoping you can make some discreet inquiries for me. Erin's dad disappeared when she was eight. I know it's been twenty-seven years, but something doesn't feel right about it."

"You want us to find him," Cruz stated.

"Yeah. At least see if you can find any information on him." Conor went on to explain all that he knew about Erin's father. He didn't have a lot, didn't have his birthdate or social security number, but knew his general age, where he'd disappeared from and when, and the name of Erin's mother.

Dax took a sip of his beer and pierced Conor with his gaze. "What aren't you saying?"

Conor's lips twitched. His friends knew him well. "I have absolutely no proof of anything. You understand what I'm saying? None. Not one iota to think anything happened other than what Erin told me, that her dad up and left one night after an argument with her mother."

"But it's not sitting well with you," Quint observed.

"Not in the least," Conor agreed. "Erin told me how much she loved her dad. How he'd take her camping, sharing his love of the outdoors with her. The man gave her his lucky flint to wear on her shoe, for God's sake. She told me her mom is a bitch and that she and her dad used to argue all the time. For him to up and disappear without another word to his daughter doesn't seem likely."

"You think the mom killed him," Calder stated baldly.

"Or had him killed, yeah," Conor agreed, stating his suspicions out loud for the first time. He looked at the medical examiner. "Come to think about it, can you check for John Does showing up around the time he went missing? Or even later? It's a long shot; if the mother did do something, it's possible the body hasn't ever been found."

"I'll see what I can find out," Calder said.

"This could backfire," TJ warned.

Conor tried to control his temper. He was getting tired of the other man being all gloom and doom. "If your beloved father went missing, and you spent the rest of your adolescent life being treated like shit by your bitch of a mother, wouldn't you want to know why your dad left? Wouldn't you want to know what happened to him?"

"Absolutely," TJ agreed immediately. "But sometimes knowing can be harder than not knowing."

"You're wrong," Conor fired back. "If one of my sisters disappeared, there's no way that not knowing what happened would be better than having the closure of knowing."

"Even if she was tortured? Raped? If she died a horrible death?" TJ responded calmly. "Because that could be her dad's fate. You think Erin can handle that?"

Conor turned to look at the woman who was fast becoming the center of his world. Erin was smiling at one of the bar's regular patrons. She had her hands resting on the bar and her light brown hair was pulled back in her customary ponytail...with a piece hanging loose by her face. That lock of hair seemed to have a mind of its own and never stayed in whatever restraint she put it in.

"She can handle it. She looks weak, but she's one of the strongest people I've ever met," Conor told TJ, looking him in the eyes as he did. "Whatever you see behind her eyes is what's made her that way. I don't know her story yet, but I will. And when I find out, I guarantee I'll want to beat the shit out of someone, or several some-ones, but whatever it is has made her able to face the truth. I'm half convinced she already has her own suspicions about what happened to her dad."

The two men stared at each other for a long moment before TJ finally nodded. "I'll do whatever I can to help."

"Thanks. Appreciate it."

"Hey," a soft voice said from next to the table.

All six men turned their heads to stare at Erin. She was holding a tray with two pitchers on it. "I thought you could use a refill."

Conor immediately stood and put his arm around Erin's waist. He could feel her trembling under him. She was nervous, but she'd overcome it and braved facing all his friends. It was the first time she'd seen them all together since they'd started officially dating.

TJ stood as well and took the tray from her. "Thanks, Erin. We were just going to see if we could have another round."

She smiled at him with a small quirk of her lips.

"Now's as good a time as any," Conor announced. "Everyone, I know you know Erin, the bartender, but I'd like to introduce you to Erin, my girlfriend."

Erin blushed, but met his eyes and grinned up at him.

"I think you know everyone, but just in case, this is Daxton, Cruz, Quint, TJ, and Calder. We might work in different fields of law enforcement, but the bottom line is we're all on the same side and help each other out whenever we can."

"It's good to see you all again," Erin said.

"So...you're dating this reprobate," Quint teased. "I could've introduced you to one of the officers from the SAPD if you'd said something."

His words were light and airy, and Conor was pleased when he felt Erin relax against him instead of tensing up.

"Oh well, thanks for the offer. I'll keep that in mind."

"You will not," Conor growled, and tightened his arm around her waist.

She giggled then and smiled at him. "Jealous?" she joked.

"Absolutely."

Her smile dimmed when she realized Conor wasn't kidding. "Conor," she whispered.

"I'll be back," Conor informed his friends even as he was turning Erin and walking her to the hallway that housed the restrooms and a back office. He wanted to take her in his arms and show her just how jealous the thought of her being with anyone other than him made him, but Conor controlled himself...barely.

He pressed her against the wall at the back of the hallway and leaned into her. "Fuck yes, I'm jealous. I don't want any other man to even think about putting his hands on you. Or kissing you. Or anything else."

"I don't want that either," Erin said immediately, unknowingly putting to rest the animal inside him that was ready to claw its way out. "I only want to be with you."

He loved that she wasn't coy. That she didn't try to make him jealous just to tie him closer to her. Her innate innocence was intoxicating. But it was the core of steel inside her that made him want to know everything about her. What she was thinking, what her dreams were, what she wanted out of her life.

"Damn straight," he belatedly replied. Then ordered, "Kiss me."

Erin looked left and right, then said, "But we're in public."

"Yup. And anyone could come down the hallway and see us making out. Kiss me anyway." Conor knew he was being bossy, but couldn't help it. Between TJ warning him off and Quint telling her he'd set her up with one of his officer friends, he needed to taste her again.

Hell, who was he kidding, he didn't need an excuse.

Without waiting for her to respond, he leaned down and took her lips with his. This time, she immediately opened to him. Her tongue came out and pressed against his lips, demanding entry. With a groan, he gave in, giving her access to his mouth. Erin was more aggressive than she'd been any other time he'd kissed her. Those other times, she let him take the lead and mimicked his actions.

This time, she took charge. Running her tongue over his, licking his lips and tilting her head on her own so she could take him deeper.

Conor was the one who finally broke the kiss, needing to get control over the situation before he came in his pants. "Fuck, you are so sexy," he told her softly.

Erin blushed, but smiled at him. "I like kissing you."

"And I like you kissing me," Conor reassured her. His eyes dropped to her shirt. "And I like seeing this." He ran the back of his hand over her erect nipple, clearly visible under her T-shirt. She inhaled sharply and her head dropped to look at her chest.

"Oh," she gasped and brought a hand up to cover her breast. "I didn't realize...I've never..." Her voice dropped off in confusion at seeing her body's reaction to his touch.

Conor reminded himself that she was new to all this. What he really wanted to do was shove his hand under her shirt and feel that erect nipple on his bare skin, but he refrained. He hugged her to him, and sighed in relief when her hands rounded his back and returned his embrace.

"It'll go down," he tried to reassure her.

"I'm not sure it will when all I can think of is how good I feel when I kiss you."

Conor groaned. "This obviously wasn't the best idea, because the last thing I want is for you to go back behind the bar and have every pervert in the place checking out my woman's tits."

Erin giggled and pulled back. "It's your fault. If you weren't so sexy, I wouldn't get so excited."

Conor rolled his eyes, then looked back down at her. "When do you get off tonight?"

"Midnight. Since it's Tuesday, the boss is letting me go home before closing because we're not that busy."

"I'd like to stay and make sure you get home all right," Conor said.

"Really?" Her head tilted.

"Yeah."

"I can get home by myself. I've been doing it a long time."

"I know."

She looked at him with an unreadable expression on her face, then smiled. "I'd like that. I've never had someone be that concerned about me before."

"Well, now you have me."

"Yeah, now I have you," she echoed, looking extremely pleased.

"Erin! Break's over!" her boss yelled from the end of the hallway.

"Coming!" she hollered back. Taking a step away from Conor, she asked, "Do I look okay?"

"You look amazing," Conor replied automatically. And she did. She might be conservative in how she dressed, but it didn't stop his imagination.

Erin gave him a small smile, then backed away and headed down the hall to do her job.

Conor sauntered out after her and went back to the table with his friends.

"You are so whipped," Dax commented as Conor settled himself into his chair.

"Yup," he agreed.

"It's good to see, man," Cruz said.

"Welcome to the club," Quint added.

"You guys are kinda pathetic," TJ said as he took a sip of his beer.

"You won't think that when you find your own woman," Dax told him.

"What if I already found her?" TJ fired back.

Everyone stared at him in shock.

"You're dating someone?" Dax asked.

TJ sighed and shook his head. "No. I fucked up. Found someone who liked me just as I was. Even with my anger issues and dealing with shit from that last tour I'd been on...she didn't seem to care. Then I fucked it up. Left. Thought she'd be better off without me."

"How long did it take for you to get your head out of your ass?" Quint asked.

TJ chuckled, although it wasn't a humorous sound. "Long enough that when I went back for her, she was gone."

"Damn," Cruz said. "That sucks."

"Yeah."

"You've got the resources, why don't you look her up? Find her?" Conor asked.

TJ turned to him, and Conor almost flinched at the look of self-recrimination on the other man's face. "Because I was a dick. Because there's no way she'd want anything to do with me after what I did to her. Besides, it's been years. She's probably married with kids by now."

"You won't know unless you try. If there was a chance she'd take you back, would you try to find her?" Dax asked.

TJ's response was immediate. "Yes."

The other man raised one eyebrow at him as if to say, "Well?"

TJ sighed.

No one said anything for a long moment before Conor offered, "Maybe she's waiting for you to fight for her. Maybe she had to leave back then because something happened to her or her family. You have no idea what occurred, and I can't believe a man like you—a man I respect and trust more than most—wouldn't even try to find out what went down between the time you left her, and got your head out of your ass and went back to her. If you never try to find her, you're an idiot."

"Well, don't hold back, tell me exactly what you think," TJ grumbled into his beer.

The other men laughed, but they obviously agreed with their friend.

"I have no idea what kind of woman would want to be with someone who examines dead bodies for a living," Calder chimed in. "But when I find her, I'm not letting her go."

"And speaking of women who want to be with us...I'm gonna get home," Dax said as he swallowed the last of the beer in his glass. "Mackenzie has tomorrow off, so we can...sleep in." He grinned evilly.

"I'm out of here too," Cruz stated. "Mickie *doesn't* have the day off tomorrow, so I need to get home before it gets too late and she's completely comatose."

The others hung around long enough to finish the pitchers of beer Erin had brought to the table, and then said their goodbyes as well. Conor wandered over to the bar and hitched himself up on a barstool. He asked Erin for a glass of water, and they spent the rest of the evening flirting with each other.

Hours later, after he'd given Erin a good-night kiss at her doorstep, Conor smiled at the text he'd received from her as he drove home. As was her usual, Erin had sent him a note as soon as he'd left her side, complete with emojis, including a pencil, a tennis ball, and a barber shop pole. They made no sense to him, but he liked to see those random pictures, because they were so her. But it was her words that burrowed into his heart and wouldn't let go.

ERIN: You make me forget that I was ever unhappy.

PUTTING his phone down to be safe while he was driving, Conor couldn't stop the huge smile. He hated that Erin had ever been unhappy, but he'd spend the rest of his life making sure she wasn't ever that way again.

8

"Come to Christmas dinner with me," Conor asked after their usual morning run. They were both sweaty, but it had been exhilarating. It was a bit chilly, but not too bad for Texas. They'd been having a mild winter so far, and running in the morning was actually pleasant rather than being too cold.

"Oh, uh...I don't know."

"I want you to meet my sisters. And my parents. They're going to love you." Conor was willing to push, but if she truly didn't want to, he'd relent.

They were walking back toward their cars and Conor reached for her hand. They held hands as they walked, and he thought she wasn't going to answer him.

"It's not that I don't want to meet them," Erin said quietly.

"What is it then?"

She stopped and turned to face him. Conor refused to let go of her hand even when he felt her grip loosen. "We've been dating for three weeks," Conor said. "We've talked on the phone every day since that canoe trip. Christmas is a big deal in my family, and I want to share it with you. I can't stand the thought of you being alone in your apartment on Christmas."

Erin bit her lip. "I told you that I don't do Christmas."

"I know you did. But you haven't said why."

She wouldn't meet his eyes. "It just doesn't bring back good memories for me."

"Let me help you make better ones then," he cajoled.

Erin looked anywhere but at Conor. He waited her out. Finally, she looked up at him. "Okay."

"Okay?"

"Yeah."

Conor pulled her to him and hugged her.

"Conor! I'm all sweaty!" she exclaimed.

"So am I. Who cares!" But he pulled back enough so he could see her face. "Seriously, thank you. This is gonna be great. Promise."

She didn't look convinced, but he appreciated the smile she tried to give him. "What time and what should I bring?"

"If it's okay, I'll pick you up around one. Mom always has dinner ready early, like four. It'll give us a bit of time to hang out with everyone before we eat."

"Should I bring presents?" she asked quietly.

Conor shook his head. "No. I'll take care of it. I'll just put your name on the stuff I got."

Her brows came down at that. "You can't do that."

"Why not?"

"Well...because."

Conor laughed. "That's not a reason, bright eyes.

Look, I asked you to come. It's short notice. You don't know my family. It's no problem saying the gifts are from both of us."

"But won't that give them ideas?"

"Ideas?"

"Yeah."

"I'm not sure what you're saying, but yeah, it'll let them know that I'm serious about you, which they'll know anyway because the last time I brought a woman to a holiday meal with my family was...never."

She stared up at him, her green eyes huge in her face. "You've never brought a woman home to meet your family?"

"Not in a long time, and never to Christmas dinner."

"Maybe I shouldn't—"

"Erin," he interrupted. "I really want you there. I want to show you off."

"But we haven't even..." She looked away from him, then brought her eyes back to his. "We haven't spent the night together, haven't done more than kiss."

Conor leaned into her and rested his forehead against hers. "So?"

"Maybe it's too soon."

"It's not too soon. We might not have made love yet, or done whatever else is going on in your brain that makes you think a man and woman are officially together, but I can tell you this." He paused for dramatic effect before he continued. "I've never wanted a woman the way I want you. So you agreeing means the world to me. Whatever your preconceived notions are for how a relationship should work, ignore them. We're us. We're making our own rules."

She swallowed hard. "Okay."

"Okay," he repeated, smiling at her. "I'm incredibly happy, Erin. *You* make me happy."

"Me too," she said immediately.

"Good. Unfortunately, I have to get going. I'm helping another officer with a poaching investigation today."

"Is it dangerous?"

Conor shrugged. "Anything can be dangerous, but this shouldn't be. We're just calling people who know the guy we think shot and left a deer in a field. Trying to get information. We'll also be looking at his social media to see if he posted any pictures or bragged about it."

"Sometimes I forget that you're a cop," Erin said softly, running her finger up and down his chest as she spoke. "You'll be careful?" she asked, looking up at him.

Conor grabbed her finger and brought it up to his lips. He kissed the tip. "Yeah, bright eyes, I'll be careful."

"Good."

"You get your grades posted?" He knew she'd been working hard to grade the final exams she'd given so she could put the grades into the university's computer system.

She nodded. "Yeah."

"So you're free until the spring semester starts?"

She smiled. "Sorta. I need to get started on my lectures for January. And I always redo my tests. Students are way too savvy and I know they pass them around in the hopes the professors are too lazy to make new ones each semester."

"Ah, to be eighteen again," Conor said. Then added, "Not."

They both laughed.

"I'm really happy you're coming to dinner, Erin."

She nodded. It wasn't lost on him that she didn't say she was happy too.

"Want to hang out tonight?" he asked. He knew she had the night off from bartending.

"I'd like that."

"Me too. I'll call when I get off, okay?"

"Sounds good."

Conor knew he had to get going. He leaned down and kissed her. It wasn't exactly a peck on the lips, but it wasn't a full make-out kiss either. He pulled back. "I'll see you later."

"Later."

He backed away as he headed for his truck. She walked in the opposite direction, headed for her Jeep parked on the other end of the street outside the entrance to the park where they usually ran.

As he headed home to shower and get ready for work, Conor couldn't help but smile. He knew she had reservations about meeting his folks, but hoped after she saw how awesome they were, she'd loosen up. He figured she was nervous simply because of her situation with her dad leaving and her mom not being the best maternal figure. He couldn't wait for her to see how a family was supposed to work. It was going to be the best Christmas yet.

∾

IT WAS GOING to be the worst Christmas ever.

Erin couldn't believe she'd agreed to go to Conor's parents' house. Not only that, but she was going for *dinner*. A special dinner that would probably have several courses and there'd be way too much food. She'd look rude if she refused to eat much, but she'd be completely miserable if she went ahead and ate what she didn't want.

She closed her eyes and tried to think of a way she could change her mind. Maybe she could call her boss at The Sloppy Cow and get him to put her on the schedule. She shook her head. No, the bar was closed on the twenty-fourth and fifth. That wouldn't work.

She could pretend to be sick! No, she couldn't do that either. She didn't want to lie to Conor, but she wasn't comfortable opening up to him yet. Intellectually, she knew she didn't have anything to be embarrassed about, but emotionally she wasn't ready to tell him about how she used to look. To explain that mealtimes were actually torture for her. Her dysfunctional relationship with food wasn't something a new boyfriend wanted to know about...was it?

That was the thing, she had no idea. Was she supposed to spill her guts before they slept together? What if she didn't and he saw her scars from her skin-removal surgeries and was repulsed? She'd worn long-sleeve shirts and pants for so long, it had become second nature to hide behind her clothes.

She rested her elbow on her desk, thankful the university was practically deserted now that all the students had left for Christmas break, and tried to think rationally about what she'd agreed to do.

After thirty minutes, Erin thought she finally had a plan. She'd go to dinner, meet his family, sample everything his mom cooked, even though it would kill her to eat that much, then after Christmas, she'd let him know about her surgeries. She had the thought that she should probably tell him before she went to his parents' house and met his family, but she simply didn't feel ready yet. And when she shared her past, she'd totally downplay how much she'd weighed. Then, if he wanted, she'd sleep with him.

Truth be told, she wanted him. Wanted to know what all the hoopla was about. She liked it when she used her vibrators, but the orgasms she had weren't anything to get too excited about. Hopefully being with a flesh-and-blood man would make it better.

She wasn't sure how it was going to work though. She wanted Conor. Wanted him bad. Wanted to see his beautiful body, run her hands all over it, but she didn't want him to see *her*. She couldn't bear to have his rock hard body next to her own not-quite-as-perfect one.

She covered her eyes and sighed. She should just break up with him now. She was a mess. A complete mess. He deserved better.

Just then, her phone vibrated with an incoming email. Picking up her phone, Erin unlocked it and clicked on the app.

Speak of the devil. She'd been thinking so hard about him, it was almost weird that she'd received an email at the same time. She clicked on Conor's name and opened the message.

· · ·

HEY, bright eyes. I wanted to send a note to let you know how happy you've made me. I know this is hard on you. I don't know why, but I hope you'll tell me someday, so I can reassure you and make it better for you. My parents are going to want to adopt you. My sisters are going love you. Mary's kids are going to want you to be their new babysitter.

The bottom line is that they're going to take one look at you and decide you're way too good for the likes of me. They'll probably spend the entire time asking why you're with a reprobate like me. Just ignore them. :)

But Erin, if at any time it gets to be too much, just say the word and we'll leave. I want you to meet my family because you've become important to me. Very important. But don't think it's escaped my notice that this will be the first meal we've shared together. I haven't pried, but I know there's some-thing to that. So if we need to bail before Mom serves the lasagna (it's not traditional, but we have turkey at Thanksgiv-ing, and Mom once said it was such a pain to cook the bird, that she wasn't doing it twice within a couple of weeks. Since we all love pasta, we agreed wholeheartedly. Lol), we will.

I hope you are having a good day. I can't wait to see you tonight.

Love, Conor

ERIN'S EYES filled with tears. How she'd managed to end up with a man like Conor for her first boyfriend, she had no idea. She'd fully expected to have to go through a couple of horrible relationships before she'd found a man she wanted to spend the rest of her life with. Nope. She could totally see herself with Conor. But until she came clean with him, she had no idea if he could see himself with *her*.

The fear of sliding and going back to what she used to be was always in her mind. It was her greatest fear. She never wanted to weigh that much again. Even though she'd done it to herself, it was awful. She'd been in constant pain, and the ridicule and censure she saw in other people's eyes on a daily basis was horrible.

She always felt as if she was one bite of food away from being Eat-more Erin again.

Putting the phone down—she couldn't email Conor back right now—she took a deep breath and pulled her keyboard closer. She had work to do. She'd get it done, *then* think about what she'd agreed to do.

THAT NIGHT, after dinner of course, Erin opened the door of her apartment to Conor. She swallowed hard at seeing him. He was so handsome, but tonight he'd obviously gone out of his way to look nice for her. He was wearing a tight pair of jeans that hugged his legs in all the right places. Her eyes went up his body, past the dark brown cowboy boots she'd only seen him wear one other time, over his muscular thighs straining at the material of his jeans, past the bulge at his groin. He was wearing a button-down light blue oxford shirt, open at his neck. The color complimented his hair and eyes. He'd shaved before he'd come over because she couldn't see any sign of the five o'clock shadow she'd halfway fallen in love with on their canoe trip.

When her gaze met his, she was startled to see desire sparkling there...for her.

"You look beautiful," he said softly, not making a move to enter.

"Thanks. You look great too," Erin told him, stepping back and motioning him inside. She was wearing a pair of loose-fitting black slacks and a forest-green blouse with three-quarter-length sleeves. She'd left her hair down and had gone out of her way to attempt to curl it.

Conor took a step toward her and caught her hand with his. He pulled her into him without a word and lowered his head. He brushed over her lips once, then twice. The third time, he pressed into her, deepening the kiss.

Erin met his tongue with her own, more than happy to have him in her space. After several moments of intense kissing, he pulled back. He turned and closed the door behind him, making sure to lock it securely.

"The rest of your day go okay?" he asked.

Erin nodded, suddenly nervous. She didn't know why. Maybe because this was only the third time he'd been in her apartment. When he'd asked to come over tonight she'd agreed, but hadn't thought about what they'd do. Since it was after dinner, she didn't even have preparing food as a distraction. She fiddled with the hem of her blouse and bit her lip, trying to think about what to say.

"Hey," he said softly, using his finger under her chin to raise her head. "What's wrong?"

"Nothing," Erin replied immediately.

"Don't do that," Conor told her. "If something's wrong, I want to know about it so I can try to fix it."

"I'm just...nervous."

"Why?"

She shrugged.

"Come on," Conor said, turning and tugging her after him as he made his way inside and to her TV room. It wasn't a big apartment, but was big enough for her. A small kitchen, medium-size room with her TV, two bedrooms, two bathrooms. It was plenty.

He walked her to the couch and sat, pulling her onto his lap.

"Relax, bright eyes. Don't be nervous with me. We can just chill here and do nothing. You don't need to entertain me."

"Did you have a good day? Did you find the poacher?" Erin asked, trying to do as he said, relax.

Conor's hand caressed up and down her thigh as if he didn't even know he was doing it. Erin shivered. It felt really good. She liked his hands on her, even if they made her uncomfortable sometimes, simply because she wasn't used to being touched.

"Nope, but we made progress. We found an ex-girlfriend who was happy to tell us about some of his past exploits. We can't nail him for those, but it does show a pattern. We're going to stake out the field where we found the deer and see if we can't catch him in the act."

"Is he stupid enough to go back to the same place?" Erin asked, relaxing more now that they were talking.

"Probably. You have to realize hunters have their favorite spots, just as fishermen have their favorite lakes to fish in. They believe they can't be caught and that there's no harm in killing one or two deer illegally. After all, there's lots more where those came from."

"There aren't?"

"That's not the point," Conor said, and Erin could tell he was passionate about the subject. "There are hunting seasons for a reason. Back in the day there were no rules about fishing in the Bering Sea or up in Canadian waters. Big companies caught as many crab and fish as they could. No one thought anything about it. Slowly but surely, the animals became harder and harder to find, simply because they'd been fished to within an inch of their lives. Luckily, rules were made and the crab population is recovering. It's the same with hunting. If there weren't any rules, then the animals would disappear. Don't get me wrong, hunting is a good thing. I firmly believe it's in the animals' best interests. It culls the herds and makes it so they aren't overpopulated."

"I understand. Some people might say that you're spending too much time trying to catch one guy who's breaking the laws, but if they aren't upheld, then everyone would think it's okay to kill whatever they want, whenever they want, right?" Erin asked.

Conor smiled at her. "Exactly. And it pisses me off that someone would so callously kill an animal for sport. Most hunters are very good about using the meat from the animals they kill. They aren't just out there shooting for the fun of it. They're doing it to bring the meat home to their families. Killing a deer and leaving it to rot just isn't cool."

"Do you hunt?" Erin asked, eager to find out more about Conor.

"Yup. I usually try to get out the first day or two of deer season. I get my allotted deer, then I can concentrate on policing the other hunters for the rest of the season."

"Do you find a lot of violations?"

Conor shrugged. "A fair amount, but a lot of what we do is education. We're not out there handing out tickets left and right. I've gotten pretty good at cutting through the bullshit people try to feed me. I can tell if they made an honest mistake, or if they know exactly what they're doing and are purposely trying to be deceptive."

Erin relaxed even farther into Conor, and he settled more comfortably on her couch. They talked for a couple of hours about his job, hers, and what races were coming up that they were participating in.

Erin wanted to tell Conor about her past. But she couldn't find the right words. When he talked about what time he'd pick her up next week to go to his parents' house, she almost did, but then he started talking about his nieces and how cute they were.

Then when he mentioned different ways to cook squirrel, deer, and wild boar, she opened her mouth to tell him that she wasn't a good cook, and why, but chickened out.

"You are so beautiful," Conor said in a lull in the conversation. The only light in the room was coming from a lamp on one of the tables next to the couch. They'd shifted until they were both lying on the cushions, Erin's back to the couch and partly draped over Conor's body. He had one arm around her and the other was playing with her hair.

Erin knew she was blushing and simply smiled at him.

Without another word, he leaned close and kissed her. The next thing she knew, she was on her back and Conor's hand was resting at her belly, playing with the hem of her shirt. He picked up his head and looked down at her. "May I?"

Swallowing hard, Erin nodded.

Slowly, as if he knew she was on the verge of leaping off the couch like a scared teenager, his fingers eased under the garment and up to her breasts. He didn't rip off her shirt or take his eyes from hers.

"I've dreamed of touching you from the first time I saw you...as you know, because I told you on our way to Big Bend." His fingers reached her right breast and he skated them over the cotton material of her bra. His touch was light, but Erin felt her nipples peak with excitement at even that soft touch.

"You're so responsive. I want you to know, I'm not going to hurt you. We'll take things as slow as you need them to be."

Erin couldn't swallow. Her mouth was as dry as the Sahara Desert.

"Does this feel good?"

She nodded. It did. He'd wrapped his hand around her bra-clad breast and was kneading her flesh gently.

He looked down for the first time, and Erin saw his pupils dilate with lust. Without asking permission this time, his head dipped and he nuzzled her erect nipple through her shirt.

"Conor," Erin croaked. One of her hands came up to

his head and pressed against the back of it, urging him on.

As if that was what he'd been waiting for, Conor pushed the cup of her bra up and over her breast. At the first touch of his fingers rolling her sensitive nipple, her back arched and she groaned.

His hand immediately went to the other side, pushing the bra off that breast as well. As his fingers went to work on that nipple, his mouth closed around her shirt—and the tight bud on the other side.

"Oh my God, Conor!" Erin exclaimed. She hadn't ever felt anything so amazing in all her life. It almost scared her. Just as she was ready to push him away because the feelings were too intense, Conor's head lifted and he looked at her.

"Beautiful." His fingers didn't stop their movement, teasing and plucking at her erect nipples. "Even without seeing you, I know you're beautiful."

He couldn't have said anything more perfect.

"I know I'm pushing it, but I want to see you come for me. Will you touch yourself while I play here?"

His thumb flicked over her nipple as he spoke, sending sparks between her legs. Erin was embarrassed, but she nodded anyway. She wanted this. Wanted him.

Conor used his free hand to grab one of hers, and he kissed her palm. Then he pressed it flat against her stomach and, keeping his hand over hers, pushed it down to the fastening of her pants. She awkwardly undid the tie even as Conor lowered his head and began to suck on her nipple through the fabric of her shirt once again.

Without urging this time, Erin moved her fingers

through the opening of her pants and under her cotton panties. She touched her clit with her index finger and jerked in response to how sensitive she felt.

Conor's hand didn't follow hers under her panties, but he did place it over her soaked folds between her legs. She wasn't sure if he could tell how wet she was through the layers, but his next words cleared that up.

"You're so wet. God, Erin. You feel amazing. Go on, make yourself feel good." Then his head dropped, and she knew he'd been going easy on her before now. Because now he wasn't messing around. His mouth opened wide and he took in as much of her breast as he could. He plumped up her mound with his hand under her shirt and...feasted.

Erin threw her head back and lost herself in the feelings coursing through her body. She usually took quite a while to orgasm, but she knew without a doubt that wouldn't be the case at the moment. She was halfway there before she'd even touched herself.

Conor's mouth and hand at her chest kept her on the edge, and her own finger flicking over her clit pushed her right to the point of no return.

"Conor!" she cried, not knowing what she needed.

But he did. He pressed the heel of his hand hard against her pussy lips and bit down on her nipple through her shirt. The combination did the trick. She jerked against him and came. When she would've moved her fingers away from her clit, he grabbed her wrist and held her in place. He used his strength to move her hand up and down, prolonging the intense feelings coursing through her.

It could've been an hour or thirty seconds. Erin wasn't sure, but when she opened her eyes, Conor was smiling down at her. His hand was lying motionless over her right breast and he still held her wrist in his hand. Seeing she was back with him, he pulled on her hand and she winced as her finger rolled over her clit one more time as he removed it from her pants.

Not dropping his eyes from hers, he pulled her hand up to his face and only then did he look away from her. He eyed her glistening finger as if it was a lollipop, and before she could protest, he'd taken her finger deep into his mouth.

They both groaned at the same time.

Erin wanted to pull away, but the feeling of his tongue wrapping around her finger and licking every drop of her juices off the digit was erotic as hell, and she couldn't seem to move.

Without a word, Conor pulled her finger from his mouth with a pop and laid it on her stomach once more. He covered her hand with his and took a deep breath.

Now that Erin wasn't lost in the feelings he'd provoked, she realized that he was rock hard against her hip. She shifted, feeling awkward and unsure about what she was supposed to do.

"Can I?" she asked, trying to move her hand to the front of his pants.

Conor stopped her by putting pressure on her hand, keeping it where it was.

"I'm good," he told her softly.

"But you didn't...you're still hard," she protested.

"I am," he agreed easily, his body completely relaxed next to hers.

"Don't you want me to?"

He lifted his head at that. "I want you, Erin. Make no mistake. But this isn't a tit for tat kind of thing. I know you're new to this, and I'm not going to rush you. I got just as much pleasure from watching you come, feeling you against me and tasting you, as I would from having an orgasm myself."

Erin's eyebrow went up at that. "Really?"

"Okay," he conceded. "Maybe not exactly the same amount of pleasure, but close. That was a gift, bright eyes. Thank you."

"You're welcome." Erin wasn't sure what else she was supposed to say to that. She yawned huge and blushed when she saw Conor smirking down at her.

"Sorry."

"Don't apologize. Sleep."

"It's late."

"I know. I'll show myself out in a bit."

Erin snuggled against Conor's chest. He moved his hand out from under her shirt and grasped her hip. He turned her until they were chest to chest. She tucked her head under his chin. "Wake me up when you go," she ordered sleepily.

"I will."

Erin's eyes were closed, but she wanted to tell him one more thing before she was out. "Conor?"

"Yeah, bright eyes?"

"There's stuff I need to tell you about me. But I'm afraid you'll not like me anymore when I do."

"I'm going to like you no matter what you tell me."

"Promise?"

"Promise. Now shhhh. Sleep."

"You're the best thing that's ever happened to me," Erin mumbled. She was asleep before she heard his response.

But later, after he'd kissed her on the forehead and let her know he was leaving, she dragged herself to her bed and snuggled under the covers, remembering how amazing the night had been. He'd had his hands on her and she hadn't freaked out.

Her phone vibrated with a text and she reached out a hand to grab it. The words there made her smile in relief and excitement.

CONOR: *You're the best thing that's ever happened to me too. Talk to you later. Sleep well.*

9

ERIN FIDGETED in the seat next to Conor. They were on their way to his parents' house and she *so* wasn't ready. She was well aware that he thought she was mostly uneasy about meeting his family, but that wasn't it, at least not all of it.

The last time she'd actually sat down at a formal meal was...she couldn't remember when. At home, she grabbed something and ate it standing up. If she had something at The Sloppy Cow, it was the same—she ate it standing and on the go. Functions at the university were typically informal and only had finger foods. It was easy enough to carry around a small plate with one hors d'oeuvre on it. People assumed that she'd already eaten and didn't give her grief about trying this or that.

But sitting at a table with Conor's family was a whole different thing. She couldn't exactly pretend to eat, but she knew if she forced herself to consume too much, she'd regret it. Her stomach had stretched out since her surgery and she could eat more than the couple of bites she used to be able to, but she absolutely couldn't gorge herself. And Erin was deathly afraid that she'd have to eat way more than she was used to, just to be polite.

It was stupid. She should've just told Conor what was bothering her, but it was way too late now.

He pulled his truck into a well-kept neighborhood and Erin tried not to hyperventilate. She'd had a nightmare last night about Conor's mom putting a plate in front of her when they were all seated around a huge oval table that was piled high with food. So much so it was falling off the sides.

The older woman had smiled huge in the dream and told her to "eat up." Then she'd added, "No one leaves the table until their plate is empty." Erin had woken up in a cold sweat and hadn't been able to fall back to sleep for the rest of the night. It wasn't that she thought Conor's family would be mean, but food was such a hot button for her.

It wasn't until Conor had parked and taken her hand in his that she realized she was shaking.

"Hey...look at me, Erin."

She turned her eyes to his.

"It's going to be fine. I would never bring you into a situation that would cause you harm. Got it?"

She nodded. She knew he wouldn't, but he didn't know about her issues simply because she hadn't told him.

He beamed and leaned over and kissed her on the lips. "Come on, let's get this over with. Once you see how great they are, you'll relax."

Conor gave her face one last caress with his hand,

then turned and climbed out. Erin followed suit on her side and reached into the back and grabbed two of the gift bags Conor had brought with him.

She met him at the front of his truck and he immediately snagged her hand and held it tightly in his as they walked up to the front door.

It opened before they got there, and Erin stepped back in alarm as a woman flew out of the house at Conor.

He laughed and caught her while they hugged as if they hadn't seen each other in months.

"Chill, Mary," Conor ordered. "You're gonna scare my girlfriend."

At that, the woman, who Erin knew to be the middle sister, turned to her. "It's so good to meet you!" she exclaimed, and engulfed Erin in a huge hug.

Startled, Erin couldn't move, but she did manage to mumble, "It's good to meet you too," before the other woman let go. Mary grabbed the gift bags out of Erin's hand and shoved them at her brother. "Come on, the others are dying to meet you. We can't wait to get to know everything about you. I have no idea what you see in my brother, but I won't hold that against you." She beamed and started dragging Erin inside the house.

"Jesus, Mary," Conor grumbled. "You gonna let her breathe before you start trying to get all the juicy details about our relationship out of her?"

Mary stopped in her tracks just inside the front door of the house. "Are you still here? Why don't you go help Dad with the grill?"

"The grill?" Conor asked. "Aren't we having lasagna?"

"Of course. But it's been so mild, Dad decided that we needed some brats as well."

Erin shuddered. More food. Figured.

"I'm not leaving Erin with you guys until she's at least met everyone," Conor proclaimed, putting his hand on the small of Erin's back as they entered the house.

Erin liked that. She turned her head and mouthed, "Thank you," to him as Mary continued to tow her toward what sounded like a huge group of people.

Conor simply smiled at her.

That gave her the courage to carry on. She could do this. These were Conor's people. His family. He was amazing, and so his family had to be also, Erin reasoned.

Mary pulled her through a set of double pocket doors and stopped. "Hey, everyone. Conor and Erin are finally here!"

Erin knew the smile on her face was forced, but she couldn't help it. Conor took her hand from his sister and led her from one person to another, introducing his family to her.

"This is my youngest sister, Karen, and her boyfriend, George Parks. You met Mary at the door, this is her husband, Alfred Wells. And their kids, Honey and Sarah." Conor kept moving after she shook each person's hand. "And this is my mom and dad, Pauline and John."

Erin licked her dry lips and said, "It's nice to meet you."

"Oh, sweetie, it's so great to meet *you*. We were afraid Conor would never find a girlfriend."

"For God's sake, Mom. Stop it."

John stepped forward and shook her hand heartily.

"Merry Christmas, Erin. We're thrilled you could join us. Especially since you don't have close family to spend this wonderful holiday with. Please consider our house, *your* house." And with that, he turned to his wife, kissed her on the cheek and mumbled, "Gotta get back to the grill." Then he smiled at her, ran his hand over his youngest granddaughter's head, and moved toward a sliding glass door.

After he'd left the room, everyone started talking at once. Erin blinked. She watched as Conor's mom and Mary headed through a door she could tell led to a kitchen. The two kids tugged on Karen's hands and brought her back to the couch. One clicked on a remote and a movie with a talking dog started up on the television.

Alfred and George wandered out the door to help Mr. Paxton at the grill.

That left Erin standing with Conor. She looked up at him with what she knew were big eyes.

He chuckled and kissed her lightly on the lips. "You're not running screaming out the door. I take it that's a good sign?"

"I'm still considering it," she said softly. "But I'm not sure that would make the best impression."

"Thank you," Conor said solemnly.

"For what?"

"For coming over today. I know I kinda coerced you into it, but I appreciate it. In case you didn't notice, I like you." He grinned to let her know he was teasing. "And I really wanted you to meet the most important people in my life...because I consider you one of those people."

Erin knew she should've been freaked out. They'd only been dating for a month, but they'd known each other for a lot longer than that. And honestly, she wasn't that nervous about meeting his parents or sisters. He was awesome, so it figured that they would be too. That wasn't what was making her a nervous wreck.

"I...you're important to me too," Erin said.

"Good. Come on, let's go sit." He led her over to a love seat next to the couch and settled her before sitting next to her. *Right* next to her.

As they made small talk with his nieces and sister, Erin realized something she'd been too overwhelmed to make note of earlier.

Most of his family was overweight.

And not just a little bit. His mom had to be pushing three hundred pounds, his sisters probably two-fifty. His brother-in-law was also a big man, probably two-fifty himself, but as he was tall, the weight was distributed pretty evenly. The only person, other than the kids, who wasn't carrying more weight than he should was his dad.

Before she could really think about it, Conor's mom brought out a tray of snacks. She placed it on the coffee table, smiled at everyone, then went back into the kitchen.

Erin watched as Sarah and Honey each helped themselves to a Santa cookie. Karen leaned forward and grabbed a miniature pig-in-a-blanket and held it out to Conor.

"Con?"

Conor reached for it and popped the whole thing in his mouth at once. "Thanks," he mumbled as he chewed.

Karen picked up the tray filled with cookies, the miniature hotdogs, assorted chocolates, and cupcake papers filled with Chex mix and held it out toward Erin. "Help yourself." The smile on the other woman's face was open and friendly.

Erin swallowed hard and shook her head, words failing her.

Karen merely shrugged and put the tray back on the tabletop. She grabbed some of the Chex mix and sat back, happily munching as she turned her attention back to the television.

Erin couldn't take her eyes from the tray of food. She felt as though she'd entered the twilight zone.

George and Alfred wandered back into the room, Alfred sitting next to his kids and George taking a seat in a recliner on the other side of the couch. Everyone was smiling, laughing, and generally having a good time.

But she was in the middle of a nightmare. She'd been so careful to avoid situations where there would be food served, but here she was, staring at the plate on the table in front of her, knowing it was expected of her to snack, smile, and be social. Not only that, but looming in the not-so-distant future was the huge dinner Conor's mother had probably been slaving over all day.

The food on the tray in front of her seemed to represent every pound of weight she'd worked so hard to lose. Her throat was tight, and Erin knew if she tried to eat even one bite, it'd come back up. Wouldn't *that* be a good first impression to give Conor's family?

Erin glanced at her watch. Twenty minutes. She'd been here for twenty minutes and it felt as if it'd been hours. She would never make it through the afternoon and evening. What a disaster.

CONOR SAT at the table later that afternoon and couldn't help checking on Erin. She'd been nothing but polite throughout the day. She'd allowed Honey and Sarah to give her a tour of the house. She'd even gone into the kitchen and helped his mom and sisters in the final preparations for the dinner.

But she wasn't all right.

He didn't know how he knew, but Conor knew to the marrow of his bones that something was terribly wrong. He wanted to leave, but when he'd brought it up to Erin after he'd pulled her aside, she'd refused, saying she was having a good time.

But she'd lied.

And Conor wasn't the only one who'd noticed. His mom had been giving him worried glances throughout dinner, and even his sisters had begun to look concerned.

Erin hadn't said a word after the meal had started. She'd stared down at her plate as if the food on it was going to come alive and attack her. She'd nibbled on the lasagna, but had refused a brat when he'd offered it as the plate was passed around.

Conor didn't give a shit what she ate, but he *did* care about the faraway look in her eyes. Right in front of them, she was going cold and remote and it scared the shit out of him.

It was when his mom came into the dining room with

the two pies she'd made earlier that morning that whatever was eating at Erin finally became too much.

Conor felt her hand on his arm and looked at her. She was looking back at him, but her green eyes were dull, not the beautiful jade he'd gotten used to. She said quietly, "I'd like to go now."

He wanted to protest. Wanted to say that they were going to open presents after dinner. That he wanted to see what her reaction would be to the small gift he knew his parents had wrapped up for her. But he didn't. He'd promised.

He'd told her before they'd even entered the house that if she'd had enough, all she had to do was let him know and they'd leave. He wasn't going to renege on that now. Not when whatever she was feeling was clearly overwhelming her.

Lifting his hand, he put it on her cheek and brushed his thumb over her lips in a brief caress. "Okay, bright eyes, we'll go."

He turned to his family. "Mom, Dad, I'm sorry, but we need to get going."

Everyone protested, but Conor ignored them, standing and helping Erin get to her feet as well. He put his arm around her waist and led her away from the table. She was stiff under his hand as they walked toward the front hallway.

Conor was getting their light jackets out of the front closet when his mom came up to them.

"I'm sorry you can't stay." To her credit, she didn't try to cajole them into staying. She held out a plate covered in aluminum foil to Erin. "I made these special just for you."

But Erin didn't move. Her eyes were locked on the plate as if it was a snake that was going to reach out and bite her if she touched it.

Conor took the plate of what he knew were his mom's special cookies. They were amazing, and she only made them during the holidays. Chocolate, caramel, peanut butter, and even Butterfinger pieces. They were delicious, and eating just one could put even the hardiest person into a sugar coma for hours.

"Thanks, Mom," he said softly.

"Don't forget this," his dad said, entering the small foyer. He handed a small package wrapped in festive paper to his son.

"Appreciate it," Conor told him. He leaned forward and hugged his dad, then did the same to his mom.

"Take care of her," she whispered as they hugged.

Conor squeezed her harder. He wasn't surprised that his mom knew something big was up with Erin. He appreciated that she wasn't holding it against her though. But then again, he knew she wouldn't. His parents were the best.

"I'll call you later."

"Love you," his mom said, stepping back.

"Love you, son," his dad said, clapping Conor on the back.

Conor shoved the gift into the pocket of his jacket and balanced the plate of cookies in his other hand. He wrapped his free arm around Erin and said, "Thanks for everything. Tell Karen and Mary I'll talk to them soon.

Oh, and make sure Honey and Sarah know Erin picked out their presents." He leaned forward and whispered, "After I told her the girls liked to camp, she picked out flint and paracord shoelaces just like she has. I added the gift cards."

He smiled at Erin, but she didn't seem to be paying any attention to him. She was standing there, but her head was a million miles away.

"Take care," his mom said, sounding extremely worried as Conor walked them out of the house toward his truck. He opened the passenger door and Erin dutifully climbed in. He shut it behind her and walked around to the other side. He waved at his parents, who were standing in the doorway, their arms around each other, and climbed in.

"Talk to me, bright eyes," he implored Erin.

She turned to him, and with that blank look in her eyes, said, "I'm really tired, Conor."

He sighed. He needed to get through to her, but sitting in the driveway at his parents' house wasn't the time or place. "Can you hold this while I get us back to your place?" He held out the plate of cookies.

She stared at it for a long moment before her hands came up and she gingerly took it from him. Then she sat with her back ramrod straight, holding the plate as if it were a bomb that could explode at any moment rather than a simple stack of cookies.

Wanting nothing else but to get her home and to the bottom of what was wrong, Conor started his truck and backed out of the driveway.

He tried to make small talk as he drove to Erin's apartment, but she didn't respond. Her eyes stayed glued to the aluminum foil in her lap.

As soon as he stopped, Conor threw the truck into park and turned to the woman who was scaring the shit out of him. "Erin, please. What happened? Was it something I said? Did someone else say something to you? Talk to me."

"I'm fine, Conor," Erin told him in a wooden voice. "I'm just really tired. I'm going to go inside. Thank you for inviting me."

She was saying all the right things, but that hollow look was still in her eyes and she was breathing too fast. Conor had a lot of practice in being able to tell when people were lying, and Erin was definitely lying to him right now.

Whatever was going on, she obviously didn't want to talk to him about it. And that hurt. A lot. As much as he liked her, if she wasn't going to open up and be honest with him, he couldn't force her to. He opened his door and walked around to help her out. She hopped down and started for her apartment without looking at him.

Conor grabbed the cookies she'd left on the seat of the truck and hurried after her. He walked with her until they got to her door. She unlocked it and turned to him. "Thanks again."

"Don't forget these," he said softly, holding out the cookies. "My mom makes them special during the holidays. They're full of sugar and totally not good for you, but they're really, really good. It looks like she made you a special batch. Even I didn't get any this year."

Once again, she stared at the plate for a long moment before holding out her hands.

Conor put the plate in them and took the present out of his pocket. "They also got this for you for Christmas." He shrugged, not at all sure now about what he'd encouraged his parents to do for her. By the way she was acting, she wouldn't appreciate it. Hell, he wasn't sure he'd ever see her again after tonight. Whatever had happened had made her act like a stranger toward him. He hated it.

He had his own present he was going to give her when they got home from his folks' house. It wasn't anything tangible, but he hoped she'd enjoy it all the same. Now definitely wasn't the time to let her know about it.

"Thanks."

That was it. Just thanks. Conor mentally winced. Refusing to give up, he leaned toward her and took her face between his hands. He tilted her head up to his. "I'm worried about you, bright eyes. It's killing me to leave, but I know that's what you want me to do."

She nodded. The movement small and stilted.

"It's too early...but I love you, Erin. You've made my life exciting and happy over the past month. You're the first thing I think about when I wake up in the mornings and the last when I go to sleep at night. I want to spend all my days with you by my side. Please...whatever happened tonight, don't give up on us. On me."

"Good night, Conor," Erin whispered.

With nothing left to say—he'd spilled his guts and she'd continued to stare at him in that blank way—Conor dropped his hands and took a step back.

"*I'm* not giving up on us," he informed her. "I work tomorrow, but I'll stop by before my shift starts at ten."

She didn't say another word, just closed the door. Conor heard the lock engage and the safety chain pull across its track.

He sighed and stared at the closed door for a long moment then turned and walked back to his truck. Before he left, he pulled out his phone and sent the woman he loved a text.

CONOR: *I love you.*

10

CONOR COULDN'T SLEEP. He'd dropped Erin off two hours ago, and he hadn't stopped worrying about her since. His mom had called and he'd talked to her about what had happened. Neither of them could figure out what had made Erin disappear into herself.

Pacing his small living room, he racked his brain trying to remember everything that was said and done that day. She'd seemed to be okay—uncomfortable, but all right—before dinner. It wasn't until they'd sat down that she'd gotten stiff.

He nodded to himself. Dinner. That was it. He remembered that she'd told him the first time he'd asked her out that she didn't do meal dates. It had to be it.

Conor had no idea what had happened to Erin in the past, but whatever it was had to be connected to meals. Just as he made up his mind to head back over to her house because he couldn't stay away, his phone vibrated.

Praying harder than he ever had in his life that it wasn't work—the worst thing that could happen would be for him to get called in *now* for an investigation or to back up one of his fellow wardens—Conor looked down at his phone.

He didn't even have to unlock it to see the text. The fact that there were no emojis attached to it said almost as much as the words did.

Erin: I need you. Can you come over?

His legs were moving before his brain caught up. He typed out a quick text even as he was climbing into his truck. Conor didn't remember locking his house, but at the moment, all he could think about was Erin.

Conor: On my way.

She needed him. The three words echoed in his brain. Was she all right? Had she hurt herself? Ignoring the fact that it was dangerous, Conor typed out another text as he raced down his street.

Conor: Are you hurt? Do I need to call an ambulance?

He didn't have to wait long for her response. It only made him feel marginally better.

Erin: No

Short and to the point. He didn't know which question she was answering, but it didn't matter if the answer was the same to both. Putting his phone on the seat next to him, Conor concentrated on the road and getting to the woman he loved.

He pulled into her parking lot in record time and raced up to her door. He knocked and said, "Erin? It's me, Conor. Let me in."

He heard the lock click and the next thing he knew, he had Erin in his arms. She was shaking and had obviously been crying, but she didn't seem to be hurt. Conor took a step into her apartment, taking her with him. He shut the door behind him then pulled back so he could look her up and down.

Running his eyes over her, he didn't see any blood and she physically looked fine. But she was obviously *not* okay. Her eyes were red and bloodshot and she had dark bags under them. Even as he looked her over, she sniffed once more. He saw her eyes fill with tears, making the green even more vivid. Then she buried her head into his chest and shook.

He leaned down and put an arm under her knees and hauled her up into his arms. She curled tighter into him and wrapped both her arms around his neck. He walked into her living room and dropped onto the cushions of her couch with Erin on his lap.

As she cried, Conor looked around, searching for what, he wasn't sure. There weren't any pill bottles indicating she might've tried to harm herself. Nor was there anything remotely out of place. Her apartment was neat and tidy, as usual.

But the plate his mom had made sat on her coffee table, the edge of the aluminum foil peeled back just enough so the cookies could be seen...and smelled. The present they'd given her was also on the coffee table, opened. The wrapping paper sat off to the side of the picture frame.

Rocking slightly, Conor stayed quiet and let Erin cry in his arms. He hated that she was upset, but was ecstatic that she'd reached out to him. He honestly hadn't been sure she wanted to see him again when he'd dropped her off.

Finally, her tears tapered off and she lay exhausted in his arms. She cleared her throat and said in a croak, "Not much of a merry Christmas, huh?"

"I don't know. I'm with the woman I love and we're both uninjured. I'll take it."

She was silent, and Conor fought the urge to fidget under her.

"I owe you an explanation. No, several explanations, actually."

"Erin, you don't owe me anything. All I want to know is if you're okay. Everything else can wait."

Her voice wobbled, but she opened up to him. "I've told you a little bit about my childhood. As you can guess, it wasn't great. No...that's a lie. It was awful, at least after my dad left. My mom yelled at me all the time. I couldn't handle it, I missed my dad and didn't understand why he'd left. So...I started eating. It comforted me. The more my mom yelled, the more I ate. Then as I gained weight, she just yelled at me more. It was a vicious cycle.

"I hated myself, but I couldn't stop eating. I'd hide food in my room and eat it at night under the covers where my mom couldn't see me. I'm ashamed to admit it, but I stole food from kids at school when I could too. When my belly was full, I felt happy...or at least content. But it was fleeting. So damn fleeting. I needed more and more food to feel full. I got called names in school. The worst was Eat-more Erin. The more depressed I got, of course, the more I ate."

"Erin—" Conor began in a soothing tone, but she interrupted him.

"Let me finish. Please. If I stop now, I don't know that I'll ever be able to continue."

"Sorry, bright eyes, go on. Get it all out," Conor said tenderly.

"I graduated from high school and moved out. I haven't seen my mom much since then. She calls me at work every now and then and tries to insinuate herself into my life, but for my own sanity, I try to have as little to do with her as possible. But moving out didn't stop my eating, it only made it worse, since I wasn't accountable to anyone. I got a job as a middle school gym teacher, but got fired when I couldn't walk more than the length of the gym without huffing and puffing. I wasn't exactly a good role model for the kids. I don't blame the school district at all. I had money saved up, but things got scary when I had to move out of my apartment because I didn't have rent money. I'd spent it all on food."

Erin took a deep breath and tucked her head under Conor's chin. He tightened his arms around her, feeling awful for all that she'd been through.

"I was over four hundred and fifty pounds at that point. I knew if I didn't do something, I was going to die. So I went to a doctor. It took a long time, and a lot of hard work, but I was able to lose thirty pounds on my own, in part to prove that I was serious about losing the weight. Then I had gastric bypass surgery. My stomach was divided into two parts, with the section holding the food I eat becoming about the size of a walnut. Because it's so small, I can't eat as much as I did before...and if I try, I usually get sick."

"Jesus, Erin," Conor breathed.

"No, it's good. It's great, actually. I was able to lose the weight. Of course, then I had a ton of extra skin. So I had to have surgery to remove it. *That* was the hard part. It hurt. A lot." Erin shrugged. "But this is the thing...even though I look completely different now, most of the time, I don't *feel* different. I feel like the same person I've always been. I saw a therapist for a while, and that helped, but it's so weird to look in a mirror and see someone I don't recognize when I feel exactly the same *inside*. I'm still the same person who cried herself to sleep every night after my dad left. I'm still the same Erin who used food as a crutch."

Conor wasn't sure what to say to that, so instead he asked, "What happened tonight?"

She took a deep breath. "I'm not comfortable eating in front of other people. It just...I can't eat a lot still, and it makes me feel weird. I can't remember the last time I sat at an actual table and had a meal."

"Oh, Erin, you should've told me. I would've introduced you to my family a different way."

"I know. But you were so excited and I really did want to meet them."

"It was more than the dinner, wasn't it?"

Erin nodded against him. "For my entire life, food has been the enemy. I used it as a crutch when I was younger, then after my surgery it was a nuisance. Something I had to do to stay alive. I've never felt any pleasure in eating. Not after my dad left. But your—" Her voice cracked, and she cleared her throat and continued. "In your family, food is love."

Her words seemed to echo around them.

"Food has always been the antithesis of love for me. Conor, your mom is overweight. So are your sisters. But no one harped on them for how much they had to eat tonight. For snacking. Your dad couldn't stop touching your mom, it's obvious how much he loves her. And George and Alfred don't seem to see the extra weight on your sisters, either."

She looked up at him then, her green eyes piercing in their intensity, but Conor could see the sadness lurking below the surface. "I'm a virgin because no one wanted to get anywhere near Eat-more Erin. I was the laughing stock of high school and college. And now I have scars. Big ones. On my inner thighs, my arms, across my stomach. Stapling my skin back together after they cut off the excess isn't an easy thing to hide. How did your sisters find someone to love them, weighing what they do? And your dad stays with your mom even though she's fat." Her face crumpled in sorrow. "If my dad didn't want me when I was skinny, I knew there wasn't any chance for me... especially after *I* got fat."

Conor couldn't keep quiet anymore. "Oh, bright eyes, I'm so sorry you had to go through all that."

"I was trying to hang in there, but at the end, when your mom gave me those cookies?" She motioned toward them with her head. "It hit me. Hard. No one ever *gave* me food in my life. My mom constantly hid it or took it away. Then I bought it myself. Since I was fat, no one dared give me something that might make me fatter. Then when I started trying to lose weight, there was no way I would eat something like that. After the surgery, I couldn't eat solid food for the longest time, and when I did, it wasn't cookies. I can't tell you the last time I even *ate* a cookie."

"I can take them with me when I leave," Conor reassured her.

"No!" Erin cried, shaking her head. "I...your mom gave them to me. Food is love for her. You said they were special. That she doesn't make them all the time. Why'd she make them for *me*, Conor?"

"Because *you're* special, bright eyes. My mom knows how much you mean to me. And she wanted to show you in one of the only ways she knows how. Cooking for you. And you're right. She and my sisters are overweight, but their men see them for who they are inside. If you asked my dad, he'd tell you that there's just more of my mom to love."

"Why the picture?" Erin asked quietly.

Conor knew she was talking about the gift his parents had given her. He leaned forward and picked it up. It was a picture of him when he was about ten. He'd been fishing with his dad and was so proud of the first fish he'd caught that day. It was big, and he'd barely been able to hold it up.

"Mom wanted to know what she could get you for Christmas. She has thousands of pictures of me and my sisters around the house. I thought you'd get a kick out of seeing what a dorky kid I was."

"I love it," Erin told him. Then she sat up and shifted on his lap. She used her fingers to wipe her cheeks and took a deep breath. "I'm sorry about tonight. Your parents have to think I'm a head case."

"Actually, they're really worried about you. I talked to

my mom about an hour ago, and she told me I should get my butt over here and take care of whatever was hurting you. Oh, and be warned, I think she and my sisters are planning on coming to The Sloppy Cow in the near future."

Erin gaped at him. "What?"

"Yup. Erin, they loved you. Nothing you did tonight was a turnoff for them. You were nervous, they could see it. But more than that, they could sense that you're a good person."

"But I'm not."

Conor barked out a laugh. "Erin, you're way too good for me, and they know it. If it was up to them, they'd kick me out of the family and adopt you instead." He was happy to see her lips quirk as if she wanted to smile. He took her face in his hands, much as he had earlier that night. "I love you, Erin Gardner. *You.* Whether you weigh a hundred pounds or four hundred and fifty. That isn't going to change."

She bit her lip and whispered, "Even if I gained back all the weight, you'd still love me?"

"Damn straight. I love what's in here," Conor said, moving one of his hands to her chest over her heart. "And as much of an asshole as it makes me, I love that you're untouched. I hate the reasons why, but that doesn't diminish the chest-beating asshole inside of me who wants to scream 'mine and only mine' at the top of his lungs to any other man who even looks at you. And I don't give a shit about scars. I have them too. I was shot once; did you know that?"

"You were?" Erin gasped. "What happened? You're okay though, right?"

"I'm fine. Long story and I'll tell you later, but my point is that I have my own scars. I heard a saying once... scars are tattoos with better stories."

He was relieved when she smiled at that.

"From this moment on, I want to make food be love for you too, bright eyes. Not something to be ashamed about, or to hide under the covers. I'm not going to try to change your eating habits and I won't force you to any other meals at my parents' house, but I want to show you that there's absolutely nothing wrong with indulging every now and then. That when my mom makes you a pile of cookies, it means that she's accepted you."

Erin stared up at him for a long moment, then leaned over sideways. Conor immediately moved his hands to brace her as she leaned halfway over the couch. She grabbed one of his mom's cookies from the plate, then sat back. She rested her head on his shoulder and brought the cookie up to her nose. "What's in these?"

"What isn't?" Conor said quietly, feeling hope rise in his chest. "Sugar and more sugar. Chocolate, caramel, candy, and more sugar."

Erin didn't respond, but brought the cookie to her lips and took a nibble.

Conor held his breath.

She swallowed, then took an actual bite of the sugary confection. Then she handed the rest to him. Conor took it and shoved the entire thing in his mouth, not really thinking, more concerned about what was going on in Erin's head.

When she looked at him with huge eyes, he mumbled around the cookie in his mouth, "What?"

"What if I wasn't done? You just shoved it in without thought."

He smiled and chewed until he was done. He swallowed and said, "There's more where that came from."

She stared at him then sighed. "Thank you."

"For what?"

"For not running out of here screaming. For not being appalled at how much I used to weigh. For making it seem normal for me to take one bite of that cookie then give the rest to you."

"Bright eyes, in the future, if there's anything you don't want to finish, or can't, rest assured, I'll have your back."

She grinned. "Then *you'll* weigh four hundred and fifty pounds."

"Nah," he returned. "We'll go running every morning together and help each other keep things in perspective."

"I'd like that."

Conor shifted then, pulling her down on top of him as he stretched out on the couch cushions. "How was the cookie?"

"Sweet," Erin said.

"I warned you."

"You did. But it was also the most amazing thing I've ever eaten in my life. And if you touch my stash, I'll have to hurt you."

He smiled. "They'll go bad if I don't help you eat them," he cajoled.

"I have a freezer," Erin said. "I'll freeze them and eat one when I feel my sugar levels dropping too low."

Conor closed his eyes and lay back on the cushion.

"Conor?"

"I'm good," he said without opening his eyes. "I'm just relieved. I was so worried about you. I'm glad you reached out to me. And that your big bad secret wasn't big or bad."

"Um...finding out I used to weigh almost a quarter ton isn't bad?"

"Absolutely not. You telling me you had cancer would be bad. Or telling me you didn't ever want to see me again would be bad. Learning your bitch of a mother tried to make your life a living hell and that you clawed your way back to the other side is a miracle. You're *my* miracle, Erin. I thank God every day that me and my friends found The Sloppy Cow and I met you." He wrapped his arms around her and his hands flattened on her lower back. "I'll tell you something else too."

"What?" she asked, her brows furrowing in concern.

"If anyone dares insult you again, they'll have me to deal with. Those days are done, bright eyes. You're not alone anymore. I don't know if you realize this or not, but you've got a whole host of people at your back now. Me, my parents, my sisters and their men, my law enforcement friends, their girlfriends, and even my firefighter friends and their other halves. You're a part of something way bigger than you probably realize."

She propped herself up on his chest and looked down at him. She swallowed hard before saying, "I don't know what love is. I thought my dad loved me, and he left. I'm pretty convinced my mom never loved me. I haven't ever had any friends like you've had." She stopped and bit her lip.

"And?" Conor prompted.

"I haven't ever loved myself; in fact, I've hated myself for most of my life, so I don't know that I even know how to love someone else. But I want to."

"There's no pressure, Erin. I know I probably jumped the gun, but I want you to know that I absolutely care about you. This isn't casual for me. You're the first person I've brought home to meet my family in a really long time. If I have to teach you how to love again, then that's what I'll do. In the meantime, I'll be at your side, protecting you while you come out of that shell you've buried yourself in for so long."

Without a word, Erin lowered her head and kissed him.

Conor let her take control of their kiss. He loved every second of her mouth on his and did his best to lie still and let her explore.

After several moments, she leaned back. "You taste like sugar," she said quietly.

Conor chuckled. "I'm sure I do," he agreed. "Those cookies have at least a cup in each one."

"Can I try again with your family?"

"What do you mean?"

"I liked them. They're funny and I want to get to know them better."

"Absolutely."

"Maybe without the pressure of a huge holiday meal though?" she asked.

"Yeah, we can do that."

"Conor?"

"Right here, bright eyes."

"Will you stay?"

"Nothing would please me more," Conor told her emphatically. "You want to stay here or go to your bedroom?"

"Here," was her lazy reply.

Conor could feel her deadweight on his chest and closed his eyes in contentment. He never would've guessed in a million years what Erin had been through, but instead of turning him off, it only made his resolve to make her his own stronger. She'd been on her own for too long.

He made a mental note to ask Dax and Cruz if they'd made any headway in finding out anything about her father.

After hearing her story about her mother, he was even more convinced the woman had had something to do with her husband's disappearance. It would hurt Erin, but maybe more than that, she could understand that her father hadn't willingly left her. That he'd honestly and truly loved her. They could deal with the consequences of her mother's actions and move on. Hopefully together.

Before long, he felt Erin's breathing even out and her limbs relax. She'd trusted him enough to fall asleep on top of him. He just hoped he could get her to trust him that much while she was awake.

Conor's eyes went to the plate of cookies on the coffee table. He wasn't happy the simple gift had hurt her, but he was thankful, nevertheless, that they'd been the catalyst for Erin to open up to him.

Her words echoed in his brain. Food is love.

It was true. All his life, his mother had cooked for him and he'd known how much she loved him as a result. Food was never hidden, never shameful. He'd always had enough, never gone hungry. He'd never thought of his mom as fat until they'd been in the grocery store one day and he'd heard a woman mumble something rude under her breath about his mom's weight. It had surprised and shocked him, but his mom had just shaken her head and told him to ignore the woman.

His sisters had dealt with bullies too. He'd hated it then and he hated it now. Even today, people made snide comments about their weight. He'd done his best to protect them when they were kids, but he knew there were times when both Mary and Karen had considered suicide. That was why he'd acted the way he had when the boys on the camping trip had made the offhand comments about overweight people.

Conor hadn't realized it, and might not've until much later in their relationship if she hadn't come over for dinner, but he suddenly came to the conclusion that, while he and Erin might've been raised very differently, by very different parents, they'd still been through similar experiences.

He might not have been overweight, but he'd witnessed the difficulties his sisters had suffered with their extra weight while growing up, and understood on a level many others wouldn't what Erin had gone through as well.

Conor wouldn't ever be able to look at food the same way again. He'd do what he could to make food equal love for her too. Eventually.

Slowly and carefully, Conor shifted Erin until her back was against the cushions, and he was lying next to and partly under her. He kissed her on the forehead and relaxed. This was the first night they'd spent together, but it wouldn't be the last. Not by a long shot.

11

ERIN THOUGHT things would be weird between her and Conor when they woke up, especially since this was the first time they'd woken up together, but she should've known better.

"Hey, bright eyes, wake up."

She opened her eyes to see him looking down at her.

"Good morning. I hate to do this, but I need to go."

"What time is it?"

"About four."

"No wonder I'm exhausted," she said sleepily, sitting up on the couch.

"I got called in. I'm sorry we can't run this morning."

"It's okay." She looked down at her lap.

Conor put his finger under her chin and raised her head so she had no choice but to look at him. "No matter what happens the rest of the day, the best part of it was waking up with you in my arms."

Erin relaxed. "For me too."

He leaned down and kissed her gently. "Go back to sleep. I'll text you later."

"'Kay."

He'd left and she had slept for a while, finally getting up around five-thirty. She was working at The Sloppy Cow later but wanted to make sure she got in a nice long run first. Not only because she wanted to burn off some of the calories she'd eaten the night before, but because it would give her time to think.

She wandered into the kitchen to turn on her coffee maker, only to find that it was already on and the coffee was hot and waiting for her. She turned and froze.

Sitting on her counter was a banana...and a note.

As if the note was a snake that would bite her if she got too close, Erin stared at it for a long moment. Ever since her gastric bypass, she'd had a banana for breakfast. It was high in protein and did a good job of filling her up. She hadn't said anything about it, but Conor had obviously noticed while they were on the canoe trip. She'd made hash browns, bacon, and eggs for the guys, but had stuck to her banana each morning.

She reached for the note and slowly unfolded it.

I'M sorry I'm not here to eat breakfast with you. I hate missing out on our first morning together. Enjoy your banana and run. I'll talk to you soon. Love, Conor

SHE HADN'T BEEN wrong last night when she'd told him that in his family, food meant love. Here was more proof.

Inhaling deeply through her nose, Erin looked up at the ceiling, searching for control over her emotions.

After several moments, when she didn't feel the urge to burst into tears, she managed to peel and eat her banana. Then she carefully refolded the note from Conor and brought it into her room. She kneeled on the floor of her closet and pulled out her fireproof safe. She unlocked it and placed the note on top of the other items.

She had the safe mostly to protect things like her social security card, passport, and birth certificate. But she also had a few precious notes from her father. Before he left, he used to leave them for her all the time. In her lunchbox, on her pillow, propped against her cup in the bathroom so she'd find it in the morning when she got up. She'd long since lost most of them, but the ones she still had, she cherished. It was silly, he'd left her without a second glance, but she couldn't bring herself to get rid of those notes.

Erin had told Conor that she didn't know what love was, but she'd lied. She knew what it was and how it felt to lose it. Her dad had loved her, and she him. She'd never come close to that feeling again after he'd left, but she felt it now.

Erin wasn't fully convinced Conor loved her, but she *wanted* to believe it. She knew deep in her heart that she loved *him*. But until he saw all of her...she wouldn't fully commit herself. He'd said all the right words when it came to her scars, but it was another thing altogether to see them and truly understand the person she used to be. If he made love to her then left, it would destroy her. She had to protect herself at all costs.

Closing the safe, Erin tucked it back into its spot in her closet and stood. She grabbed her shorts and long-sleeve shirt on the way into the bathroom. Maybe she'd double her usual 5K run this morning.

Later that evening, while on break at The Sloppy Cow, Erin checked her phone and saw she'd missed a call and a couple of texts from Conor.

CONOR: *Looks like I'll be working a double shift.*
   Conor: *I'm sorry I won't be able to see you today.*
   Conor: *I miss you.*

THE LAST ONE was followed by a bunch of random emojis. She'd brought him to the dark side of those silly little pictures. Erin wasn't sure this was how most relationships worked, but she wasn't going to look a gift horse in the mouth. She smiled for the rest of her shift.

The next day, when she got back to her apartment after her morning run, there was a plastic bag hanging from her doorknob. She peered inside and saw a banana and another note. Grinning like a lunatic, Erin grabbed the note to read even as she was pushing open her door. His handwriting was decidedly messier than in the last note, as if he was in a hurry when he wrote it.

I GOT *about four hours of sleep last night and am back patrolling. Since the end of deer season is approaching, more and more people are doing what they can to try to skirt around the hunting laws and bag a last-minute deer. Anyway, I was thinking about you and hoped to see you this morning, but forgot that you'd be on your run. Whoops. I was hoping for a good-morning kiss, but it'll have to wait. Have a good day. Love, Conor*

LATER THAT NIGHT, after another shift at the bar and while lying in bed, exhausted but strangely wired, Erin thought about Conor. She hadn't spent much time thinking about what the man's faults might be, but she was rapidly realizing the biggest—the man was a workaholic. She thought *she* was bad with her two jobs, but Conor worked more than she did...and that was saying something.

He was doing a great job in making sure she knew he was thinking about her, but she missed seeing him. Missed hearing his low, rumbly voice. And, surprisingly, missed touching him and being touched.

She—Eat-more Erin—missed being touched. There had been a point in her life when she went out of her way not to make any kind of bodily contact with anyone. And here she was, lying in bed, sated after using her vibrator, thinking about Conor and wishing he was there to replace the battery-operated boyfriend.

But from what she could tell, he was an excellent game warden. She hadn't really thought about that branch of law enforcement before Conor. She wasn't a hunter or fisherman, and hadn't ever come into contact with one. But after some Internet research, she realized that Conor's job was way more complex than she ever thought.

Well, she couldn't change his workaholic tendencies, nor would she want to. But she also couldn't help but wonder where she might fit into his life. If things did work out with them would she constantly be wondering when he'd be home? Wondering if she'd always feel like she played second fiddle to his job?

But as soon as she had the thought, Erin dismissed it. Conor was amazingly thoughtful. He texted her all the time, called when he had a small break, not to mention the bananas.

No, Conor might work too hard, but she had a feeling she'd never feel neglected.

She fell asleep hoping she'd get to see him soon.

THE NEXT WEEK or so was much the same. Lots of communication via the phone and messages, a couple of mornings where they ran together, a few nights where he popped into The Sloppy Cow, but no real quality time with the man she was quickly becoming extremely attached to. It was frustrating.

Two weeks after the disastrous Christmas dinner, Erin had the entire day to herself. Classes were about to start up again at the university and her free time would soon be drastically reduced. She'd hoped to spend the day with Conor, but he'd texted the night before and said there was a special investigation into a marijuana grow field that he'd volunteered to assist with.

She wanted to be upset, but she couldn't be. She'd merely told him to be careful and had agreed to text him later.

Around eleven-thirty in the morning, Erin's doorbell rang. She looked through the peephole and was surprised to see Conor. She unlocked and opened the door. "Hey."

"Hey, bright eyes." Then he took a step forward and wrapped his arms around her. His head dropped and he proceeded to kiss her as if he were a starving man and she was his last meal.

After a moment of surprise, Erin returned the kiss. She had no recollection of Conor closing the door and backing her into her apartment. The next thing she knew, he was saying, "Up."

She blinked and looked around. They were in her kitchen and he had his hands on her waist.

"What?"

"Jump up and sit on the counter."

"Why?"

Conor grinned then. A naughty smile that made her nipples peak in desire.

"Trust me."

And because she did, Erin hopped up onto the counter. Conor used his hands to spread her legs and he stepped between them. He then pulled her ass to the edge of the counter and against him. She was spread before him and all Erin could think was, *Finally*.

As if he could read her mind, Conor mumbled, "God, I've thought about this every day for the last week."

"I'm not the one who hasn't been around. You work more than me, Conor."

He froze and looked her in the eyes. "I know," he said slowly. "And I honestly didn't realize just how much I did work until this past week. I wanted to see you so badly, more than just here and there, but I'd promised myself to so many special investigations at work, I couldn't do it. I'd like to say I'll change, but I'm thirty-five, bright eyes. And I love my job. But you should know, even when I was working I was thinking about you. Wondering if you were saving me any of those cookies my mom made you. Wondering how your planning for the next semester was going. Wondering if you were being hit on at the bar."

He growled then, a low, sexy sound that Erin felt between her legs. "No one hit on me," she reassured him, putting her hands on his sides and petting him, trying to soothe him.

"Right. You wouldn't know if they did or not, because you're clueless when it comes to that shit."

"Conor!" she exclaimed. "Men don't hit on me."

He leaned forward and nuzzled the side of her neck. His warm breath wafting over her skin making goose-bumps pop up on her arms. "They do. And I love that you don't notice."

Erin thought for sure he was lying...wasn't he? Then any thoughts she had flew out of her head when she felt his hands on her thighs. They were rubbing up and down her jeans lazily. With each pass upward, his thumbs brushed her inner thighs...almost touching her core, but not quite. She found herself shifting in his grasp on the next pass. Both wanting him to see for himself how wet she was for him, but feeling embarrassed about it at the same time.

"Anyone other than you ever touch your pussy and make you come, bright eyes?"

Conor never took his eyes from hers as he asked the question. Erin was flustered, but so turned on, she almost didn't care. She shook her head and clenched his T-shirt at his waist.

"Do you trust me?"

She did. "Yes."

"I love you, Erin. I know we're moving fast, but you're all I thought about this week. I've dreamed about being your first. First to make you come. First to suck your pussy and the first, and hopefully only, man to show you how wonderful making love can be with the right person."

His words made her inner muscles clench and she felt a gush of wetness dampen her panties. She wanted to affect him just as much as he did her. "I've watched some porn. I know it's not exactly something boyfriends and girlfriends talk about, but I wanted to know what I was missing. What sex was all about. I want you to be the first real man I see naked. The first cock I suck. The first to take me from behind. I want to do everything with you."

"Fuck," Conor swore, taking one of her hands in his and placing it over the rock-hard dick in his pants. "I want that too."

Erin gently massaged his erection. He was so hard. *She* did that. The power she felt in that moment was almost overwhelming. She always thought having sex would be about the man having all the control over the situation, but she'd been wrong. Seeing how much Conor wanted her was empowering. But she knew without a doubt she wasn't ready to strip off all her clothes and go at it on her kitchen floor.

"I...I'm scared for you to see me without any clothes on, Conor."

"I know," was his calm response.

"You do?"

"Yeah, bright eyes. I got that from our conversation the other night. I'm willing to take things as slow as you want. We can touch each other with our clothes on, just like this, for as long as you need. But you should know, I'm gonna want to see all of you. Every inch. I want to touch and kiss you all over. Every scar. Every wrinkle. Every roll of skin. And I know you're going to be beautiful, know why?"

Erin was speechless. She shook her head, words beyond her.

"Because you're mine. Because I'm yours. Because at the end of the day, you're the person I want to spend time with."

Tears sprang unexpectedly to her eyes. For a woman who had been alone and isolated for most of her life because of her weight and feelings of inadequacy, Conor's words were overwhelming.

"But for now, how about we start with one of those firsts? Hold on to me," he ordered, moving her hand away from his hard cock and back up to his waist.

When she gripped his shirt in both hands, Conor placed his palm between her legs and used the other to press against the small of her back, urging her to arch toward him. "All you have to do is feel. I'm not going to undress you, and I'm going to keep my hands on top of your clothes. Let's give this kitchen some memories other than just food, shall we?"

Before she could do more than nod, Conor's hand was moving. He used the heel to press against her clit and massage her hard. Her hips bucked up and she groaned. She was primed and ready to come with just that simple touch.

Except it wasn't simple. It was complex and confusing and oh so amazing.

For several minutes, Conor caressed her. Erin felt herself getting more and more wet and, amazingly, she wanted him to touch her. Skin to skin.

She opened her mouth to ask him to undo her jeans when he switched tactics. One hand went to her chest, where he roughly kneaded her breast over her T-shirt, and he used the thumb of his other hand to center on her clit.

As if he had a road map and knew exactly where and how to touch her, Erin went from being aroused to the verge of coming within seconds. "Conor!" she called out frantically, letting go of him and propping herself up with her hands behind her.

"Yes, bright eyes. Come for me. Let go. I've got you."

And that was all it took. She exploded in Conor's arms right there in her kitchen. The one room in her house that she never took any pleasure being in. On her countertop, legs spread, Conor standing between them. Her back arched, hands braced on the granite.

And while she shuddered and shook through the first

orgasm she hadn't given herself, Conor didn't say a word. He continued to massage her and prolong the amazing feelings coursing through her body.

When she was coherent enough to open her eyes, Erin looked right into Conor's dark ones.

"Beautiful," he murmured, then leaned forward and kissed her harder than he ever had before. His tongue plunged into her mouth, sharing his excitement with her. When he pulled back, they were both breathing hard.

Erin snaked her hand between them and brushed over Conor's erection, which was pulsing against her inner thigh. He grabbed her hand in his and brought it up to his mouth. He kissed the palm then held it against his chest.

"But you didn't...I want to please you," Erin said, uneasily.

"You please me more than you'll ever know," Conor reassured her. "My time will come...pun intended." He smirked. "Believe it or not, I didn't come over to ravage you."

She smirked. "You didn't?"

"Nope. I wanted to invite you to lunch with me and my friends. And no, don't tense up. I know you don't like to have meals in public, but there's no pressure here. I've..." He stumbled over his words for the first time that Erin could remember. "This is kind of a business meeting. I did something, and I don't know if you're going to be pissed at me or pleased. So I'm using my friends— your friends too, since you know them from the bar—as a buffer, and to help me explain."

Erin tensed in his arms. She knew he felt it, but didn't

apologize. He'd...done something? She racked her brain to try to think about what it might be, but came up blank.

He brushed a lock of her hair behind her ear and said softly. "It's not bad, bright eyes. At least I don't think so. I think it's a good thing, but you have every right to be upset with me for going behind your back. But that's why I want to come clean. I don't want there to be any secrets between us. You trusted me earlier, can you trust me about this too?"

"You're worrying me."

"I know. And I hate that." He smiled then. A mere quirk of his lips. "But I'm hoping I can distract you with wondering what the hell I did and you won't think about the fact that you're sitting at a table...having a meal."

Erin shook her head at him. "You're incorrigible."

"I know. And to sweeten the deal, I have a present for you afterwards."

"A present?"

"Yeah, I never got to give you the gift I got you for Christmas."

"You didn't have to get me anything."

"I know, but I did. And the time wasn't right after dinner at my folks' house to tell you about it. And I've been so busy for the last couple of weeks, it just didn't seem like the right time."

"It's been a long time since I've gotten a present," Erin said softly. "Other than the one from your parents, of course."

"So you'll come? Have lunch with our friends. Hear me, and them, out. Then I'll take you somewhere special to me and give you your gift."

She scrunched her nose. "That's kinda blackmail."

"I know," Conor responded without any remorse.

"Is this how our relationship is gonna go? You handling me and blackmailing me not to be mad at you?"

His smile died. "No. I couldn't 'handle' you if I tried. I want to give you nothing but good things, Erin. I never want you to think my job comes before you...even if sometimes it feels like it."

"Okay, Conor. I'll go with you. But don't be surprised if I'm not that comfortable."

"Noted. Now...I'm assuming you want to clean up before we go?"

She shifted on her perch on the counter and winced. Yeah, everything felt damp down there. She definitely wanted to change her undies and pants.

He chuckled and took a step back. He kept her hand in his and held it as she jumped off the counter, holding her steady. "I'll wait out here."

"Yeah, you will," she told him with an eyebrow arched.

Conor reached for her and tugged her into him, wrapping his arms around her. "I love you, Erin. Don't forget that today, okay?"

"Now I'm *really* worried," Erin mumbled into his chest. Whatever he'd done had to be big because he was genuinely concerned about her reaction.

"Go change. I'll wait," he ordered gruffly, as if he hadn't just been vulnerable.

Erin nodded and turned to go to her bedroom. She was worried, but she was also extremely curious. She knew Conor well enough to know he wasn't a man who acted without thinking. He wouldn't be a good officer if he did. So she had no doubt that whatever he'd done had been after he'd thought about the consequences. And one of those was obviously her being upset with him. But he'd still done it. That told her he'd felt it was important.

She'd give him the benefit of the doubt and hear him, and their friends, out.

Their friends. Erin liked that. She hadn't really thought about the men and women who hung out at The Sloppy Cow as her friends before, but they were.

She quickly changed, her curiosity getting the better of her. Not only about whatever mysterious thing Conor had done, but for her present. She loved the photo his parents had given her, but somehow she knew that whatever Conor had planned would blow that out of the water.

12

AN HOUR LATER, Conor held Erin's chair for her as she sat. They were at a small restaurant near Fire Station 7. He'd chosen it partly because the owners were incredibly grateful for the firefighters and police officers who frequented their establishment, but they were also more than willing to go out of their way to make whatever dishes he and his friends wanted...whether they were on the menu or not.

He'd talked with them earlier and had arranged for Erin's meal. He'd done a lot of research over the last couple of weeks about gastric bypass surgery and had learned a lot about what kinds of foods were best for patients who had gone through the procedure, even a decade later.

He'd tried to keep the lunch to the minimum number of people needed to tell Erin what they'd found out about her dad, but when word had gotten out amongst their friends what was going on, everyone wanted to be involved. So instead of an intimate lunch with four or five people, there were eleven.

Dax and Cruz were there, as they'd done a lot of the initial investigation, but Mackenzie and Mickie also insisted on coming with their boyfriends. Beth had also agreed to come, which was somewhat unusual. She had done an amazing job in dealing with her agoraphobia, though she still struggled some days. But she was there, as was her man, Cade. Not only that, but when Sophie had heard about what was going on, she'd insisted on being there to support her friend. TJ also showed up, along with Calder.

Conor was touched and pleased with the support both he and Erin had, and was glad the rest of the gang hadn't also joined them, but he was worried about how Erin would handle the large group.

On the outside, she looked completely relaxed, but Conor knew her well enough to know she wasn't as stoic as she appeared. One hand was clenched in her lap while the other fiddled with a fork on the table.

Conor placed his hand over hers on her thigh and squeezed. "Thank you everyone for coming. It means a lot to me, and I know to Erin as well."

"It'd mean more to me if I knew why I was here," Erin said a bit snarkily.

"You want to discuss business first, or eat?" Dax asked.

"Dax," Conor warned, but Mackenzie beat her boyfriend to the punch in responding.

"Conor, you can't expect the poor woman to sit there and make nice with everyone while she's worried about what we're going to talk about. Not to mention trying to eat. I mean, if it was me, I'd probably choke on anything I tried to shove down my throat. We get that you want to protect her, believe me, all your threats to us about spilling the beans before you can explain to Erin made that more than clear, but seriously, I vote we talk about it, get it out of the way, then we can relax and have lunch."

Conor sighed. Mackenzie made sense, but he was still irritated. He turned to Erin and was surprised to see a small smile on her face. "What?" he asked.

She gestured toward the woman who'd come to her defense. "Just...she's just so...Mackenzie."

Conor knew what she meant. Mackenzie was one of a kind. She could ramble on and on and on about just about anything.

"I agree," Beth piped up. "And not because of anything more than the fact that I want to go home."

"Oh," Erin said on a surprised breath of air.

"Not because I don't like you or anything," Beth reassured her in a tone that sounded pretty monotone. "I just didn't have a good night. Cade didn't even want me to come today, but there was no way I was missing this because I knew Conor would screw up the explanation somehow."

"Hey," the man in question protested.

Beth waved a hand dismissively. "I took an extra pill this morning, and while it's dulled my anxiety, I'll feel better if I can hole up in our house again. So don't take it personally if I don't stay for lunch. Okay?"

"No problem," Erin told her. Then she turned to Sophie. "You know what this is all about?"

The other woman nodded.

"Am I going to be mad?"

Instead of immediately nodding or shaking her head, Sophie thought about the question for a long moment. Finally, she said softly, "M-Mad? No, I don't think s-so. S-Surprised? Yes. Upset? M-Maybe. But I s-suspect you'll also be relieved too."

"Oh Lord. Can someone just get to it?" TJ grumbled. "Jesus, you're stressing *me* out and I *know* what the fuck is going on."

Conor held up his hand, then turned his chair to face Erin. He reached out and turned hers too, so they were facing each other and their knees were touching. He grabbed both her hands in his and leaned forward.

"Here's the deal. After you told me about your dad, I asked Dax and Cruz to look into his disappearance. I wanted you to have the closure that you obviously didn't have after he left. I wanted you to be able to know once and for all what happened."

Erin stared at him with her mouth open, obviously in shock.

He tightened his grip on her hands when she tried to pull away from him. "I gave them what basic information I had, that you'd told me, and they went from there. They asked Beth to help when what they found was highly suspicious. You may or may not know, but Beth is an expert on finding information on the Internet."

Erin turned her head to look at Dax, Cruz, and Beth, then turned back to him. "Did she find him?"

"Yeah, bright eyes. We think she did."

"Can I see him?" Erin asked. "Does he know I'm looking for him?"

Conor took a deep breath. He hated this. He really did. "Cruz checked through government records with his contact at the FBI...and your dad hasn't submitted any kind of tax returns since the year before he disappeared. Then Dax searched the Texas database for any John Does who hadn't been claimed."

"No," Erin whispered, obviously understanding what Conor was trying to tell her.

Calder spoke up, preventing Conor from having to tell her the bad news.

"As a medical examiner, I have *legal* access," he emphasized the word, and raised his eyebrows at Beth when he did, "to all autopsy reports. I searched through the reports for all male bodies that were brought in and never identified. Beth sent me your dad's stats from his driver's license, and his medical records. Erin...a body was brought into the Houston medical examiner's office three years after he disappeared. I identified him using dental records and x-rays that were taken at the morgue. I'm so sorry, Erin. It was your father."

Conor watched as Erin's eyes filled with tears and spilled down her cheeks. She gripped his hands as if he was the only thing holding her together.

If he could've kicked his own ass, he would've. He shouldn't have brought her here to tell her. He should've sucked it up and told her by himself at her place. Where she'd have the privacy to fall apart.

"How'd he die?" she asked softly. "Do you know?"

"The autopsy revealed that he'd been shot several times," Calder said equally as softly. "Once in the chest. Twice in his head."

"Shot?" Erin asked in confusion, turning to Conor.

He nodded. "The report stated that it looked like it was the second shot to his head that killed him."

Conor hated what that report meant. It meant that Erin's dad hadn't died right away. The first shot in his chest had knocked him down, made him vulnerable. The second had missed, merely grazed the side of this head. But the third, in the middle of his forehead, was definitely deliberate...and deadly.

Erin's eyes met Beth's, then Dax and Cruz's. "You're sure?"

All three nodded solemnly.

Conor had no idea what was going through Erin's head. He wanted to pull her into his arms, but he needed to be able to see her face. Gauge her reactions. Figure out if he needed to whisk her away so they could deal.

She turned back to Conor. "Where did they find him? Calder said the *Houston* medical examiner. We lived near there."

"To the east of the city is a large body of water called Lake Houston. A group of college-aged kids were partying in the area. They saw what they thought was a skull on one of the remote banks. They called the police. They were right."

"When?"

"When what, baby?" Conor asked.

"Calder said his body had been brought in three years after he left. When did he die?"

This was the hard part. "They can't be sure. Because of the water and the heat, there wasn't much left to be able to tell when exactly he died."

"Erin," Beth interrupted. Her voice was monotone, but Conor knew it wasn't because she didn't care. It was more because of the anti-anxiety pills she'd taken. Cade had told him how, when Beth had found out the information she was probably about to tell Erin, she'd lost it. Cried for all that Erin had lost. "There wasn't any clothing found with the body, but whoever put him in the lake didn't expect he'd ever be found. They weighed him down with chains and several construction blocks. But this is the thing—construction companies don't like it when their material is stolen. For years, they've marked their building materials so if they're taken, they can possibly be returned if found."

Erin's eyes went to her friend's. "Marked?"

"Yeah. With the date and location of where the construction project takes place. The blocks found with your dad were dated the month before he disappeared."

Erin bit her lip. "What does that mean?"

"It means," Conor said, turning Erin's face to him with a finger under her chin, "That your dad didn't leave you, bright eyes. He was murdered."

Erin's eyes widened.

Conor repeated himself. "He didn't *willingly* leave you. He loved you, Erin. I have a feeling you were the best thing in his life."

"He didn't leave me," Erin said softly. Then she turned to look at the table of people sitting around her. "He didn't leave me," she repeated louder.

The women around the table smiled at her. The men continued to scowl, but the lines around their tense mouths eased a bit.

"We've turned all the information we've gotten over to the investigators. It's unlikely they'll ever prove who killed him, but the bottom line is that your dad didn't abandon you," Cruz said as gently as he could.

Erin sat up in her chair and faced the others around the table. "My mom told me my dad left because I was 'an annoying little shit.' She said he told her he didn't want anything to do with me anymore. She let me think the reason he left was all because of me. For years, every time I did something she didn't like, she'd tell me it was no wonder my dad had left."

Conor couldn't stand it anymore. He pulled Erin onto his lap, even as she was still talking.

"When I started to gain weight, she said my dad would've been embarrassed by me. When I graduated from high school, she didn't bother to come to the ceremony. She said I didn't deserve to have anyone there supporting me because I'd made her husband leave her. The more I think about everything...the more likely I think it is that my *mom* probably killed my dad. She never liked how much attention he paid me. Never liked it when he would take me camping. Never liked it when we spent time together. I think she's a jealous bitch of a woman who probably got so mad that she couldn't control him, she killed him. Then, out of spite, she made my life a living hell for the rest of the time I lived with her."

Silence greeted her words, but Conor couldn't have been prouder of her than he was at that moment.

"Are you pissed at us?" Beth asked. "I mean, Conor went behind your back and told Dax and Cruz about your dad's disappearance, and how mean your mom was to you. Then I dug deeper to find out more info about your dad so we could try to find him for you."

"Jesus, Beth," Conor complained. "Lay it all out, would ya?"

"Erin's not s-stupid," Sophie said quietly. "S-She knows that Daxton and the others would need as m-much information as possible to find her dad."

"You know about *me*, too?" Erin asked Beth.

Beth met her eyes straight on. "Yeah. I know about you."

Erin kept her eyes on the woman across the table from her. It was more than obvious to her that Beth had looked into her history. She probably knew everything about her. If she was as good at finding information as the others said she was, she most likely knew about her being fired from her first job after college and all about her surgeries.

After everything else she'd learned today, the thought that Beth knew about her didn't seem so awful anymore.

Conor ran his hand up and down her back.

She took a deep breath—and did something she'd never done before in her life. Talked about herself with a group of friends.

"I thought it was my fault my dad left. I coped by eating. I gained a lot of weight. So much that I couldn't walk very far without being out of breath. Things came to a head when I lost my job, and I made the decision to change my life. I had gastric bypass surgery and when all was said and done, I lost three hundred pounds." The words were said in a rush, as though, if she didn't hurry up and say them, she'd chicken out. Erin huffed out a breath and leaned back into Conor, feeling his lips touch her temple as if rewarding her for her bravery in opening up to her new friends.

"I think it's so cool," Mackenzie said, sitting back in her chair and crossing her arms over her chest. "I mean, if you think about it, you lost about three people from your frame. It's amazing and freaky and I bet your dad would be so darn proud of you right now, he'd bust."

"Proud?" Erin asked.

"Yup. Proud. You had to deal with his bitch of a wife, and she treated you like shit. You did what you had to in order to protect yourself—eat. Which I get, by the way. I mean, what woman doesn't indulge in chocolate, ice cream, and junk food when she's upset? But you had like, ten years of being upset and not having anyone to talk to about it. It's not surprising you gained all that weight. But you didn't just lay down and die. You fought back. You had the surgery, but it's not like *that* would've done anything if you hadn't changed the way you ate. You had to completely change everything about how you coped with shit thrown your way...and that's a hard thing to do. I admire you, Erin. You're my hero."

Erin stared at the other woman, obviously stunned.

"You haven't thought about yourself that way, have you?" Conor asked softly.

Erin shook her head.

"Right. Now that M-Mack has word vomited all over the table...who's hungry?" Sophie asked dryly.

Everyone laughed, and just like that, the tension was broken. They started talking at once about what they wanted to eat and what they had going on for the rest of the day.

Conor kept his eyes on Erin, trying to gauge where her head was at.

"Did the subject of how much I used to weigh seriously just get brought up then dismissed just like that?" Erin asked Conor quietly.

He grinned. "Yup. You see, bright eyes, all the women in our circle of friends are strong. They see you as being one of them. Strong enough to overcome the shit life throws at you. Even if you gained back all the weight, they wouldn't see you any differently. In fact, Mackenzie would probably gain weight in commiseration so you wouldn't feel so bad about it."

"Is this what it feels like to have friends?" Erin asked him.

"As if you could rip off all your clothes and dance naked on the table and they'd not only *not* laugh at you or call the police, but they'd take off their own clothes and join in so you wouldn't have to spend the night in the pokey by yourself? Yeah, this is what it feels like to have friends," Conor finished with a big smile.

It grew when Erin grinned back at him. He relaxed for the first time under her. "Are you upset that I went behind your back?" he asked.

She immediately shook her head. Her fingers wrapped around the nape of his neck and she leaned into him. "No. Some people would tell me I should be, but you gave me the best gift I've ever received. My dad didn't leave me. You have no idea what that means to me. I'm angry and sad that he was murdered, but all I can think of at the moment is that I wasn't the reason he left."

"The best gift you've gotten until later today, when I give you your belated Christmas gift," he teased, more thankful than he could ever say that he was actually joking with her right now instead of pleading with her to forgive him.

Erin leaned her forehead on his and they stayed like that for a moment before Calder interrupted. "Hey, you guys gonna order? I'm starving. All this drama really worked up an appetite."

Conor pulled back and looked Erin in the eyes. "Trust me?"

"Yes."

"Enough to let me order for you?"

She hesitated, but finally nodded and said, "For you, food is love. I trust you."

Conor wanted to stand up with her in his arms and take her directly home to his bed and make love to her right then, but he refrained, barely. He turned to the waitress and said, "The cook knows what my order is. Just tell him to make what Conor asked for."

The young waitress didn't even blink. She simply nodded and turned to head into the kitchen to place their orders.

An hour later, Conor walked next to Erin as they left the restaurant. He waited patiently as each of the women gave her a big hug and as the men gave her their customary chin lifts. Beth and Cade had left not long after the food had arrived, promising to catch up with Erin later.

When they were alone in Conor's truck, he turned to her. "Are you sure you're okay with everything? I didn't want to tell you what I was doing in case it didn't pan out. It seemed like the lesser of the evils to keep quiet about Dax and Cruz making inquiries. If they found your dad, they would've contacted him themselves to see what happened all those years ago and if he wanted to see you. If he was a dick, you never would've known I'd found him because there's no way I'd let you go through that kind of rejection a second time. But we all kinda had a feeling the outcome would be something like it was."

"I'm okay with it, Conor. I'm grateful. I never wanted to try to find him myself, one, because I didn't know where to start, but also two, for the reason you just said. If he said he didn't want to talk to me, it would hurt just as badly the second time. So let it go. Okay?"

"Okay, if you're sure."

"I'm sure. Now...how did you know what to order for me?"

"Part of it was research. I looked up the best foods for you and what a gastric bypass patient should be eating. But another part is the simple power of observation. We haven't had a lot of meals together, but I've seen you eat, Erin. On the canoe trip, at the bar, I even scoped out your fridge and cabinets at your house when you weren't looking."

"The grilled chicken was amazing. And the side of plain, no-butter-or-salt-added broccoli was cooked to perfection. And the portion was exactly right."

Conor smiled over at her. "I know you said your stomach has stretched, but I didn't think you'd be in the mood to fill yourself until you were full, so I simply asked the chef to keep the meat to around five ounces and only a couple florets of broccoli. It was enough?"

"Yeah, it was actually more than enough."

"Which is why I kept stealing bites of your chicken."

"I noticed."

Conor got serious. "I don't ever want you to be afraid of telling me to butt out. Or to fuck off if it comes to that. You're not a child and you've spent more time than most people learning what your body needs and what it can and can't do. So if I start to push too hard, tell me to back off. Yeah?"

"I will," Erin told him immediately. "And I'll say it now...I don't mind you eating off my plate, but keep away from my cookies. Your mom gave them to me. If she wanted you to have some, she would've made them for you." She smiled, letting him know she was teasing.

Conor grinned. Then he leaned forward and whispered, "I saw her last week and she gave me my own plate."

"And you've eaten them all, haven't you?" Erin asked with a smirk.

"I'm pleading the fifth on that one," Conor said.

"Thank you," Erin said seriously.

"For what?"

"For everything. I feel as if I hit the lottery with you."

"I'm going to remind you that you said that when you're bitching because of my work schedule and how you never see me," Conor said. "Now...are you ready for your present?"

"Yes! Although I feel bad I don't have anything for you."

He reached out a hand and ran the backs of his fingers down her cheek. "You have something for me, bright eyes. The best present a man could ever be given." He loved the blush that bloomed over her cheeks. He dropped his hand and reached for the ignition. "We have to drive somewhere before I can give it to you."

"Well...get on with it," Erin told him, crossing her arms. "The buildup to this present has been so huge, I'm almost afraid it's not going to live up to my expectations."

Conor laughed. "It's not a ring," he warned her. "I mean, I love you and want to spend the rest of my life with you, but that's a bit fast, even for me."

She laughed, as he hoped she would. "I wasn't thinking anything like that."

"Whew." Conor pantomimed wiping his brow. "Off the hook."

Erin smacked his arm. "Drive."

"Yes, ma'am," he told her and started the truck. He hoped she *would* like the gift. It wasn't conventional, but he had a feeling it was just what they needed to really move forward with their relationship.

13

ERIN KNEW they were driving out of San Antonio, but she wasn't worried about it. Her mind reeled with everything she'd learned at lunch. Her dad hadn't split, he'd been murdered, and Conor had made sure she had what she felt comfortable eating for lunch.

She looked over at him. He drove with an ease that didn't surprise her. One hand on the steering wheel, the other clasping one of hers and resting on her thigh. As if he could feel her eyes on him, he turned to her. "What are you thinking?"

"That if I had to go through everything I've been through in my life all over again to end up at this point right here...sitting next to you in this truck, you holding my hand, saying you love me...I'd do it. Right down to my dad leaving and everything I went through with my weight."

"Erin—" he began, but she interrupted him.

"I know that's dramatic, but I'm feeling pretty good right now. Don't ruin it," she warned.

Conor smiled. "Okay, bright eyes, I won't. But for the record, I'm pretty fucking happy myself."

"Good."

"Good," he echoed.

They rode in silence for the rest of the trip. They'd gone northwest of San Antonio to Bandera. Then south on State Road 1077 until they passed a sign that said Hill Country State Natural Area. Erin glanced at him, but he refused to meet her eyes. She grinned and kept silent.

Conor waved at the ranger manning the entrance booth and they entered the natural area. Instead of following the road to the campground section, Conor turned left on a dirt road. He kept going a couple of miles down the twisting and turning road and only stopped when they couldn't go any farther.

Without a word, Conor climbed out of the truck and walked around to her side. He opened her door and held out a hand. Erin grabbed it and he helped her jump out. Then, keeping hold of her hand, he walked them to a slight trail that Erin knew she probably would've missed if she was by herself. They walked in silence for what she thought was about half a mile.

Just as she was going to ask where in the world they were going, Conor stopped and pulled her close to his side. He put an arm around her as she gaped at the view in front of her. They were on some sort of rise over-looking what had to be most of the natural area.

Conor finally broke his silence.

"This is one of my favorite places in Texas. It encom-passes most of what I love about the land. There are hills, like the one we're on, desert areas," he pointed to some light tan areas off to the left, "and thick trees that house a slew of different kinds of animals. There are walking trails for everyone. Some easy, and others that are tough because of elevation drops and gains and the steepness of the trails in some areas. But more than that, this area has some of the best camping I've ever encountered. There are no full-access hookups, which means no big RVs. There are walk-in sites, equestrian camping sites along with fifty miles of horse trails, and even wilderness-area camping sites for backpackers."

"It's beautiful," Erin told him honestly.

Conor turned her in his arms. "It's probably not very original, but for your Christmas present, I thought we could spend some time out here together. Camping. You used to love it with your dad, and I'd love to share the love of the land that I have with you."

Erin was speechless.

Conor obviously took her lack of saying anything as a bad sign, because he hurried to try to convince her. "It'll be fun. It'll be like the canoe trip, but without the canoe or river and no audience." He smiled. "I was thinking around spring break. That way you wouldn't have to worry about grading papers or anything while you were gone. We don't have to stay the whole week. We can camp for as long or as short as you want. I figure by March, we'll have gotten to know each other better so it wouldn't be weird being stuck in a tent together. And the weather then is usually pretty mild. I know it's a crapshoot, but last year it was in the seventies during the day, which is perfect hiking weather. You know? And if you think it's a horrible idea, we can always—"

Erin reached up and put her hand over Conor's mouth to shut him up. "You sound like Mackenzie," she teased, smiling when he flinched. "I'd love to go camping with you."

Conor breathed a sigh of relief. "Thank God."

"This place looks amazing," Erin said, turning back to look out over the land.

"The park has over five thousand acres and about forty miles of trails. Every time I've been out here hiking, I've seen less than five people. To me, it's an undiscovered gem of Texas, and that's how I'd love to keep it."

"When were you here last?" Erin asked.

"Last fall. A little boy got lost. He wandered away from his campsite."

"Isn't this outside the area that you work?" Erin asked, looking over her shoulder at him.

"Yeah. But when something like that happens, the game wardens usually try to help when they can. Sometimes we're more capable when it comes to tromping around in the wilderness than regular beat cops."

"That makes sense," Erin mumbled, turning back to the beautiful view in front of her as he continued.

"The kid was five, so we had hopes he'd be able to look after himself, at least for a while. If he was any younger, it would've been a different situation. Alamo Area Search and Rescue was called out and we tagged along. AASAR is an all-volunteer search and rescue team based out of San Antonio. They brought their air-scent canines to help look for the little boy as well."

"Did you find him?"

"Yeah, bright eyes. He was on his own in the wilderness for about fourteen hours, including overnight. He'd found a bush and crawled under it. He heard everyone shouting for him but he told his parents he was afraid he was in trouble for getting lost. If it hadn't been for the search dogs, we wouldn't have found him. At least not as quickly as we did."

"But he was okay?"

"Dehydrated, scared, and covered in your favorite, ant bites, but generally okay," Conor told her.

"It doesn't really look like it'd be that hard to get lost out there," Erin noted.

"The land is really deceiving. From up here, it looks like it's all scrub bushes and thin cover, but when you're down there hiking it, there are places where it's really thick. It's easy to get turned around. Also, northwest of the park is all completely undeveloped. There are some steep drop-offs and a few streams. Of course, the water is pretty low right now, only a couple of feet deep because we haven't gotten a lot of rain recently, but it could still be dangerous if you got lost and started wandering around aimlessly."

Erin shuddered and turned to face Conor. "I like the outdoors, but honestly, I prefer to stay near a tent and other people. I don't do well by myself."

"You'd be fine, bright eyes," he told her. "I have no doubt you'd make meals out of berries and sticks and fix up hurt animals while you were at it."

"Where's the wood to knock on when you need it?" Erin mumbled even as she was rolling her eyes.

Conor laughed, then sobered. "I'm so glad I said yes to that canoe trip."

"Me too."

"I want you to know, I'm gonna work on putting less priority on my job and more on you."

Erin put her hand on Conor's arm. "You don't need to. I know you love what you do."

"I do. But I love you more."

Erin's breath caught in her throat as he continued.

"I haven't had a reason to *not* work fifteen hour days before now. There was no reason to pull out of a stakeout and go home, because there wasn't anything for me there. My mom and sisters have complained to me a lot over the years, telling me I'd never find a wife if I didn't stop working so much and get out there and look for her, but I always blew them off. But I'm making you a promise right here and now, in front of God and the land that I love. I'm gonna make that effort. I won't always succeed, and I hope you'll let me know when I don't pay you the attention you deserve. I want you to know down to your toes that you are more important to me than my job."

"Conor," Erin protested softly.

"There are times of the year where I'll have to work longer hours than others, especially deer season, but I'll make up for it at other times...like spring break...when we can have the entire week to ourselves out here under the stars and sky. I'm not perfect, Erin. Not even close. But what I feel for you makes me want to be...for you."

"I'm not looking for a perfect man," she reassured him. "I'm so far from that it's not even funny. I'll never be able to eat like a normal person, and I've got more than my fair share of insecurities. But I want to be with you, Conor. I want to see where this relationship can go. I want to share my hopes, dreams, and eventually, my body with you."

"And I'll cherish those hopes and dreams and protect your beautiful body with everything I have."

They smiled at each other, and Erin finally broke the comfortable silence. "Is it wrong that I want to rip your clothes off and make love to you right here?"

Conor choked as he inhaled and Erin laughed. "Okay, not really. I can't imagine how it would feel to have fire ant bites on my ass. And then you'd have to rush me to the hospital, which would suck. But you should know, the more time I spend with you, the more comfortable I am with you seeing me without my clothes on...and the more I want to see all of you."

"Another reason to make sure I don't work too much," Conor said with a wicked smile. "How about making out? You up for that?"

"Absolutely!" Erin said enthusiastically.

As his head dropped toward her, Erin realized that she really had changed over the last month or so that she'd been seeing Conor. She used to worry, when she did finally get to kiss a man, about what she should do with her hands, and what her tongue should do, and whether her boobs would touch his chest and if her stomach would get too close to his. But in reality, the only thing she could think about when Conor kissed her was how good she felt.

She wasn't an idiot, she knew there would be some awkward times in the future and that she'd have to work really hard not to flinch away from him when he touched her bare skin, but for the first time in her life, she wanted to be with another person. With Conor.

The day had been weird. Heartbreaking and a relief at the same time when she'd found out about her father. And touching when she realized what it was Conor had "gotten" her for Christmas. She couldn't wait to spend more time with him...in general and when they were camping.

She hadn't lied when she'd told Conor earlier that she'd go through everything she had in her life all over again if it meant she still ended up with him. She might be a virgin, but she wasn't naive. She knew their relationship might not work out in the end, but he'd given her more gifts than he even knew. Mainly, her self-esteem. With him, she felt pretty. Maybe not beautiful, but at least not like the Eat-more Erin she'd been back in the day.

Lord knew she wasn't perfect, but hopefully with his help, she'd get to start experiencing life rather than having it pass her by.

She smiled as she continued to kiss Conor, happy with her life and happy with the man in her arms.

14

THE REST of January went by in a flash. The new semester started and Erin was almost as busy as Conor. She'd thought long and hard about what Conor had said about cutting back on his work hours so he could spend more time with her, and she'd made the decision to do the same. She was only working two nights a week at The Sloppy Cow now, so she could spend as many evenings as possible with Conor.

Deer and duck season was over at the end of January, and they were concentrating on quail hunters now... along with all the other investigations that were never-ending. He'd had a few calls about alligators, which surprisingly were becoming more and more prevalent in their area. The investigation into the marijuana grow was still ongoing, as well as illegal sales of pythons, under-cover stings related to the sale of illegal reptiles on Craigslist, and a dozen other things related to the land and wildlife that Erin had no idea were even issues.

Conor had kept his word, telling his boss and fellow

wardens that he wanted to cut back on overtime because he had a girlfriend.

Except for the nights Erin worked at the bar, they'd spent every evening together. They would eat together— he usually ate a high-carbohydrate meal with lots of meat, and she ate salads with grilled chicken on top. Then she'd do schoolwork at his kitchen table while he either lifted weights in his guest room turned workout room, or he'd do work on his computer next to her. She'd leave around ten and then they'd meet up again most mornings for their daily five-mile run.

One night, after they'd gotten their work done, Conor grabbed her hand and towed her to his couch. He sat, pulling her down onto his lap.

"Stay the night," he blurted before they were even settled.

"What?"

"Stay the night," he repeated. "You're over here almost every evening as it is, then we meet up in the mornings. It would be easier if you just stayed here. With me."

"You want me to sleep here?"

"Yeah, bright eyes. I want you to sleep here. In my bed."

Erin bit her lip and looked down at her lap.

"Hey, look at me," Conor ordered, for once not using his finger to lift her chin.

She looked into his eyes.

"I dread this time of night because I know you'll be leaving. I love having you here. Even when we're both doing our own thing, there's something so soothing knowing all I have to do is look up and you're there. I love the sounds you make in your throat when you're grading papers and one of your students is an idiot. I love walking by on my way into the kitchen for a water refill and being able to kiss the top of your head as I pass. Having you in my space, laughing with you, watching TV with you…it makes me want more. Stay. Please."

"I want to. I'm just…nervous," Erin told him.

"I'm not going to tell you nothing will happen, because I'm a guy, I hope something *does* happen. But I'm not going to pounce on you in the middle of the night. We're still taking things slowly. I want you to be completely comfortable with me before we make love. I can't deny I want to touch you, but we'll go at your speed. But I absolutely want to hold you in my arms until we both fall asleep. I want to wake up and roll over and see you next to me. I want to brush my teeth, shower, and eat breakfast, with you by my side."

Erin swallowed hard. "You make it sound so easy."

"I'm sure there will be adjustments we'll both have to make. I'm used to living on my own, leaving the toilet seat up." He grinned at her. "But for the first time in my life, I want to be around someone else. When you're not here, I'm thinking about you. Wondering when I can see you again, looking forward to it. We don't have to jump into living together full time. Just every now and then. Please?"

"I guess it would save time in the mornings," Erin mused. "You wouldn't have to come all the way to my apartment to pick me up before our runs."

Conor frowned and he loosened his hold on her. "If you don't want to, it's okay."

Erin quickly put her hand on Conor's scruffy cheek. "I didn't mean it like that. If you want me to stay, I'll stay. But don't blame me when you're surprised at how awful I look in the mornings."

"Oh, bright eyes, you couldn't disappoint me if you tried. And the thought of you with messy hair, a sleepy look in your eyes as you turn over to look at me after waking up in my bed, on my sheets...yeah, awful is the last word I'd use."

"I have one question before I agree," Erin said, keeping her face blank of any emotion.

"What?"

"Do you snore? Because if you do, that's a deal breaker."

Conor snorted and began to tickle her. "You little snot," he said.

"Stop! I'm so ticklish!" Erin cried as she squirmed and wiggled to try to get away from Conor's fingers. She laughed and pushed at his hands.

Before she knew it, Conor had maneuvered them onto the floor so she was straddling his waist and he was under her. He plunged his fingers into her hair and held her head still as he said softly, "I want you in my bed, Erin. Even if all we do is sleep. I love you."

"I'll stay," she told him, holding on to his wrists.

They stayed like that for a long moment. Erin knew it was the beginning of a shift in their relationship. Over the last month, Conor had been sweet. They hadn't done much sexually since that amazing orgasm in her kitchen except kiss. But somehow, she knew that was about to end.

Conor stretched and put his hands under his head, as if he was completely relaxed. "Touch me," he said, although it came out more as an order than a simple request.

"Where?" Erin asked.

"Anywhere. Everywhere. You said you hadn't seen a man before, well, now's your chance. I'm yours, Erin."

Her eyes narrowed. "Are you trying to manage me?"

He chuckled. "Maybe a little. But I figure if you're comfortable with me, touching me, seeing me naked, then it'll be easier for you when the time comes."

"Nothing is going to make it easier to let you see me without my clothes on."

"If it takes ten years, that's what it takes. There's no time limit, bright eyes."

It was the perfect thing to say and exactly what Erin needed to hear. She wasn't thrilled at all about having Conor see her—hell, she couldn't even comfortably look at herself—but she wanted him. All of him. She really wanted him to make love with her. And in order to get that, she had to let go of some of her preconceived notions about what was and wasn't beautiful.

She decided at that moment to ignore the nasty voice inside her head that said she was hideous and ugly. She'd try to listen to Conor when he said she was pretty and amazing more often. It wouldn't be easy, but she'd lost over three hundred pounds and she hadn't thought she could do *that* either.

Without a word, she placed her hands on Conor's stomach and ran them up his chest to his shoulders, then back down. She did it several times and, on the fourth pass, moved so her hands were under his shirt when she stroked upward.

His warm skin felt wonderful against her palms. He inhaled deeply as she rubbed over his nipples, but he didn't move his hands from under his head. On the way back down, Erin stopped at his nipples and began to play with them, as he'd done to her several times before.

His pupils dilated as he stared up at her.

"You like this," Erin said in awe.

"No, bright eyes. I *love* this." He moved then, reaching for the hem of his shirt and arching his back so he could rip it off. Then he resumed his earlier position, his fingers linked together under his head.

Conor lay under her, completely bare to her gaze. Erin almost didn't know where to look or touch first. She resumed their exploration. She ran her hands over every inch of his chest, learning what he liked and what made him squirm. "What do they call this? A happy trail?" Erin asked, more to herself than Conor as she ran an index finger over the hair visible above the waistband of his jeans.

"God, yes," Conor moaned as her finger traced the edge of his jeans along his stomach.

She scooted back a bit and marveled at the size of the bulge in his pants. Being brave, Erin put her hand over his erection. "You've given me an orgasm, but I didn't get to return the favor," Erin said softly, asking permission without coming right out and asking if she could undo his pants.

In response, Conor's hands slowly moved down his

body, and he undid his button and the zipper on his jeans. "Lift up," he ordered.

Erin came up on her knees and watched with wide eyes as Conor shoved his jeans and boxers down without hesitation. She couldn't believe he'd exposed himself to her as easily as he had.

His pants were only at his thighs, but he settled his ass back on the floor and looked up at her calmly. "I've dreamed about your hands on me, bright eyes."

Erin swallowed hard. She could feel her pulse beating overtime at her throat and knew she was probably blushing bright red.

"Does it hurt?" she asked softly as she settled back down on his thighs. His cock was bright red and the smooth mushroomed head was shiny with his excitement. It curled upward toward his belly button and the hair around the base was trimmed short. She wasn't sure if it was beautiful or scary.

"Not like you think. Touch me. Please."

Erin looked away from his dick for the first time. Conor was watching her closely. She swallowed hard and looked back down his body. She slowly reached out a hand and lightly gripped his dick. He was warm against her palm. She stroked him from the base to the tip and back down again.

Conor groaned.

Erin glanced up and saw he'd thrown his head back and was grimacing.

She loosened her grip on him, but kept stroking.

His eyes opened and he looked up at her. Then he reached down and wrapped his own large hand around hers on his cock. Erin's heart was beating so hard she had the brief thought that if she looked down, she'd be able to see it pulsing under her shirt. Her thoughts returned to the large, hard man under her when he moved his hand, taking hers with it until they were both stroking his rock-hard dick.

"I've never felt anything as amazing as your hand on me," Conor said softly. "You don't have any calluses and it's so tiny compared to mine."

"My hand isn't tiny, you're just...big," Erin protested.

He chuckled. "Thanks for the compliment. I just meant, I'm used to my own hand, feeling yours on me is a dream come true. I've gotten myself off so many times in the last few months, imagining this moment right here, that I couldn't have held back that moan if my life depended on it. Don't be afraid when you have your hands on me. Unless you strangle my dick or dig your nails in, anything you do will feel good. Holding me this tightly doesn't hurt, bright eyes. In fact, the only thing I can imagine that would feel better is pushing inside your tight, hot body."

Erin couldn't take her eyes off their hands. Conor was squeezing them around him much harder than she ever would have. Each time their hands reached the tip of his cock, he moved her palm over the pre-come leaking out of his body so on the down stroke, his natural lubrication eased their way.

"Use your other hand to caress my balls," he ordered, not slowing his movements. "But be careful, they're really sensitive at the moment."

Erin was glad he was helping her. She wanted to give

him pleasure, but had no idea how. She took the fat globes in her other hand and again, was surprised at their feel. They were warm and soft. She gently squeezed them, and Conor's ass came up off the floor and he moaned again.

Erin didn't panic this time, just smiled as she did it again and got a similar reaction.

"I'm going to drop my hand," Conor told her as he did just that. "Keep going. Faster. Yeah, bright eyes, just like that. God, you're amazing," he praised as she continued to stroke him.

"I'm not going to last. You feel too good and I've dreamed about this so often. Faster, just at the tip. Oh yeah...right there...press against the base of my dick... fuck...yeah...right there, harder...I'm coming," Conor groaned.

He didn't need to tell her, Erin could tell. She was watching him carefully and felt his balls tighten up in her palm. She felt the blood pulsing in his cock and she pointed the tip at his stomach right as he started to come.

It was erotic as anything she'd ever seen, much more so than the videos she'd watched online. Conor's entire body stiffened as he exploded in several small spurts. His nipples were hard little rocks on his chest and as he pulsed in her palm, Erin slowed her strokes. Eventually she just held him tightly as his chest moved up and down and he tried to catch his breath.

His eyes were closed, and while he wasn't watching her, she let go of his balls and brought her index finger up to his belly. She swiped through his release and brought it up to her mouth. Tentatively, she stuck out her tongue and tasted him. After a moment, she put her entire finger in her mouth and sucked his release off. It wasn't exactly good, but it wasn't horrible either.

"Verdict?" Conor asked, the humor easy to hear in his voice.

Erin's eyes swung up to his face and she blushed, realizing that he'd seen her taste him. She tried to be nonchalant. "It's not terrible."

He chuckled, then closed his eyes and took a deep breath. After a moment, he opened his eyes again and said, "Thank you. That was amazing."

"Yeah," Erin agreed. "But now you're...messy."

"I need to go clean up."

"I'll go get a washcloth," Erin told him. "Don't move."

She was somewhat surprised when Conor didn't argue. He put his hands back under his head and nodded.

She stood on shaky legs and turned to head down the hall to his bathroom. She grabbed a washcloth and waited until the water warmed to get it wet. Then she headed back to where she'd left Conor.

He was still lying on the floor next to the couch. His pants were still around his thighs and his body was on display. Erin stood above him for a long moment, admiring him. He really was built. From his rock-hard thighs to his flat, muscular stomach and broad shoulders. Conor Paxton was every woman's dream man—and he was here with her.

His cock was lying between his legs, soft and sated. It looked completely different flaccid, but no less fascinating. The come on his belly glistened in the light of the room and Erin kneeled next to him and hesitated.

"It's okay. I won't bite."

Erin nodded and wiped the evidence of his orgasm away, noting the various scars as she went. Now that she wasn't distracted by...other things...she could easily see them. A long, jagged wound here, a small circle there. He hadn't lied, he did have scars.

She realized that she hadn't even noticed them when he'd undressed earlier. It wasn't that they were hidden or subtle, they weren't. But all she'd seen was beauty laid out underneath her. It was somewhat of an epiphany. Would the same happen to Conor when he looked at her body? Would he be too concerned about seeing her boobs and...between her legs...to even care about her scars? They were bigger than his, but after ten years, had faded quite a bit.

While she'd been sitting next to him, the washcloth in her hand, Conor had pulled up his jeans and boxers. He stood and held a hand down to her. "Come on, bright eyes, it's time for bed."

Without thought as to what would happen when they got there, Erin placed her hand in his and let Conor pull her upright. He led her down the hall to his bedroom, turning off lights as he went. It was early, but Erin had no problem with going to bed already.

He let her have the bathroom first and Erin used an extra toothbrush she found under the sink, and then washed her face. Conor had given her one of his T-shirts and a pair of boxers to wear to bed. She came out of the bathroom and Conor immediately entered, giving her time to herself to get under the covers.

She crawled into Conor's king-size bed and waited nervously for him. He came out minutes later, dressed in nothing but a clean pair of boxers. Without making a fuss, he turned out the light and climbed under the covers with her. He gathered her into his arms, kissed her briefly, and relaxed under her.

Erin waited for him to move. To touch her. To do something. But when he hadn't moved several minutes later, she tentatively asked, "Aren't we..." Her voice trailed off.

"As I said earlier, just because we're in the same bed doesn't mean I'm gonna jump you, bright eyes. We're gonna take our time, get to know each other physically. If you want to touch me, you're welcome to. Anytime, anyplace. But I'm not going to force you to do anything. I just had the best orgasm I've had in a really long time because it came from my girlfriend. I feel mellow and relaxed. Your touch was everything. I'm gonna lay here and enjoy having you in my arms. Feeling your bare legs against mine, your body heat soaking into mine. I'm more excited than I probably should be that your smell will permeate my pillow and sheets, so on the nights when I can't hold you, I can still have a reminder of you in my bed. Sleep, Erin. There's no pressure here. None. Thank you for what you gave me out there. I'll remember it for the rest of my life."

She had no words for that. Erin realized she'd been nervous about what he'd want to do when they got in bed because in her limited experience, she thought that once the line had been crossed of her touching him, he'd want more. She should've known better.

Tilting her head, Erin kissed the underside of his jaw. She wrapped her arm around his warm, bare belly, surprised at how comfortable it was to sleep next to someone. Within moments, she slept.

She never felt Conor's kiss on top of her head or heard his whispered, "I'd walk through fire to fight your demons, bright eyes. I love you."

15

A MONTH LATER, they had their first fight.

Erin was supposed to go over to Conor's house for the night. He was going to call her when he got home to let her know she could come over.

But he'd had a shit day at work. He was grumpy and didn't want to talk to anyone, so instead of calling to tell her he wasn't up for company, he sent a short text that merely said, *Had a rough day. I'll call you tomorrow.*

Around eight, his phone rang. Conor had been working out in his guest room. He thought about ignoring it, but knew he couldn't.

"Hello?"

"Conor? It's me, Erin."

"Hey."

"Um...are you home?"

"Yeah, but I'm not in the mood for company tonight."

"You're not in the mood for company," Erin repeated.

Hearing the censure in her tone, Conor answered

more brusquely than he'd ever spoken to her before. "Yeah, Erin. That's what I said."

"What's wrong?"

"Nothing."

"Conor, I can tell something happened. Is it your family? Are they okay?"

"They're fine."

"Then what?"

"I just don't want to deal with anything tonight."

"Deal with anything?"

"Yeah."

"So seeing me would mean you have to *deal* with something."

Conor sighed. "That's not what I said."

"Actually, it's exactly what you said."

"Then it's not what I meant. I just had a crappy day at work. I'm not in the mood to be sociable. This isn't about you, and pressuring me to talk about my crappy day isn't helping."

Erin was silent for a long moment. "I see."

He sighed. "I'm just in a bad mood. I don't want you around me when I'm like this."

"So every time you're in a bad mood, you don't want to be around me?"

"Yes. No...it's just not a good time, Erin."

"When that asshole at the bar told me he thought I'd gained weight, and I was miserable about it, I shouldn't have called you to comfort me?"

"No, I just—"

"When I learned that I couldn't apply for tenure at

the university and was ready to quit, I shouldn't have told you all about that either?"

"Erin—"

"And when that asshole rear-ended me and I went to the emergency room because my neck hurt, I shouldn't have told you? I should've kept that to myself until I was in a better mood?"

"Dammit, Erin! It's not the same."

"It's exactly the same, Conor." This time, the hurt in her tone was loud and clear. More so because she wasn't yelling at him. She was using logic, and every word speared through his heart as if they were knives. "You take care of me every day, and while I'm not used to it and it sometimes makes me uncomfortable, I still love that you do it. All I'm trying to do is the same for you. But, I'm glad you told me how this relationship is supposed to work. Thank you. Next time I have a bad day, I'll be sure to hole up in my apartment like a five-year-old and send you a bullshit text. Enjoy your sulk, Conor." Then she hung up on him.

His fight with Erin didn't improve his mood or his day at all. Conor spent the next thirty minutes justifying his actions to himself, then the following thirty minutes pacing in agitation when he realized what a dick he'd been. Then he called Erin half a dozen times, but she didn't answer.

As his worry for her increased, he understood what he'd done. And she was right. Being in a relationship didn't mean they only shared good times together. If they stayed together, got married, and had kids, he couldn't pout in his room every time he had a bad day.

He needed to talk about it with her like the adult he was. He knew without a doubt that if asked, Erin would give him the space he needed to work through his feelings.

Except, he suddenly realized, he didn't *want* space. Being around Erin always made him feel better. Happy.

He'd been wrong. A dick. And he needed to apologize. And it couldn't wait.

After taking the world's quickest shower, Conor got into his truck and drove to her apartment. It wasn't too late, but he knew she usually went to bed early. Ultimately, it didn't matter. It could've been three in the morning and he still would've groveled for her forgiveness.

He knocked on her door and waited. He heard footsteps on the other side, but she didn't open it.

"I'm sorry. You were right. I was sulking. I want so badly to be everything to you, that I forget that you being everything to *me* means letting you in when I've had a bad day."

The door opened a crack and Erin peered out.

He didn't hesitate. "We raided a property today and found dozens of abused and neglected reptiles. Snakes with their skin sloughing off. Turtles with broken and cracked shells. Alligators who were so skinny it was horrifying. I know people tend to only care about cute dogs and cats who are found with animal hoarders, but the filth and lack of remorse from the man who owned the property got to me. I didn't want my bad mood to touch you."

Erin opened the door all the way. The look of sorrow

on her face was hard to bear, but Conor stayed quiet so she could have her say.

"I'm sorry, Conor. But if you think I only want to be around you when things are good, this relationship isn't going to work. I know so far I've done a lot more taking than giving, but I need to feel as if you need me as much as I need you."

"I need you," Conor told her immediately. "So much it scares me. I was afraid you'd see me in a bad mood and have second thoughts about continuing on with this relationship."

"Conor, for God's sake. It's entirely possible my mom murdered my dad and you know about how I almost ate myself to death. A bad mood here and there doesn't even land you in the same stratosphere as *my* issues. I freaked out the other day when I stretched and you saw my belly. Good God. I'm in love with you, and you're worried about being in a freaking bad mood around me. That doesn't exactly bode well for any kind of successful relationship between us."

Conor knew she was right, but he couldn't think past those five words. "You love me?"

Her bottom lip quivered and she choked out, "Yes. So much, it scares me to death that you're going to change your mind and decide a thirty-five-year-old virgin who has more mental issues than she knows what to do with isn't worth the hassle."

"I'm coming in," Conor declared, pushing her door open and forcing Erin to take a step backwards. He shut the door behind him and took her face in his hands. "I love you. I treasure every minute we spend together. I'm sorry I made the wrong decision tonight. It won't happen again. Thank you for calling me on it and not just taking my shit. I'm *not* going to change my mind about loving you, bright eyes. Just don't give up on *me*, okay?"

"I won't," she said, tears brimming in her eyes.

Conor pulled her to him and they stood in the front hallway of her apartment, hugging for several long minutes. Finally, he pulled back and asked, "Can I stay?"

"Of course," Erin replied immediately.

"You still want to go camping with me next week?"

She huffed out a breath. "Yeah. You're not canceling on *me*, are you?"

"No. But..." He stopped.

"But?"

"I can't go on Monday. I need to go to court and make sure the guy from today doesn't get his animals back. It's not a formal thing, but we go in front of the judge and the accused makes his case, and we make ours. The ASPCA has all the animals now and my testimony will help their case. But I have the rest of the week off as we planned."

"How long will it take?"

"What? The hearing?"

"Yeah."

"It's scheduled for two o'clock. It shouldn't take more than two hours."

"Why don't I meet you out there then?"

Conor frowned and she continued.

"I could drive out there and set up the tent and stuff. Then by the time you get there sometime after six, everything would be ready and we could just relax."

"I'm not sure," he said.

"Come on, I haven't had a week off in a really long time. I could make that Dutch oven lasagna recipe I've been wanting to try. It'd be ready for you when you got there," she cajoled.

"I suppose that could work. You don't mind?"

"Of course not. I didn't look like I minded setting everything up when we were on that canoe trip, did I?"

He shook his head. "Nope. You had everything under control."

"Exactly."

"Okay. It's a plan then. Thank you."

"No need to thank me. I want to get out of town just as much as you. My classes at school are driving me crazy. Some semesters my students are great, and others they're just...ugh."

"No, I mean, thank you for forgiving me for being an ass tonight."

"Conor, we're not perfect. I suspect you're going to be an ass again at some point. Just as I'm going to be a head case about my body, about eating, and probably about something else stupid. If this relationship is going to work, we need to communicate. When you told me about the bullying your sisters went through, and how it affected you, I realized then you would understand my pain and issues better than most people in my life. Because you saw firsthand how ugly people can be to each other. But I want, and need, to be there for *you* as much as you're there for me. Please don't shut me out."

"How'd you get so smart when you're the virgin in the relationship?"

She smiled. "Because I'm a woman. We're smarter, don't you know?"

With that, Conor bent and put his shoulder to Erin's stomach. He stood with her hanging over his shoulder.

"Conor! Put me down!"

He ignored her and strode toward her bedroom. "Put you down? Sure." He shrugged his shoulder and carefully dumped her on her ass on her mattress.

She sat there, looking up at him, her hair in disarray around her head. She hadn't ever been prettier to him. More so because he realized at that moment that she'd managed to lighten his mood. He'd been an ass earlier. He should've recognized that being around her was the one thing he needed to feel better. Not shutting her out. He wouldn't make that mistake again.

"Get changed, bright eyes. I'm gonna do my thing in the bathroom, then I want to show you how appreciative I am of your forgiveness."

Her eyes got big. He ran his hand over her hair and leaned down and whispered in her ear, "I want to taste you. Show you the difference between an orgasm I give you with my hand, and one I give you with my mouth."

"Conor..." she said breathlessly.

He could see the excitement, and trepidation, in her eyes.

"We'll keep the lights off, baby. All you'll have to do is feel. I'll do the rest." He waited with bated breath for her acquiescence. "It'll be good, bright eyes. Promise."

"Okay."

That one word made his cock spring to life. "Okay. I'll be back." He kissed her swiftly, already imagining how she'd feel and taste under his mouth, and headed for the bathroom. He always gave her plenty of time to get changed and under the covers. As much as he craved seeing her body, he wanted to make her comfortable more. Conor had no doubt the day would come when she'd be all right with having his eyes on her, but until that day came, he'd do everything in his power to protect her...even from himself.

His thoughts turned to the upcoming night and he licked his lips. Oh yeah, making her come on his face had been his fantasy for the past month. Making her feel good was the least he could do after what he'd put her through tonight.

Conor exited the bathroom wearing nothing but a pair of boxers. He immediately went to the light switch and flicked it, throwing the room into darkness.

He made his way back to her bed and settled on the mattress next to her. She held herself stiff next to him, and he smiled. He couldn't wait to taste her. To feel her explode under him. He couldn't deny he wanted to see her, all of her, but being with her like this, in the dark, heightened all his other senses.

He could hear her increased breaths and feel her slight trembling. Leaning forward, Conor put his nose behind her ear and inhaled the slightly sweet smell of whatever shampoo she used. "Relax, bright eyes," he murmured as he nuzzled the sensitive skin of her neck. "This is going to feel good. *Really* good."

"I know...I'm just nervous."

Conor didn't respond. He knew she wasn't completely comfortable with what he wanted to do, but that made him all the more determined to make it an experience she'd never forget. He picked up one of her hands, which had been pressing into the mattress, and kissed the palm. Then he placed her hand on his naked chest. "Touch me."

He figured if she was concentrating on his body, maybe she'd pay less attention to what he was doing to hers.

As she brought her other hand up to his chest, he leaned over her and kissed her, deep, wet, and lazy. He made love to her mouth as she explored his body. Her hands caressed his chest, then roamed down his arms. He shifted and straddled her thighs, without taking his mouth from hers. He felt her small hands move to the small of his back and trace the indentation of his spine.

His cock jumped behind the cotton of the boxers he wore and Conor felt a spurt of pre-come leak out the tip. He wanted the woman under him more than he'd wanted anything in his life, but tonight was about her, not his own sexual satisfaction.

Ending the kiss, Conor moved to Erin's neck. He sucked and kissed every inch of skin there, grinning as he felt her turn her head to the side, giving him room. Slowly, so he didn't alarm her, he inched his way down her body. She was wearing one of his T-shirts, and aside from nuzzling her breasts as he went, he didn't try to remove it, knowing she'd feel more secure and comfortable with her clothes on.

Her belly was soft, and Conor would give anything to see her, all of her, but the scent of her desire distracted him. He sighed in relief as he settled between her thighs.

She opened for him, allowing him access to her pussy. His hands smoothed down her stomach and he stopped when he reached her hips.

She wasn't wearing panties.

No wonder he could smell her arousal so easily.

"I figured it would be stupid to keep my underwear on if you were going to...you know," Erin said tentatively.

Conor didn't respond with words. He leaned down and ran his nose up the crease where her leg met her torso. She moved under him, lifting her ass a fraction of an inch, before relaxing against the mattress again.

He shifted until his fingers rested on her hips and his thumbs caressed the coarse hair above her clit. "You smell amazing," Conor said. "So fucking perfect."

Not giving her time to respond, he leaned down and licked her slit ever so slowly. Groaning at his first taste of her, he did it again. Then a third time. After the last pass, he concentrated on her clit. Running his tongue over it lazily.

"Conor...oh my God!" Erin said. Her hands came to his head and she gripped him tightly. Her fingernails dug into his scalp, increasing his pleasure.

He couldn't see the perfection in front of him, but there was something to be said for making love in the dark. He liked it. A lot. He shifted, forcing her legs wider around his shoulders. Without warning, he fastened his mouth around her clit and sucked—hard.

She bucked under him and he used his hands to hold her down as he increased the suction around the small bundle of nerves. Conor breathed in and out fast through his nose, whipping his tongue over and over her clit even as he sucked.

His nose was buried in her trimmed pubic hair, and he felt Erin begin to twitch under him in the beginnings of an orgasm. She was incredibly sensitive...and she was all his. No other man had seen or felt her this way. Only him.

The possessive feelings rose up in Conor until he couldn't think about anything but making her come. Of giving her something no one ever had.

"Conor...please...I'm so close!"

He could tell. Shifting one hand to rest on her lower belly and keeping her in place, he lifted his head and licked her slit once more. She was soaked now, dripping with excitement. He parted her folds with his hand and leaned in once more. Conor pushed his tongue up inside her as far as it could go, relishing her taste.

He moved his free hand between her legs and lazily played with her. One finger coasted lightly over her sensitive clit, making her jump, before tracing her opening. She moaned and lifted her feet until they were resting flat on the mattress.

"You're beautiful," he murmured as his finger continued to touch and play in her wetness without ever entering her.

"You can't even see me," she protested.

"I don't have to see you to know you're beautiful, bright eyes," he said honestly. "The way your body weeps for me is gorgeous. The moans coming from your mouth are exquisite. You trusting me and spreading your legs farther apart is stunning." He slowly—*ever so slowly*—eased one finger inside her body as he choked out, "And the feel of your tight, wet pussy strangling my finger is so goddamn magnificent, I could come just imagining how my cock will feel once it gets inside you."

"Conor..." Erin wailed as she tightened against his finger.

Conor didn't know if she was trying to keep him out, or was just overwhelmed with sensation. "Easy, bright eyes, I'm not going to hurt you. Relax and let me in."

"I need...I want...please, Conor," Erin begged.

Realizing she was on the edge, and wanting to feel her go over, he didn't prolong either of their agony any longer. Keeping his finger nestled inside her, not moving, Conor leaned down and roughly tongued her clit. He had no mercy, didn't start slow and build, he attacked the bundle of nerves and lashed at it as fast as he could.

Within seconds, Erin was bucking against his mouth and he could feel her inner muscles squeezing his finger. Her hands gripped his shoulders so hard he knew she'd leave marks, but he didn't care.

She arched her back, and he could just imagine the look of ecstasy on her face as every muscle in her body tensed right before she exploded. Conor was so turned on, he was amazed he didn't come right along with her. The musky smell of her increased as she came, and he slowly eased his finger in and out of her incredibly tight sheath, doing what he could to prolong her orgasm.

When she was coming down, he fastened his mouth over her clit again and sucked, hard. Erin let out a high-pitched screech and immediately came again. Conor reveled in her pleasure. Loved knowing *he'd* done that for her. His mouth. His fingers. Him.

As she came down from her second orgasm, Conor had pity on her and released his mouth from her clit and eased his finger from inside her body. He couldn't resist bringing his come-soaked digit up to his mouth. He closed his eyes as her essence exploded on his taste buds. Without thought, he leaned down and used his tongue to lick her folds clean.

Erin trembled as he reluctantly pulled away and got up on his hands and knees to crawl up her body. He turned onto his back and pulled Erin into him. Her knee immediately bent and eased over his thigh and one hand curled around his chest to hold him closer.

It was a minute or two before she spoke. "Thank you."

Conor smiled in the darkness. "You're welcome."

"I...I had no idea it was like that."

"It's not always," Conor said honestly. "You're just a natural."

Erin smacked him lightly on the chest. "Shut up."

He turned his head and found her forehead in the darkness and kissed her. "Seriously. You're incredibly passionate, Erin, and I'm honored and blessed to be the man to bring it to the surface. I should be thanking *you*."

She shifted uneasily next to him and said, "Are you... you didn't get off."

Conor tightened his arms around the woman at his side. "Holding you as you came was a gift. Tonight was all for you."

She moved her hand slowly down his chest toward his still rock-hard dick. "I can—"

Conor caught her hand and brought it up to his mouth. He kissed the palm and laid it on his chest. He kept his hand on top of hers and pressed it tightly against him. "Shhhhh. Relax. Despite what some men claim, a guy won't die if he doesn't come. I can't deny I'm harder right now than I've ever been in my life, but I'm feeling mellow despite the condition of my dick. Knowing I was the first man to make you come with my mouth is the most intimate thing I've ever experienced. It was amazing. *You* are amazing, bright eyes."

He felt a splash of wetness against his chest and stiffened in alarm.

"You're pretty amazing yourself, Conor," she said softly, and he relaxed.

"Sleep, Erin."

She took a deep breath against him, then went boneless. "Good night, Conor." Her lips touched his chest before her cheek rested against him once more.

It took a while for him to fall asleep, but it wasn't his uncomfortable erection that kept him awake. He couldn't sleep because he didn't want to miss a second of the satisfied feeling coursing through his veins. Holding Erin in his arms, having her trust him to satisfy her in such an intimate way after everything she'd been through, made him feel ten feet tall.

16

"I'll see you probably around six-thirty," Conor told Erin over the phone.

"Sounds good. I'm leaving here in about thirty minutes. I'll get the campsite set up and lasagna will be ready and waiting for you when you get there."

"I'm more than excited about this trip."

"Me too," Erin agreed. And she was. After their fight, and their incredible night together when Conor showed her how amazing oral sex could be, she was ready to move forward with their sexual relationship. And this week was the perfect time to do it. They could concentrate on each other, and she wouldn't have to worry about the harsh lights of the modern world.

For the first time in her life, she wanted a man to see her. All of her. Conor had proved himself time and time again. He wouldn't be repulsed by her scars. He wouldn't care that she still had a stomach pooch that she couldn't seem to get rid of or that her boobs sagged a bit more than she thought they should. She loved him and he loved her. The week was going to be perfect.

They'd chosen a campsite all the way at the northern end of the park called Hermit's Shack Camp Area. It was actually still closed to campers this early in the season, but Conor called in a favor from the game warden who worked in that area. They'd graduated from the same class, and the woman had called the person in charge of reservations to make special arrangements for Conor and her to be able to camp there. They'd have the area all to themselves. She couldn't wait.

"Drive safe, and shoot me a text when you leave and when you get there," Conor ordered. "I won't be able to answer most likely, but I'll see it and know you're safe."

"I will. Good luck today."

"Thanks. From what I understand from the ASPCA coordinator, they have enough pictures to make sure the guy doesn't get the reptiles back."

"Good."

"Yeah. I'll see you tonight, bright eyes."

"Later."

Erin hung up and couldn't keep the smile off her face. She had another surprise for Conor that night. Not only was she going to tell him she was ready to make love with him, she wanted to do it without condoms. She'd been to her gynecologist last month and had started on birth control. She knew Conor was clean because he'd told her he'd gotten tested, just to put her at ease since they were "playing" in bed more and more. He wanted her to know that he wouldn't put her in danger.

She wanted Conor with nothing between them.

Wanted her first time to be as memorable as possible. It wasn't often a woman got to make love for the very first time with the man she wanted to spend the rest of her life with.

Whistling, Erin made sure she had plenty of fruit and salad packed for her. The meat was already in the cooler. She thought she had everything she needed. She tightened the laces of her boots, smiling at seeing the flint her dad had given her so long ago.

Conor had given that to her. Instead of feeling sad when she looked at the paracord shoelaces and flint, she could finally focus on only the good memories. She hoped her dad would be proud of her if he could see her today.

It took three trips to her Jeep to get everything packed, but finally Erin was on her way. She shot off a quick text letting Conor know she was leaving and pulled out onto the road, not able to keep the goofy, excited smile off her face.

CONOR DROVE SLOWLY DOWN the narrow road that wound through the Hill Country State Natural Area, his brows drawn down in worry. He tried to tamp it down, but the sick feeling in his gut churned, making it impossible to concentrate.

He'd texted Erin right before he'd left San Antonio. The ASPCA had won the right to keep, rehabilitate, and rehome the reptiles taken from the animal hoarder. Conor's testimony about what he'd found and what a healthy alligator, turtle, and snake should look like went a long way toward the judge ruling in the animal shelter's favor.

She'd responded immediately, sharing his excitement with half a dozen emojis, and including a picture of the lasagna she was just then putting into the pit she'd dug in the ground. She'd lined it with charcoal and told him it would cook for an hour and a half on the low heat and should be perfect by the time he arrived.

Conor had looked forward to the camping trip for the last couple months, but especially over the past week as the date had neared. After the fight, and making up with Erin, he'd been more than ready to spend some quality time alone with her in one of his favorite places on the planet.

It was crazy, but the fight had only seemed to bring them closer. He hoped after this week, Erin would feel comfortable enough to let him make love to her. He wasn't going to hold his breath for getting any while camping. Even though they'd be isolated from the other campers, he wasn't sure a woman would think making love in a tent was sexy. Especially for her first time.

But he wasn't counting out other intimate things they could do. They'd played quite a bit, and had both given and received orgasms. And each and every time only made Conor love and want Erin more.

He'd stopped to top off his gas tank and had shot off another text, letting Erin know where he was and updating his ETA, but she hadn't responded. Then he'd tried to call her when he'd gotten close to the park...but she hadn't answered. The phone had rung six times and gone to voicemail.

Conor tried to tell himself it was because she was busy, but deep down he had a bad feeling.

Pulling up to the Hermit's Shack Camp Area, he sighed in relief. Erin's Jeep was sitting in the designated parking spot for the camping area. He parked alongside it and threw his bag over his shoulder. He jogged the hundred or so feet down to where the campsites were. He immediately saw that Erin had set up their tent at the far end of the small field. There were bluebonnets blooming everywhere, as was typical for this part of Texas this time of year.

As he got closer to the campsite, Conor frowned. He didn't see Erin anywhere.

He put his bag down on the picnic table next to the fire ring. There was a plastic tablecloth hooked to it, but she hadn't gotten any plates or silverware out yet. Looking around, he found where Erin had dug a hole to make the in-ground oven for the Dutch oven.

"Erin?" he called, but got no response. He strode over to the tent and unzipped it, looking inside, hoping she was simply taking a nap. Empty. She'd blown up an air mattress and made what looked like quite a love nest for them. She'd used real sheets, along with the comforter he recognized from her own bed. The pillows were lying neatly at the head of the bed. Her duffle bag was on the floor, still zipped.

Conor went back to the hole in the ground and used the nearby shovel to dig up the dirt covering it. As soon as he did, he could smell burnt food. Pulling the iron pot out of the ground by its long metal handle, he carefully lifted the lid. The pasta on the edges of the pot was black and smoke rose in a big plume.

He was really alarmed now. Erin would never have let the food burn like this. She'd known when he would be arriving and had said herself that she'd have the meal waiting for him. Erin wasn't one to waste food, and she knew what she was doing when it came to camp cooking.

Putting the lid back on the pot, he placed the Dutch oven on the ground and didn't give it another thought. He immediately went into officer mode.

The area was eerily quiet, he could only hear one bird chirping overhead. The tent had been placed on a grassy area off to the side of the picnic table and on the edge of the empty field. His eyes scanned the area, every sense alert. He didn't see anything amiss at first glance. He walked over to the edge of the area where the scrub bushes and trees started. He called her name again. "Erin?" Nothing but silence followed.

He pulled out his phone and called the game warden who had helped them with the campsite.

"Hello?"

"Hey, Winston, it's Paxton."

"Hey. You set up yet?"

"That's the thing. I'm here, but Erin's not."

"What do you mean?" Juliette Winston asked, the concern clear in her tone.

"Just that. The tent is here. Her Jeep is up at the parking area. The food was still cooking, burnt. But she's not here."

"Let me make a quick call to the ranger on duty at the gate. See if he saw anything."

"Call me right back."

"I will."

Conor hung up, feeling a little more settled now that he'd talked to a fellow officer. He narrowed his eyes, somehow sensing that he was missing something. His gaze went from the tent, to the fire pit, to where she'd buried their dinner to cook, and back to the picnic table. Everything looked normal. He dropped his chin and stared at his feet, trying to gain his composure.

That's when he saw it.

The dirt at his feet was scuffed.

Taking a giant step back so as not to disturb anything more than he already had, Conor concentrated on the ground.

As if the dirt could speak, he immediately saw what had happened—and it chilled his blood. It looked like Erin had been standing next to the table, probably clamping the tablecloth down, and someone had come up behind her.

Erin was tall at five nine, and strong, but if taken by surprise, she could easily be overwhelmed.

He could tell where her feet had tried to gain purchase in the dirt, there was one long scuff that went under the seat of the picnic table, and a lot of disturbed dirt directly behind it. Since they were the only people who had been in this area since the fall, the dirt should be pristine, like it was on the other side of the table.

Conor carefully made his way around the table and did another sweep of the area.

There. A footprint. Too big to be Erin's, and he hadn't walked in that area. Conor took pictures with his cell phone. He turned his head this way and that, trying to figure out where whoever had caught Erin unawares had taken her. The grass in the field only showed two sets of footprints...his and presumably Erin's. It looked like she'd taken at least two trips back and forth with the supplies.

But whoever had taken her had to have come from somewhere. He concentrated harder, finally finding footprints in the dirt in the trees behind the table. He'd snuck up on Erin from the wilderness side. No wonder she hadn't seen him coming. Who would think someone would enter the camp from that side?

His phone rang.

"Paxton."

"The ranger said only two vehicles have entered or left in the last hour. Your truck and a minivan with a family. Mom, dad, and three small kids. Oh, and a dog. No one else."

"Someone's taken her," Conor told the other warden. "Snuck up through the scrub, caught her by surprise from behind."

"You sure?"

"Absolutely."

"What do you need?"

Conor was relieved his old friend didn't question him or otherwise tell him he might be wrong. He knew deep down he wasn't. Someone had taken Erin. He had no idea what they wanted from her, or wanted to do *to* her, but whatever it was couldn't be good.

"Call Alamo Search and Rescue. And SAR in Boerne. The sooner we get looking, the sooner we'll find them."

"You think he walked with her out of there?"

"I'm not sure. But whoever he is, he knew what he was doing. He got in and out without leaving any obvious traces. Erin isn't a small woman. She's tall, and while not overweight, she's not exactly a lightweight. He had to have some sort of vehicle nearby to transport her."

"On it."

"I'm staying here. Just in case she manages to get away from him and comes back here or to her vehicle. Send everyone back here to the Hermit campsite."

"I will. We're going to find her," Juliette said.

"Damn right we are," Conor answered. He couldn't afford to be pessimistic. Not when it was the woman he loved whose life was on the line.

"I'll call when they're on their way."

"Ten-four." Conor clicked off his phone. He hesitated then turned to the last text he'd received from Erin.

ERIN: *YAY! I knew you'd kick that guy's ass. Lasagna has another hour & a half to go. It'll be perfect when you get here. Drive safe. Love you.*

SHE'D INCLUDED a picture of the Dutch oven and half a dozen emojis of different kinds of reptiles. His gut twisted.

Not letting himself wonder whether she was hurt or

what she was thinking, Conor clicked on a name in his address book.

"Hey, Conor. Aren't you supposed to be going off the grid with your woman this week?"

"Listen, Beth. Something's happened to Erin. I need your help."

"Talk to me," Beth said immediately, all business.

Conor explained what he knew and felt better when Beth said she'd get back to him after tracking Erin's phone.

"Want me to call the others?" she asked before hanging up.

"Yeah, I have a feeling I'm going to need all the help I can get," Conor told her. He had no compunction about calling on every resource he could think of to help find Erin. FBI, Texas Rangers, firefighters, SAPD...it didn't matter how many markers he owed by the time this was all over. As long as Erin was safe and sound, he wouldn't care.

Backing away from the crime scene, Conor's eyes took in the campsite that should've held memories of one of the best weeks on his life, but instead was the beginning of a nightmare. He wanted to believe Erin would pop out from behind a tree, blushing as she told him she'd wandered off to pee and had simply gotten lost. But he knew she wouldn't. Someone had taken her.

He wouldn't get away with it. Conor would find her and they'd get on with their lives...together. He had to believe that, otherwise he wouldn't be any good to anyone.

Spinning on his heel, he stalked back toward the

parking area. He needed to check Erin's Jeep and see if by chance there were any clues there. Then he'd wait for the search teams to arrive.

"Hang on, bright eyes," Conor whispered as he strode toward the two lone vehicles in the parking area. "Hang on."

17

ERIN GROANED as she tried to turn onto her side. She was stopped short with a sharp tug on her wrist. She frowned and pried her eyes open. Her lids felt as if they were ten times their normal weight.

She was lying on a cot under what looked like a green tarp converted into a tent. She turned her head and saw a man sitting across the small area. His head was shaved and his skin was deeply tanned...either that or extremely dirty. He had on a pair of camouflage pants and a shirt. They looked like what soldiers in the Army used to wear before the uniform was digitized.

It was dark, a single lantern all that lit up the inside of the shelter.

She shifted and tried to move her legs, but groaned again when a sharp pain shot through her ankle. Erin looked down and blinked in confusion. Both her ankles had rope tied around them. She tugged again, realizing that she was tied to the cot. Her ankle hurt, not from the rope around it, but in a more internal way, as if it was sprained.

She shivered—and suddenly realized that it wasn't simply because it was chilly. She was wearing nothing but her bra and panties. As if it wasn't bad enough to be tied to the cot with a man she'd never seen before, she was practically naked.

Feeling more vulnerable than she ever had before, she began to frantically tug on her bindings.

"You're awake."

The deep voice scared her and Erin flinched. Her eyes flew upward, and she saw the man who had been across the tent was standing over her. He was tall and intimidating.

"W-where am I?" she croaked, the cotton feeling in her mouth preventing her from swallowing.

"Here, have some water," the man said quietly, grabbing a cup from a makeshift table next to her and bringing it to her mouth.

Erin turned her head and refused, even though she was dying of thirst. "Who are you? Where am I?" she asked again.

The man sighed as if annoyed. "You don't need to know either of those things. All you need to do is concentrate on healing."

"Healing?"

"Yes. You hurt your ankle earlier tonight. It was my fault, really, I underestimated what a wild creature could do when confined."

Erin wrinkled her brow. She couldn't think straight. She had no idea what he was talking about.

The man took a sip of the liquid in the cup then said, "See? It's not drugged. You need to stay hydrated. It's important."

He held the cup back to her mouth and lifted her head with his other hand, assisting her. The need for liquid overrode any other objection she had at the moment, so Erin drank. She finished the cup and the man gently put her head back down on the cot.

"Where are my clothes? Untie me," Erin demanded.

The man ignored her and walked back to the table where he'd been sitting. He picked something up and returned to crouch at her side. She saw then he was holding an MRE, a military meal-ready-to-eat. He scooped up a spoonful of food and held it out to her.

Erin recoiled in horror. MREs were notorious for having a ton of calories. They needed to in order for the soldiers who ate them to be able to continue to function while out in the field.

"You must eat. Keep your strength up."

Erin was starting to be able to think more clearly now. She closed her eyes for a moment. Camping. Dinner. Lasagna. Conor. Her lids flew up and she struggled against the ropes at her feet, ignoring the pain that shot through her right ankle. "Let me go!"

"You need to eat," the man repeated as if she hadn't spoken, and held up the spoon once more.

Erin gathered as much spit as she could, which wasn't enough for what she wanted to do, and spat at the man. "Get away from me," she hissed.

Instead of being upset, the man merely sighed again. He put the MRE to the side and stood.

Erin glared up at him defiantly.

He went back to the table he'd been sitting at and fiddled with something. Erin pulled harder at her bindings. The rope around her wrists chafed, but she ignored it. She needed to get free. Needed to find Conor. Had this man hurt him too?

Her captor walked back over to her with a piece of fabric in his hand. He moved lightning fast, and before Erin knew what he intended, he had his hand over her nose and mouth, the fabric held firmly in place.

He was going to smother her. Erin struggled as hard as she ever had before—to no avail.

"Shhh," the man soothed calmly, holding her still as she struggled. "At least I got some water into you. Got to keep your strength up. Once your ankle heals a bit more and you can run properly, I'll let you go. It's no fun to hunt wounded animals. Where's the challenge in that?"

Erin didn't understand what he was saying, but it didn't matter. Her eyes drooped. Whatever chemical he had on the fabric was doing its job. The last thing she heard before losing consciousness was, "I love your fight. You'll be my most worthy hunt yet."

AFTER SEARCHING ALL NIGHT, the only thing they'd found was faint tire tracks from some sort of all-terrain vehicle. Whoever had taken Erin had carried her to where he'd stashed the ATV and had driven off. They'd tried to follow the tracks, but they'd lost them in the wilderness.

Beth had called Conor back an hour or two after he'd

first talked to her and let him know that she'd tracked Erin's phone and, as he suspected, the last time she used it was to text him. She also said that the phone wasn't currently transmitting a signal.

Conor allowed himself a moment of despair. The sun was just peeking over the horizon, giving the area a pretty golden glow. It would've been a hell of a sunrise to experience with Erin on their first morning camping, but instead he was sharing it with around two dozen men and women who were eating a rushed breakfast provided by the search and rescue support team.

"We're going to find her," Hayden said quietly. She and the rest of his law enforcement friends had come as soon as they'd heard Erin was missing. Conor hadn't had to ask, they'd just appeared about the same time as the SAR teams. He knew Beth had called them.

Conor didn't answer Hayden verbally, he just nodded. He didn't know if he believed her. People disappeared without a trace all the time. Hell, look at Erin's father. He'd been there one day and gone the next.

He didn't want to believe that would be the case with Erin, but even with the most experienced search and rescue teams in the state, they hadn't found hide nor hair of her. The dogs had picked up human scent, of Erin or her kidnapper, but where he'd climbed into the ATV, the dogs had lost them.

Hayden put her hand on Conor's arm. "Don't give up. She's smart, Conor. She knows we're looking for her."

"Yeah." It wasn't much, but it was all he could muster at the moment.

His phone rang, sparing him from any more forced positivity from his friend.

"Paxton."

"It's Beth. Any sign of her? Any other information?" Beth's voice was rough, as if she hadn't slept all night, which she probably hadn't.

"No. I was hoping *you* would have more information. But it's obvious you don't. So is this it? There's nothing more we can do to find her?" Conor asked in frustration.

"I didn't say that," Beth clipped. "Look, it's not like she was snatched on a street in the city where there's a camera on every corner. I can only work with technology, and without her phone, and without the number of the phone of whoever took her, I don't have anything to go by. I *am* searching satellite images to see if I can't catch a glimpse of the ATV you said you found traces of. I'm also searching the databases for the make and model of its tires using the pictures you sent me of the tracks."

Conor could feel the pulse frantically beating in his neck. He felt kind of sick from all the adrenaline coursing through his body for the last eight hours. But he knew perfectly well how little they had to go on. It was great they had Beth on their side, but she was right. Her expertise with technology wouldn't help Erin in this situation.

"Thank you," he told her sincerely. "I appreciate anything you can do."

Beth cleared her throat before saying, "When I was taken, I had no hope whatsoever that anyone was looking for me. No one knew I was missing. But Erin's different. She knew you were going to join her soon. She knows you'll do whatever it takes to save her. Don't give up on her. No matter what's going through your head, don't give up. You'd be surprised at how tough us women are."

"No, I'm not surprised at all," Conor told Beth softly. "And thank you. I've been sitting here thinking about how scared and helpless Erin must be feeling, but you reminded me that while she might be scared, she certainly isn't helpless. Between you, Mackenzie, Corrie, Laine, hell, even Adeline and Sophie...I've got amazing role models of strong, resilient women all around me. And you're right, I'm not going to give up until I've found her."

"Right. So I'm going to go hack into the top-secret military satellites. The Google one is a piece of shit. Later."

Conor wanted to laugh at Beth, but he didn't have it in him. He clicked off his phone.

"Beth might be a techie geek, but she's one of the smartest women I know."

Conor jerked in surprised and looked up to see Hayden still standing next to him. He'd forgotten all about her. "Yeah."

"Come on. You're not eating that breakfast burrito on your plate, so let's go over the maps again," Hayden urged.

Conor was more than happy to chuck the now cold sausage-and-egg burrito he'd been given. He wasn't hungry, not in the least. He didn't think he'd be able to keep anything down anyway. He needed to find Erin.

∽

WHEN ERIN WOKE UP AGAIN, she was quicker to remember what had happened to her. The same man from earlier was sitting on a stool at her feet. He had her injured ankle in his hand and was gently rotating it and pressing on the swollen tissue on the side. The air around them smelled pungent, as if he'd used some sort of lotion on her injured ankle.

She tried to jerk her leg away from him so she could kick him in the head, but he held her calf with an iron grip she couldn't break away from.

"You're awake again," he said.

Erin pressed her lips together tightly and refused to talk to him. She pulled on her arms, but they were just as secure as they were the last time. She was well and truly trussed up and wasn't going anywhere until the man let her go. She had no idea how long she'd been out of it, time was impossible to tell since he kept drugging her.

His free hand brushed up her shin then back down. He did it over and over, as if he were trying to gentle a horse. "Shhhhh, easy. You're okay." His words were mumbled into her leg, as though he didn't want to look up at her face. "I think another day and you'll be good to go."

"Please," Erin croaked, not able to keep quiet any longer. "Let me go. I have a boyfriend, he's looking for me. I bet he has half the state of Texas trying to find me too. It's in your best interest to set me free."

"Interesting choice of words," the man drawled, looking up at her for the first time.

Erin didn't like his eyes on her nearly naked body, but

she was less concerned about what she was or wasn't wearing at the moment. The man's eyes were gray. A dark, cold gunmetal gray that held no compassion whatsoever. She shivered.

"I can't let you go until your ankle heals. And you need your strength." He made sure her ankle was secured back to the cot before turning and picking up another MRE.

Erin watched as he filled the pouch with water and stirred it up. He took a bite and swallowed, probably proving that it wasn't tainted.

He scooted to the head of the cot and held out a spoon filled with what looked like some sort of pasta. He didn't say anything, which was super creepy. Erin wanted to knock the spoon into his face, but her stomach growled right at that moment.

She was hungry. She didn't know what time it was but the inside of the makeshift tent was bright, with sunlight coming through the large gaps in the material. Hating herself, but knowing if she was going to escape this crazy asshole, she needed her strength, as he'd said, she opened her mouth.

The man's lips quirked upward, but he didn't say anything. He spooned the rather disgusting food into her mouth, and Erin jerked her head back from him as soon as he pulled the spoon away. She swallowed with diffi-culty and kept her eyes on the man in front of her.

She tried to memorize everything about him so she could tell the cops later. From the scar bisecting one eyebrow, to the mole on the left side of his neck, to the way he smelled...like body odor and dirt.

Erin accepted another half dozen spoonfuls of the meal, then turned her head away from him. She couldn't choke down any more, no matter how hungry she was.

She felt something on her head—his hand, petting her—and jerked as far away from the man as she could.

Turning angry eyes his way, Erin saw that he was grinning at her.

He stood and went to the other side of the tent and the table he'd set up. When he turned, and Erin saw he was holding another piece of fabric, she went berserk.

"No! Get away from me. Don't touch me!" She thrashed against her bindings, terrified that he'd suffocate her this time instead of merely drugging her.

When he kept walking toward her with that evil half grin on his face, she truly began to panic. She wasn't afraid the man was going to touch her or do anything sexual to her. He'd had plenty of time to do that already, but her body felt fine. He hadn't molested her even though she was lying on the cot nearly naked.

No, he had something else in mind, something which didn't bode well for her. Not at all.

She flung her head from side to side, trying to prevent him from being able to put the cloth over her face, but tied down, she was no match for him.

As the slightly sweet smell penetrated her nose, Erin once again had to listen to him murmuring in her ear right before she passed out from whatever he'd drugged her with.

"Tomorrow, wildcat. Our fun starts tomorrow."

∼

CONOR WANTED TO PUNCH SOMETHING. Preferably whoever had taken Erin from him.

Earlier that afternoon, one of the dogs had found a pile of clothes—Erin's clothes. More specifically, her three-quarter-sleeve T-shirt and a pair of jeans. The same clothes he'd seen her put on yesterday morning.

They had been cut with a knife. The bastard had cut off her clothes.

Daydreams of what was happening to Erin plagued Conor. He imagined her in a cave, lying on the dirty ground, naked. When she saw him enter the cave, she picked up her head and said, "Why didn't you come for me?" before turning into a pile of dust in front of his eyes and blowing away.

He'd barely held back a cry as he jolted back to reality, and had refused to think about her fate for the rest of the afternoon.

He stared at the man standing over a large map. They were in the parking area at the campsite except now it was teeming with people. There were large RVs housing the search and rescue teams, a food truck had arrived earlier, as well as at least a dozen other vehicles.

Tuning out the man—and the newest plan for searching for Erin—Conor turned his back on the table and wandered away. He crossed the field of bluebonnets to the campsite that Erin had so carefully set up more than twenty-four hours earlier. Keeping his back to the hustle and bustle, he climbed up onto the picnic table and sat. He leaned his elbows on his knees and stared out into the wilderness.

Not surprised, he heard the wooden table groan as he was joined by two of his friends.

"What're you thinking?" Cruz asked.

"You don't want to know," Conor told him, then turned to Dax. "How did you do it?" he asked his friend. "How did you keep your shit together knowing that Mackenzie was hurting and you couldn't do a damn thing about it?"

The Texas Ranger didn't answer for a long moment. Finally, he said, "The only thing that kept me sane was knowing if I *did* lose it, she'd have that much less of a chance of being found."

Conor swallowed hard. Yeah, he knew that. It was the only reason *he* wasn't destroying anything and everything in his sight. "He took her clothes off." The words were forced out from his tight throat. "*Cut* them off. He's got her somewhere, and she's not wearing any fucking clothes."

"She's tough," Cruz murmured.

"You don't understand," Conor said, shaking his head.

"Tell us," Dax commanded. "You'll feel better to get it out."

Conor didn't want to. It wasn't his secret to tell. But Dax was right, the thought of what Erin was going through was eating him alive. He needed to share it with his friends.

Before he could open his mouth, they were joined by Quint, TJ, Weston, Hayden, and Calder. No one said a word. They were all there, silently supporting him.

Conor swallowed hard, then talked about Erin. His

friends knew about her struggle with food and obesity, but he wanted them to know more about her as a person. She was more than her past.

He told them about her love of silly gameshows on television. How much he'd been looking forward to trying her Dutch oven lasagna. What a great leader she was, and how she'd been so patient and easygoing with the students on the canoe trip. He told them how much she enjoyed teaching, most of the time, and how she was working toward tenure at the university. And he told them how important she was to him, and how he wanted to spend the rest of his life with her.

When he was finished telling his best friends everything he loved about Erin, he went on to explain why he was so tortured.

"She can't bear to show *me*—the man she admitted she loves, and who loves her back—her body. She just recently started wearing one of my short-sleeve T-shirts to bed. The woman has never made love...and that was going to be mine. I was going to show her how beautiful she is, inside and out. And now she's out there somewhere with a man who *cut off her clothes*. She hasn't been naked in front of anyone her entire life...and I'm afraid if we do find her, she's not going to be the same Erin I fell in love with."

"She won't be," Dax said, not harshly. "Mackenzie is different in a lot of ways after what she went through. But, Conor, different isn't necessarily bad."

"I said this to Quint when we were on the way to find Corrie," Hayden said quietly. "Don't underestimate your woman, Conor. You're all alpha men. Used to being in charge. Used to being able to slay dragons with a flick of your wrist, but what you don't understand is that many times us women can hold our own sword. We might need your help when it comes to making the final kill, but the fight is ours."

Conor looked at the only woman in the group. "She was a virgin, Hayden. She was going to be *mine*."

One second, Conor was looking at Hayden, and the next he was trying not to fall off the picnic table from the force of the blow she landed on the back of his head.

"Pull your head out of your ass, Paxton," Hayden said in a low, deadly tone. "If that's your attitude, then she's better off without you."

Conor sat up and glared at Hayden. She was supposed to be making him feel better, not pissing him off.

"She's right," Quint added. "Erin is *still* yours. Would it make you feel better right now if she'd been with two hundred guys before you?"

Conor stilled and stared at his friend. "No," he whispered.

"Right. So yeah, it sucks that she's never been with a man, but that doesn't make what happens to her any more awful than if she'd been with hundreds of men before now," Quint said.

"And you saying 'she was going to be mine' is just stupid," Hayden said with her arms crossed. "What you're implying is that you no longer want her because of what you're imagining is happening."

"That's not true," Conor was quick to say. "She's mine no matter what."

"Right. Here's my take on the situation," Hayden said. "Your woman went through a lot of shit. She managed to make it to age eighteen with a bitch of a mother trying to eat away at her soul. She was strong enough to change her eating habits...by *herself*, with no family support. That makes her one tough broad. She might be suffering, but she won't quit, Conor. I can guarantee it."

"You and her run together all the time, right?" Calder asked out of the blue.

"Yeah."

"She's in shape. If she can get away from whoever took her, she could run a long time."

Conor nodded. "True."

"And we didn't find her shoes or lingerie, right?" Cruz asked.

"That's right, only her T-shirt and jeans," Conor confirmed.

"Right, so if she does have to run, maybe she's not completely naked and, most importantly, she's got her shoes," Weston confirmed.

Conor stood and went to the edge of the campsite. A couple steps forward and he'd be engulfed into the wilderness of the area. He took a deep breath. His friends were right. He needed to stop thinking about how weak Erin was, and start remembering just how fucking tough she could be. And yeah, he hated to imagine what she might be going through, but his Erin wouldn't give up. She'd do whatever it took to escape and get back to him.

"Give me a sign, bright eyes. I'm going to find you, but you need to help me." His words were low, but not so soft his friends didn't hear them.

"We'll be on the lookout," Hayden said, putting her hand on his arm. "She's smart. She'll figure out a way to let us know where she is."

"Yeah, she will. We just have to recognize it for what it is when she gives us the signal."

18

ERIN'S HEAD HURT. She tried to lick her lips, but had absolutely no moisture in her mouth. It took her no more than a couple of moments to remember everything. She immediately tugged on her arms, expecting to find them secured to the cot, just as they had been every other time she'd woken up from whatever drug the man had been using on her.

But this time, she could freely move her arms.

She tested her legs and found that they were similarly unbound.

She immediately turned on her side and curled into a tight ball. It felt so good to be able to move and not be stuck on her back, at the mercy of the man she'd begun to call "cyborg" in her mind. With his bald head, his penchant for talking to himself and not to her, and his coldness, he was what she imagined an unemotional, robotic cyborg might be like.

She opened her eyes—and blinked in surprise. She

wasn't inside the tent anymore. She was lying on the dirt out in the open. Well, sort of.

Sitting up, Erin kept her knees drawn up to hide her body. She was inside a cage...or maybe a corral was a better word for it. The fence around her was tall, probably around ten feet. There was a cover over the top as well, preventing her from climbing out.

Looking around, Erin didn't recognize much of anything. Trees and scrub bushes, that was about it.

"Get up."

The man's low tone surprised her, and Erin scrambled to her feet and stared at him. He looked the same as he had every other time she'd woken up. Very tall, probably about six and a half feet, and big. He was very muscular. He was wearing the same camouflage clothes as every time she'd seen him. His head shone brightly in the sunlight. Erin briefly wondered if he shaved and oiled it to make it look like that.

"You have a bucket of water there," the man said, pointing to the side of her cage. "And food. Walk around."

Erin blinked. "What?"

"Walk around," he repeated.

She shook her head and gripped the fence behind her tighter. "No."

"I want to make sure you're not limping on that ankle."

"Why do you care? What are you going to do?"

"I said. Walk. Around," the man bit out.

The change in his demeanor scared the shit out of Erin, but she nonetheless shook her head. If he wanted her to do something, it probably wasn't in her best interest to comply, no matter the consequences.

The man stared at her for a long moment, then walked away and bent to a bag on the ground.

Erin held her breath. She was looking around her jail cell, trying to find a way out, when she heard the cyborg's footsteps.

He was walking toward her carrying a pistol.

"Oh my God," Erin breathed—then started begging for her life. "Please don't kill me! Don't. I have a life, friends. A boyfriend. I don't want to die!"

He fired the gun, and Erin scrunched her eyes closed and flinched.

When she didn't feel any pain, her eyes popped open again.

The cyborg motioned to the ground at her feet. A small dart was stuck in the dirt.

"I said, walk around."

She looked up into his absolutely emotionless face. "And if I don't?"

"I'll shoot you with the dart and drug you again."

Erin licked her lips. She didn't like being at this man's mercy. So far all he'd done was doctor her ankle, feed her, and give her water. But untying her and moving her outside to this...pen...wasn't giving her warm fuzzies. She'd much rather be awake and conscious. She couldn't escape if she was passed out.

She tentatively took a step away from the back of the cage, to the side.

"Again," the man demanded.

She took another step.

"Faster," he ordered.

Erin shook her head. "I did as you asked."

Without a word, the man shot another dart at her.

Erin screeched and leaped to the side. She felt the end of the dart hit her upper arm as it went by.

The man grinned. And it was the evilest thing Erin had ever seen.

He raised the gun again. Erin quickly ran to the other side of the small enclosure.

The cyborg kept the gun trained on her and said simply, "If you stop moving, I'll hit you."

So Erin moved. She ran from one side of the cage to the other. Then to the front and to the back. She even started running in circles. Through it all, she kept one eye on the cyborg. He never changed position and kept the pistol aimed at her as she moved.

"What's the point?" she asked, still moving. "I can't go anywhere."

"There's no sportsmanship in killing an animal who can't escape, you're right."

Erin stopped at the back of the cage, the farthest away from the man she could get, and stared at him in horror. She was breathing hard, both from the exercise and adrenaline. Was he saying what she thought he was saying?

"Does it hurt?"

"What?"

"Does your ankle hurt?"

Erin hadn't even thought about her ankle. All she'd been worried about was the asshole shooting her. Even knowing she was practically naked wasn't fazing her at the moment. Interesting how, when her life was flashing before her eyes, she didn't care if the man saw her scars or her body. Hell, someone should've suggested this as a treatment long before now.

"No. It doesn't hurt."

"Good. That means it's almost time."

"Oh shit. Please, let me go. Please!"

Instead of responding to her plea verbally, the man fired the gun again.

The dart sank into her shoulder and Erin shrieked, both with pain and surprise. She grabbed the dart and yanked it out of her body, but it was too late. She could feel whatever drug was in the needle start to make its way through her bloodstream.

"Fuck, not again," she murmured, going to her knees in the dirt.

The cyborg walked up to the cage and kneeled. "One more sleep, wildcat. Then the hunt is on."

ERIN WAS GETTING VERY TIRED of waking up after being drugged. This time, however, she woke because she was being strangled.

Her eyes popped open and she automatically reached for her throat and tugged at whatever was around it.

She scrambled to get to her feet and the Cyborg smirked at her.

Erin tugged at the collar around her neck and winced when the man jerked at the leash he was holding, and clearly had been dragging her with. She lost her balance and went down to her knees.

"Stay down," the man ordered.

Ignoring him, Erin stood. He yanked on the leash again, and once more, Erin was pulled to her knees.

"*Down*. Stay."

Hating that she was being treated like a dog, Erin stayed down this time. She needed to bide her time. Looking around, she saw no evidence of the cage or tent. In fact, she saw nothing but wilderness. She was still wearing her panties and bra, but the man had put her boots and socks back on her feet.

A sloshing sound made her turn her attention back to the cyborg. He placed a bowl of water on the ground in front of her. Then a second bowl with what had to be another MRE meal...this time mushed up until it was unrecognizable.

"Eat," he ordered.

Erin stared up at him. Was he serious?

He yanked on the leash and Erin threw her hands out to catch herself so she didn't land on her face. She was on all fours now.

"Eat," he repeated. "You're going to need your strength."

Erin glared up at him, but reached for the bowl of water with one hand.

"No," the man barked, yanking on the infernal leash once more. Erin knew she was going to have a horrific bruise around her throat from the collar by the time he was done with her. "No hands."

How was she supposed to eat or drink without them?

As if he could read her mind, the cyborg snarled, "Like an animal."

"Oh, fuck no," Erin muttered and began to sit up.

But the man was too fast. He had his hand around the back of her neck before she could get to her feet. He forced her down until her face was over the bowl of food. He pressed harder, and no matter how much Erin struggled, she couldn't prevent him from pushing her face into the food.

"Eat," he ordered in a deadly tone.

So she did. With the cyborg's hand on the back of her neck, Erin ate the food in the bowl like a dog. She even licked the bowl at his command when she was done. The man let go and smiled cruelly down at her, and then he motioned to the water with his head.

Hating him more than she'd hated anyone in her entire life, Erin did as he ordered. She hated him even more than she'd hated her mother when she'd made Erin cry by telling her it was her fault her dad left. Even more than the mean girls in high school who'd called her Eatmore Erin. Even more than the principal who had fired her by saying nonchalantly, "You're just too fat to be able to do your job."

She lapped at the water in the bowl with her eyes shut, concentrating on getting the fluid into her body, rather than on what the cyborg hoped to accomplish with his attempt to humiliate her.

He jerked at the leash suddenly, surprising her. Water she'd been about to swallow shot out of her mouth and she coughed, trying to catch her breath.

"Come on, you've had enough." He pulled on the

leash, not giving her time to stand. So she crawled after him, scraping her knees and hands on the harsh, rocky ground under her. He didn't pull her far, just to the edge of a long drop-off.

Erin held her breath. Had she made it this far, only to be thrown off the small cliff? There was no way she'd survive the fall. She stayed on her knees, thinking it would be easier to try to keep her balance if she had a lower center of gravity.

But he didn't pick her up and try to throw her off. In fact, he dropped the leash he'd been holding. Erin tensed but stayed where she was. When he didn't make a move toward her at all, she cautiously sat up, keeping her eyes on the cyborg as he stood facing outward, his hands behind his back. He stood there as if he didn't have a care in the world.

Erin wanted to smash his bald head in and watch his brains splat out all over the ground, but she kept her attention on him, like the wild animal he'd accused her of being, not trusting him enough to take her eyes off him for one second.

"Your fate is in your own hands, wildcat. In a couple minutes, you're going to run. Faster than you've ever run in your life. Your goal is to evade capture—by me." He turned then, and stared down at her with his cold, dead eyes. "You won't succeed, but the chase will amuse me. You see...I'm the hunter, and you're the prey."

"Why bother letting my ankle heal? And giving me water and food?"

"To make sure you were a worthy opponent. I've been doing this for quite a while now. At first I didn't care. I let my prey run no matter what shape they were in. But the weak and injured were too easy to catch. It wasn't a challenge."

Erin was horrified, but couldn't get any words out to save her life.

"I've tried all sorts of combinations. Men. Women. Children. But most didn't last more than a mile before I caught up with them and made my kill. I've tried to make it interesting. I took all the clothes from one woman, but she didn't even make it a few steps outside my camp before coming back and begging for her life. She was too embarrassed to run naked. I made one man run without his shoes, but he was so weak, the first rock he stepped on made him falter and I caught up to him within minutes. But I've learned."

"You killed them?"

"Of course I killed them. I'm a hunter, after all. It's what I do. But I figured out that leaving my prey with their undergarments and shoes gives them a feeling of security. Makes them think they have a chance. And it allows them to evade me...for a while."

"Please, don't do this," she whispered.

He ignored her as if she hadn't spoken.

"I've perfected my methods. I've done this all over the United States. My favorite hunting grounds are in the northwest...Oregon, Washington. But the forests up there are thick, there're too many places to hide. And hunting in the snow isn't as much fun because of the footprints my prey leave behind...leads me right to them."

"You're sick," Erin told him.

He acted as if he didn't hear her. "I use campsites to

stake out my prey. I cull the strongest of the herd, and the least likely to be missed. Then I release the animal and hunt. Your goal is to evade me; you can't, but the fun is in your trying. My weapon of choice is a crossbow. It's more challenging to kill with one shot. I'm still working on that. It's soundless, so as not to alert the authorities or nosy civilians who don't understand the excitement of hunting. I've found, over the years, that animals are no longer a challenge. They can't really think, can't reason. And in order for me to feel fulfilled, I need a challenge. Are you ready?"

"What? No!" Erin said, looking up at him with wide eyes.

He stalked toward her then, leaning down. Erin fell on her butt and tried to crab walk backwards to get away from him. He jerked the leash he'd just grabbed and halted her movements. He leaned into her and she tried not to gag on the smell of body odor that wafted off him.

"This hunt is to the death, wildcat. There is no time limit. The game ends when you're dead. Ready? Set. Go!" He unclipped the leash from the collar around her neck and took a step away from her.

Erin sat on the ground, her muscles refusing to move.

The cyborg nudged her with the toe of his boot. "Go on. Git!"

Slowly, Erin pulled her feet under her, thankful that he'd let her keep her hiking boots. She hadn't really thought about it before, but yeah, not having them would seriously impede anyone running through this part of the wilderness.

She stood and took one step away from him, half

expecting him to lunge at her, laughing that he was just kidding and was actually going to throw her off the cliff. But he didn't. He merely stood there, staring at her with his arms crossed.

Glancing behind her, Erin saw nothing but scrub bushes and tall, spindly trees. The ground was uneven and rocky, but it didn't even register.

"Run, bitch," the man growled, then took a menacing step toward her.

It was all the incentive she needed. Erin whipped around and ran for her life.

19

"TELL CADE and the other firefighters not to come out here," Conor told Beth.

"They want to help."

"I know, and I appreciate it, but right now there's nothing to help with. We don't have any clues."

"So, I was talking to Tex about this," Beth said, "and he agreed that while there might not be anything I can do right now to track Erin, I can look into the past."

"What do you mean?" Conor asked, shifting on his tired feet. He was going to crash...and he hated it. He didn't want to sleep. What if he missed Erin's signal because he was sleeping? He'd stayed awake longer than this before on an important stakeout, he could keep going for a while longer.

"Someone took her. We know that. But we don't know who. But assholes generally don't start out their life of crime with stealing people. They might start out by shoplifting. Or holding up a gas station. Kidnapping is a huge risk, so whoever did it probably has either done it before, or they've at least done something to get on the wrong side of the law."

"Yeah," Conor agreed, perking up. "You're right."

"I know. So I started searching for kidnappings in the area in the last year."

"And?"

"Nothing. At least nothing resembling this."

Conor's shoulders slumped. "What the fuck, Beth? Did you just bring it up to give me hope, only to shut me down and make me feel even more shitty than I did two minutes ago?"

"What? No!" Beth exclaimed. "Jeez, all you guys are the same, jumping to conclusions. Let me finish. So, I didn't find anything in the last year in the area, but I expanded my search parameters. I thought maybe I was being too narrow. I looked not in just the last year, but in the last ten. And I expanded where I was looking...I went wide, looking across the entire country."

"Jesus. You're never going to find anything related to Erin that way. You must've had thousands of hits."

"Eighty-four thousand, four hundred and twenty-three," Beth said matter-of-factly.

"What?"

"That's how many missing person's reports there were. But I channeled my hero Penelope Garcia and started weeding them out. Taking out the people who were found, the ones whose perpetrators were behind bars...that sort of thing."

"And?" Conor asked impatiently when she finished speaking.

"It's weird. The final results don't seem to have any pattern to them, but maybe that *is* the pattern."

"Details," Conor ordered. "Come on, Beth, I've got a meeting here in a couple of minutes."

"Right. I looked at the cases that were left, and the victims are all over the map. Teenagers, an eight-year-old kid, a grandmother, men who ranged in ages from twenty-two to forty-seven. They're also all over the place. A few up in Washington, three in Oregon, two in Nevada, one from Barstow, California, and a few in the Midwest."

"So they're not related," Conor said, sighing.

"I didn't say that," Beth said, her voice rising in excitement. "Every one of the victims disappeared from a campground."

"No shit?"

"No shit. And there's more."

"What?"

"Not all the bodies were found, some are still open missing person's cases, but the ones that were found were all discovered in the same area where they disappeared. They were all killed with either a high-velocity bullet or..." She paused.

"What, Beth?"

"An arrow."

"An arrow," Conor echoed. "What the fuck?"

"Some had more than one wound. But they were all killed with a shot through the heart."

"So, what? They were accidentally shot with a crossbow by a hunter?"

"I don't think it was by accident, Conor. Some victims were naked, others weren't wearing any shoes...but *every* single one had bruises around their throats, as if they'd been wearing some sort of collar at one point, and they all had injuries indicating they'd fallen several times."

"They were being chased?"

"I don't know," Beth admitted.

"But you think so," Conor said.

"Yeah."

"Whoever took Erin wants to, what...*hunt* her?"

"I don't know," Beth said again. "But the times of death for the other victims I found were all within twenty-four hours of disappearing."

Conor swallowed the bile that came up his throat at the implication of what Beth had just told him. It had been way longer than that for Erin. "She's not dead," he said vehemently.

"I didn't say she was. If she'd been hunted and left for dead, you would've found her by now. The victims were all discovered in the area where they were taken. You've been all over that land."

"Why is Erin different? What made him delay the hunt?" Conor asked, more to himself than Beth.

They were both silent as they contemplated the question.

"What if she was hurt?" Conor finally asked. "What if, when he was dragging her off, she fought him and was injured in the process? If he does like to hunt, wouldn't he want the person to be in good shape? If Erin was hurt, she couldn't run as fast or as far."

"Right," Beth agreed, getting into it. "So he has to make sure she's in the best condition possible before he sets her free to hunt."

"Which means he gave her water and food, and probably isn't abusing her," Conor concluded hopefully. He had no idea if he was right, but he wanted to be. God, how he wanted to be right.

"Find her, Conor," Beth said softly. "I'll search the satellite images for any kind of structure where he could be keeping her, but I have a bad feeling her time is running out."

"I will."

"I'll tell Cade to stay here for now. But if you need more eyes or hands, let me know, and everyone from Station 7 will be there in a heartbeat."

"Appreciate it. Later, Beth. Thanks."

"Later."

Conor hung up and closed his eyes for a brief second. God. He couldn't imagine the hell Erin was going through if Beth's hunch was right. But at the same time, it meant she had a chance. She loved the outdoors. If some bastard thought letting her go out there somewhere would freak her out and he'd easily be able to find her, he was going to have a harsh surprise waiting for him. Conor ran with Erin, he knew firsthand how fast and how far she could go. If anyone could outrun and outsmart a psychotic killer...it was Erin.

Please let it be Erin.

He spun on his heel with renewed determination and headed for the huddle of men and women. The good news was that they were looking in the right area. The bad news? Both Erin and the kidnapper were most likely on the move.

ERIN HUDDLED down behind a tree and tried to catch her breath. She had no idea how much time had passed since she'd run from the cyborg. She'd continued until she had a stitch in her side, then she kept running. The landscape ebbed and flowed from being mostly scrub bushes with no place to hide, to thick trees. She'd seen some sort of lake from an overhang at one point, but so far hadn't seen it again.

Erin closed her eyes in despair. She didn't want to be playing this deadly game of hide-and-go-seek. She wanted to be in the tent with Conor. Wanted to have nothing better to do than sit around and watch the stars. Instead, she was running for her life, in her underwear no less.

She wanted to give up. Wanted to say "fuck it" and just lie down and wait for cyborg man to find her and put an arrow in her heart. But she couldn't. Thoughts of Conor finding her that way wouldn't leave her brain. She wanted a life with him. Wanted to be his in every way. Wanted to know what it felt like to make love. She had so many things she still wanted to do in her life. Cyborg asshole wasn't going to take that away from her.

With that thought, she stood and began to run once more. This time trying to stick to a path that wouldn't broadcast which way she'd gone to the man hunting her. She had to be more strategic. She couldn't continue to just run willy-nilly as she had been.

Conor would have people looking for her. *He'd* be looking for her. She needed to find civilization. The

Natural Area wasn't exactly near any big cities, but there were people around. Erin just needed to find them.

With renewed faith that she could get out of this, Erin ran.

HOURS LATER, Erin knew there was no way she could get out of this alive. She'd done everything she could think of, but she knew the cyborg was on her trail. She'd tried to backtrack once and almost ran right into the man. She'd only survived by dropping to her belly silently and lying in the dirt for ten minutes while she'd waited for him to get out of range.

Leaning against a tree and sliding down its rough bark, not even caring that she was scraping her skin up in the process, Erin sat in the dirt and wrapped her arms around her legs. She looked up into the sky and estimated that it was late afternoon. How long had she been running? At least four or five hours. Maybe more.

She was sweaty, hungry, and her body had begun to shake from lack of water. She stared at her shoes and thought about her dad. The flint tied into her laces caught her eye and she smiled as she remembered the trip her dad had given it to her.

"This is my lucky flint, Erin. I want you to have it. Don't take it off, you never know when you'll need to start a fire."

"Dad," she'd complained, "We live in Houston. I only go camping with you and we bring matches. Why would I need to start a fire?"

He'd laughed, and Erin could still remember the sweet sound echoing in the trees around them. "I don't know, baby, but if you did, wouldn't it be lucky to have the means to make it?"

A tear escaped Erin's eye at the memory. Her dad. God, she missed the man. Even more now that she knew the truth about his disappearance.

She froze and blinked. She held her breath for a long moment, then let it out in a silent whoosh. No one knew where she was. Hell, *she* didn't even know where she was. But the cyborg had been right, she couldn't escape him.

But what if she could create a distraction, lead the people who had to be looking for her to the cyborg's hunting grounds? To her?

It was risky. Fuck, it was dangerous, reckless, and made her a horrible person.

But if it saved her life, it might still be worth it.

Erin reached for the laces of her boot. She quickly and carefully undid them, pulling the flint off in the process. Then, holding the only thing that might save her life in her palm, she re-tied her laces, leaving one end longer than the other. She needed her boots to run, and they needed to be tied tightly. But she also needed the steel striker at the end of the lace to use on the flint.

Looking around, Erin quickly gathered a small pile of sticks and logs. She grabbed some of the dry leaves left over from last fall to use as kindling. She set up the small campfire just like her dad had taught her all those years ago.

Hearing a sound, Erin looked up, her heart in her

throat, hoping she hadn't been caught right when she thought she might have a chance.

A deer was standing about twenty feet from her. They stared at each other for a long moment.

"I'm sorry," Erin whispered. "He made me do it. Run, Bambi. Tell all your friends. Run for your lives."

And with that, she looked down and struck the flint with the steel end of the lace.

Sparks flew. She did it again. Then again. Each time, more sparks ignited as the years of gunk were wiped off the flint.

She leaned down and concentrated. Time was running out. She felt it in the air around her. As the sparks flew, Erin blew on the dry leaves.

Finally, they caught.

She cupped her hands around the small flame and prayed as she nurtured it. One stick caught. Then another. When the fire was big enough, Erin reached for the larger sticks and logs she'd found. She fed the small fire until it blazed two feet off the ground.

She took a step back, then another. With tears coursing down her cheeks for what she'd done, knowing full well the destruction it would cause, Erin turned and ran.

JULIETTE WINSTON, Conor's friend and long-ago class-mate at the game warden academy, answered her phone. She was sitting in her office in Bandera, organizing search parties and trying to keep a handle on the search for Conor's girlfriend.

"Winston."

"There's a huge fire just north of the search area," the voice on the other end of the phone said. Juliette didn't know who she was talking to, but it didn't matter. If the people searching for Erin were going to be in the line of fire, they needed to be notified and evacuated.

"Ten-four. I'll call the Texas A&M Fire Service and let them know what's going on. In the meantime, have local fire departments been notified?"

"Yes, ma'am. The call went out to Bandera, Tarpley, Pipe Creek, and Medina. Units are en route now."

"Good. Thank you for the head's up."

The person on the other end of the line disconnected without saying anything else, but Juliette's mind was already on other things. Namely, making sure her friend and fellow warden, Conor, didn't do anything that would get him killed.

"THE CREW from Station 7 are here," Hayden informed Conor in a low tone. "I heard the incident commandeer say he's going to pair them up with the local volunteers. They've fought grass fires, but not full-blown wildfires like this one. He can use the extra hands, but doesn't want a situation where they have to go in and rescue *them* because they don't understand how a wildfire works."

Conor ignored her and shrugged on the turnout coat

one of the firefighters from the Tarpley Volunteer Department had lent him.

Hayden put her hand on Conor's arm, stopping him. "You need to let the fire department do their thing. If you get fried to a crisp, it's not going to help Erin."

Conor turned then and looked down at his friend. "What are you suggesting? That I hang out here and do nothing? It's her. I know it."

"It could be a coincidence."

Conor snorted. "You don't believe that any more than I do, Hayden. It's the sign we needed. I have no doubt Erin started that fire out of desperation, but it's also going to lead us right to her—which I think she's counting on."

Hayden looked around, then grabbed Conor and dragged him over to a group of volunteer firefighters who were gearing up to head into the wilderness. Moose and Penelope were also there, obviously having been paired with the group of local firefighters.

"Moose. Penelope." She nodded at her friends, then turned to the others. There were five other men, all in turnout gear, getting ready to go. "Conor is going with you," Hayden informed them. "Make sure he doesn't get killed, okay?"

One man reached out a hand to Conor. "I'm Pops, the commander of our little group."

Conor nodded at him and shook the outstretched hand.

"The others are Dirty-D, Tank, Buff, and Short Shit." The commander looked at Moose and Penelope, then back to Conor. "Stick with us, do what we do, and everything will be fine."

Everyone nodded, and the local firefighters concentrated on making sure their packs were set and they had what they needed to fight the wildfire. Penelope turned to Conor and put her hand on his arm. "You doing all right?"

"No," Conor said tersely. He appreciated what Hayden and Penelope were trying to do, but nothing at this point would make him feel any better about this situation. Nothing except having Erin in his arms, safe and sound.

The firefighters got ready to go. Along with Pops, they looked once more at the map of the area. Taking into account the wind direction and where they thought the fire was started, they made a plan.

Conor stared at that section of the map. It was about fifteen miles from the campsite. Not too far, but it might as well have been on the moon. They hadn't searched out that far, they didn't have the resources.

But that was where Erin was. At least where she *had* been. The nagging feeling that told him Erin had started the fire in an attempt at getting help solidified in his gut. She was out there somewhere. Trying to stay two steps ahead of a madman and now keep out of the line of fire. The desperation she had to be feeling was clear.

Following along docilely behind the seven firefighters, Conor made sure he had everything he might need in his backpack. He didn't have any firefighting gear, but he wasn't along for that. He had his pistol on his hip in its holster, a few extra rounds, and a first-aid kit filled to the brim with everything he hoped he wouldn't need. He wasn't an official paramedic or EMT, but he could hold his own.

But when push came to shove, it didn't matter. Moose and Penelope, and most likely the other firefighters, *were* EMTs, they could help Erin if she needed it. All he needed was to see her alive. He could work with anything else.

They entered the wilderness area in a single-file line in silence. No one said a word, conserving their energy for the trek ahead. Their mission was to dig a firebreak along the south side of the fire, making sure it didn't spread any farther into the Natural Area.

Conor raised his head and looked at the cloudless sky. "I'm on my way," he said softly. "Hang on, bright eyes, I'm coming."

20

ERIN TRIED NOT TO COUGH, but it was impossible. The fire had worked...too well. She felt sick at the destructive force she'd unleashed, but it had definitely worked. She hadn't heard the cyborg man for a while. She'd seen him once, right after she'd lit the fire. She'd been standing on one side of a line of fire, and he'd appeared on the other.

He'd tipped an imaginary hat to her and called out, "You better run, wildcat. You're good, but not good enough."

She hadn't stayed around to hear any more. She'd turned on her heel and run. Knowing it was dangerous, but doing it anyway, she kept as close to the fire as she could. The fire would bring people, and she needed to be found by those people, not the insane man who was hunting her.

She shivered and forced herself to keep going. She was tiring, which wasn't good. As Erin walked, she thought about her life and her body. It was somewhat ironic that the cyborg had chosen *her* to kidnap. If she'd been her old self, he wouldn't have looked twice at her. An overweight woman wouldn't be a challenge to him. He needed someone in shape.

She looked down at herself as she walked. Yeah, she had scars. She still had some saggy skin, but dammit, she'd done it. By herself. The surgery had definitely been the starting point, but through pure grit and determination, she'd lost the weight, and worked damn hard doing it.

For the first time in her life, she was proud of herself and her body.

She wasn't perfect, but fuck that. She was closer to forty than thirty, she was *never* going to be perfect. But Conor liked her just how she was. He'd stuck by her side for almost four months without pressuring her to have sex. Oh, they'd been sexual together, but they hadn't gone all the way.

He wouldn't be with her just for sex. The man could get that easily from someone else. He loved her.

Erin stopped in her tracks. Conor *loved* her.

He'd said it before, but she realized there was a part of her that hadn't really believed him. Somehow, being out here, almost naked, running for her life, playing the ultimate game of hide-and-seek, everything became clear.

She smiled.

Looking down at her hiking boots, the flint a gift from her father, she leaned over and touched them, saying, "Thanks, Dad."

The second she bent over, an arrow shot above her

head and landed in the rocky ground about eight feet in front of her.

She whirled around and saw the cyborg loading another arrow into his crossbow.

"Fuck!" She took off. Running as fast as she could, weaving in and out of the trees and bushes. Erin had no idea where she was going, just that she needed to get away from the cyborg. It would suck to make it this far, only for him to kill her right when help was about to get there.

And help was coming, Erin knew that. The fire crackled as it consumed the dry trees around her.

Making a split-second decision, Erin turned right, running straight toward the fire she'd been keeping ahead of. She could lose herself in the smoke and flames. As long as she stayed away from the fire itself, she should be okay...maybe.

It wasn't a great choice, but when a second arrow grazed her arm, she knew it was her only one. She ignored the pain shooting down her arm, running pell-mell in a zigzag pattern, trying to keep herself out of the line of fire of the arrows.

She knew the man had to reload, so she had some time. Not much, but a little. Over the last couple of hours, Erin had discovered that the cyborg was in shape. He could run for as long as she could. She'd never be able to outrun him, so she had to outsmart him. He wanted to hunt an animal that could think for herself? It was time she started doing just that.

Erin glanced around as she ran, trying to come up with a plan. She thought about Corrie, and how she'd climbed a tree and hidden from the men after her. That wouldn't work, as the trees had some leaves on them but they hadn't grown in enough to fully hide her. She'd be a sitting duck for cyborg man.

The fire had been a good diversion, but she needed to do something else.

Then, seeing something she hadn't expected to see, Erin put on a burst of speed.

She reached the edge of the stream and smiled in relief. The water would help if the fire, which was way too close as it was, came even closer. It would also serve to hide her footprints. She knew she'd been leaving an easy trail for the expert hunter to follow. She hadn't had time to try to hide her prints.

She stepped into the stream, which was about two feet deep, and looked around. Which way?

Her decision could have a direct result on whether she lived or died.

Taking a deep breath and hoping for the best, she turned right...and headed straight toward the flames. It was slow going, but she refused to leave the stream. The water was obscuring her path...she hoped.

She hadn't gone more than a half mile when she thought she heard something behind her. Not stopping to look back, Erin saw a miracle in front of her. A logjam.

Well, not exactly, but close enough. A tree had fallen across the stream and formed a sort of blockade for the water. Other sticks and debris had gotten clogged behind it.

Her heart beating faster than she could ever remember it beating when she was in the gym or working out, Erin looked up at what sounded like a freight train coming straight for her.

It wasn't a motor, but a wall of fire. Bigger, hotter, and meaner than anything she'd ever seen.

She wasn't sure what she'd expected when she'd started the blaze; a slow-burning wildfire that would be easy to put out while still being a flashing beacon for anyone looking for her. But the flames that were bearing down on her weren't that. Not even close.

They were horrifying and scary. The trees in this area were bigger than where she'd set the fire. The grass more abundant. There was a lot of fuel for the flames, and it was being consumed at an alarming rate.

Knowing the flames were actually her bigger concern at the moment, more so than the hunter, Erin quickly ran around the fallen tree and knelt in the stream. The water wasn't terribly deep, but she hoped it was deep enough. It flowed around her from somewhere upstream with a surprisingly strong current. The image of boiling alive as the flames heated the water like a pot on a stove ran through her mind, but she ignored it.

Erin used her hands to frantically scoop out an area near the head of the tree so she could fit underneath it. Hiding under a pile of combustible dead tree limbs wasn't exactly the best decision when a wildfire was bearing down on her, but at the back of her mind, she knew she not only needed to hide from the flames, she needed to hide from the man hunting her as well. Either would kill her without thought. The water and this felled tree were her only hope of surviving.

She clawed her way through the stray sticks and

leaves pressing up against the large trunk lying across the stream. She took a deep breath and ducked under the tree and water, but had to come back out because, once she was under the log, there wasn't enough space between the limbs for her face to get above water for air.

Not daring to look behind her at the fire she knew was dangerously close, Erin moved to the head of the log on the bank of the stream. She wasn't sure what she was looking for, but got excited when she saw that the tree was forked at the top. She moved more debris out of the way and dug beneath the tree, closer to the bank this time, and took another big breath. She ducked under the dam once more but this time closer to shore. She wiggled her body toward the bank until her head and chest were lying in the mud, above the water line but still shielded between the limbs of the tree. Her lower body was below the surface, hidden by the downed tree and other debris.

Her upper body position made the mud and dirt on the edge of the stream start to shift, and she moved her hands over her head to try to hold the earth in place.

Erin heard the fire bearing down on her from one side and, incredibly, heard the hunter yelling from her other side.

"Where are you, wildcat? You can't survive that fire. Come back this way and I'll make sure you're safe. Time-out. You hear me? Time-out!"

She shook her head. The man was insane. Time-out her ass. Yeah, maybe he wouldn't shoot her if she went back to him, but he'd certainly drug her again, and possibly bring her to another state to start his insane hunt all over again. She couldn't forget the way he'd made her eat out of the dog bowl as if she really was nothing but an animal. Allowing her ankle to heal wasn't an act of compassion, it was the sign of a serial killer. She'd sooner be burned alive than trust him. The thought of being in his clutches again made Erin's skin crawl. She shivered.

Wait...

No. It wasn't the thought of being the cyborg's prisoner that gave her that feeling.

It was ants.

She'd found the perfect place to hide—but so had other creatures of the forest.

She felt the first bite on her elbow. Then a second followed.

Erin closed her eyes and exhaled silently. There was no time to find another hiding place. Between the fire and the hunter, she had to stay right where she was. She might survive the fire bearing down on her by hiding in the water, and she might be able to elude the hunter in the process, but she was still going to die. Fucking hell.

CONOR DECIDED that firefighters were insane. He'd rather face a man with a gun twenty times over than the flames that were slowly getting closer and closer. They were hiking along the edge of the fire. The seven firefighters were digging a trench as they went, trying to create a firebreak so the flames wouldn't have anything to feed on when they got to this point.

The heat was incredible, and Conor was sweating

profusely. The men, and Penelope, worked mostly silently, communicating through hand signals as they quickly and competently did their best to keep the fire from spreading.

A noise to their right startled Conor so badly, he turned and had his pistol out before he'd even thought about what he was doing.

"What the fuck?" Moose said as they all stopped to watch what had made the noise way out in this part of the forest.

It was a donkey. A small one. A *really* small one.

"Oh my God!" Penelope exclaimed. "It's on fire."

And it was...sort of. The donkey was smoking as it came running toward them. Its head was up and it was staring right at them. It didn't stop until it was in front Penelope. His body was literally smoldering.

"Shit, give me a water bottle," Penelope demanded to Moose, holding out her hand.

The big firefighter didn't hesitate, simply unclipped his water bottle from his pack and handed it over.

Penelope unscrewed the lid and put her hand on the donkey's head. "Easy, boy," she murmured. "You're okay. I got you." She slowly began to pour water over the donkey's back. The animal didn't move. He just gazed up at Penelope with big brown eyes. As the water hit his skin, steam rose. "Oh, you poor thing," Penelope crooned as she continued to put out the smoking embers on his body.

After several water bottles, the embers were out and the donkey was still steaming.

"It's tiny," Moose observed. "I mean, I've seen small donkeys, but this one is *really* small."

"Hmmm," Penelope responded, obviously not truly listening.

The donkey really was in pathetic shape. His mane had burned off, leaving nothing but black stubs of hair along the back of his neck. Any hair he'd had on his sides had been burned as well, and there were patches of red, burnt skin in their place. Conor couldn't tell what color he'd been originally.

Penelope rubbed the animal's nose gently. "I'm so sorry. You'll be okay now. Go on home and your owner will take care of you."

The donkey didn't move, except to nuzzle Penelope's waist, making her take a step back. Moose was there to keep her upright. He wrapped one arm around her waist to steady her, and the other reached out to lightly stroke the donkey's neck.

"I estimate him to be around thirty inches tall. Normally these guys are around thirty-six, although I've seen some as small as twenty-five," Moose said.

"Do you think he'll be able to find his way home?" Penelope asked, looking up at the man who had his arm around her.

"Yeah, Tiger. I'm sure he will."

"We need to move," Pops said. "We're right in the line of that fire and it's looking uglier than it was five minutes ago."

And he was right. The crackling and popping of wood as it burned was louder now than it was even a few minutes ago.

Everyone picked up their tools and started digging again.

They continued for several minutes, and Conor looked behind him when he heard something. It was the donkey. He was following them.

"Go on. Go home," Conor said, trying to shoo the animal away. He didn't budge, simply kept his eyes on Penelope...the human who had saved him.

Conor shook his head and gave up. "If he's too stupid to run to safety, there's not much I can do."

"I don't blame him," Penelope said as she dug. "If I was in pain and came across people who helped me, I wouldn't want to leave them either."

Conor shrugged. He didn't really care if the donkey stuck close to them. He just wanted to find Erin. He wanted to be out of the middle of this fire and wanted his girlfriend to be safe.

The group continued to parallel the flames for several hundred yards. The heat increased and the sound of the fire was intense. Just when Conor was going to voice his concerns and suggest they run like hell, the most spine-tingling sound he'd ever heard seemed to echo around the area.

It was a scream.

He couldn't tell if it was human, but it didn't matter. His feet were moving before he thought about what he was doing. He leaped across a scrub bush and ran head-long into the forest. He heard Moose call his name, but he didn't stop.

The heat of the fire was more intense now, but all Conor could think about was whether the scream had come from Erin. He stopped short and stared at a mass of pine trees in the near distance. They were crackling, and flames burst from the tips of the branches as if the trees themselves were lighters being flicked on by an unseen hand.

His eyes whipped down to the base of the trees—and he saw the source of the inhuman scream. It wasn't Erin.

It was a man. A tall man who was dressed from head to toe in camouflage. He was standing in the middle of the group of trees, boxed in by flames.

As Conor watched, the man's clothes burst into flames from the intense heat even though the fire hadn't yet reached him. Conor only got a glimpse of what he thought was the man's skin melting from his face before he was tackled to the ground.

He hit with an *umph* and his world went dark.

Pops had tackled him and covered them both with a fire shelter. It looked kind of like a sleeping bag, or a burrito wrapped in aluminum foil. Conor knew it was a last resort for firefighters caught in the line of a wildfire. But it wasn't failsafe. The shelter was designed to withstand temperatures of five hundred degrees Fahrenheit. Basically, it would protect them from the radiant heat that came from a fire, but it likely wouldn't protect them from direct flames.

The sounds inside the shelter were scary. Conor was face down in the dirt with the other firefighter on top of him. The crackling of the fire was deafening and the heat inside the shelter was stifling.

They stayed under the shelter for the longest ten minutes of Conor's life. Every time he tried to get up,

Pops would press harder against him, letting him know without words that it wasn't safe.

Finally, just when Conor couldn't stand being confined in the small, hot space any longer, Pops moved off him. Very carefully, he peeled back the edge of their shield and, after looking around, sat all the way up and shoved the shelter away from them.

Conor looked around him in horror. The fire had obviously passed right over them. The heat from the flames and residual heat would've killed them if it hadn't been for the shelter.

Conor turned to the other man and shook his hand without a word.

After the initial shock of what had just happened passed, Conor remembered why he'd been there in the first place.

Looking around, he noted that some of the trees around him were black and charred, but surprisingly there were a few that looked unscathed.

"It's because of how fast the fire was moving," Dirty-D explained, rising from his own shelter, seeing where Conor's gaze had gone. "Even though it was hot, the flames didn't have time to catch some of the trees on fire. We were lucky. The worst of it seemed to be higher up. If we'd been standing, we would've been in big trouble, but because we were on the ground and covered, the heat and flames skipped right over us."

It was amazing and terrifying at the same time. Conor looked to where he'd last seen the man who'd screamed. He was lying about fifteen feet from where their shelter had been.

Conor slowly walked over and nudged him with his foot. The man didn't move.

He kneeled and turned him over—and stumbled away in shock.

Conor had seen a lot of bad things during the course of his job. Mutilated animals, dead bodies, people who'd been hurt while enjoying the great outdoors, but he hadn't ever seen anything as gruesome and horrifying as what he was seeing right then.

The man's face had literally melted. Conor could see the bones of his eye sockets and face. It was gruesome. He heard one of the other firefighter's gagging and quickly turned the man back over. As an EMT, the man had likely seen plenty of things as well, but a melted face wasn't something the average person encountered on a regular basis.

Looking around more carefully, Conor saw a melted crossbow lying nearby, along with a quiver of what had most likely been arrows. Frowning, Conor knew that crossbow hunting season had long been over. There was no reason anyone should be hunting in this area, but definitely not with that kind of weapon.

His jaw tightening, Conor immediately knew this was probably the man who'd kidnapped Erin. Who else would be out in this area with a crossbow?

The rest of the group found them, the donkey following Penelope a lot closer now.

"Thank God," Moose exclaimed. "We weren't sure what happened to you three."

Conor shrugged. "Pops saved my life. Got the shelter over us both just in time. This guy wasn't so lucky." He motioned to the dead man on the ground with his head. "Good to see y'all are all right."

"It was close. Tiger insisted on protecting that damn animal," Moose said, shaking his head.

"What?" Conor asked, his brows shooting upward in disbelief.

"I couldn't just leave him to die. Not after he came to me for help," Penelope defended herself, patting the animal standing at her side. "I got him to lie down, then got on top of him and covered us up."

"And he fit in there?" Conor asked.

"Barely," Moose said. "Good thing they're both so small."

"Wow." Conor really didn't have any words for that. He kind of wished he'd seen it, but then again, even if he was with the rest of the group, he wouldn't have seen a thing because he'd have been under his own shelter.

He glanced at Moose. The man looked pissed and dumbfounded at the same time. It was a well-known fact that Moose had feelings for Penelope. But he'd been taking his time, as Penelope was still dealing with the aftereffects of being kidnapped by terrorists overseas. But the tender expression of longing on Moose's face as he watched her bond with the donkey made it even more obvious. Of course, Penelope was clueless—or pretending to be.

"That the guy who kidnapped your woman?" Buff asked.

"Don't know, but if I had to guess, I'd say yes," Conor said, then looked around. For a brief moment, he wanted to go back to the command post. He didn't want to find

Erin, not if she'd been caught in the wildfire as they had been. But he dismissed that thought. He loved her. If she was dead, he needed to be the one to find her.

He took a step past the dead man on the ground toward the black, charred forest behind him. Then another. He stopped and turned to the others. "I need to find her. I understand that you have a job to do."

"Fuck that," Pops said. "The fire is way beyond us now, we'd have to go all the way around to get back in front of it. You said yourself that you thought Erin started this fire to either get away from whoever had kidnapped her or to bring attention to where she was. If that's true, it's possible she could be nearby. Especially if he was here. It'll be easier to search with eight than with just one."

Conor swallowed hard and nodded, more grateful than he could say for the support. He was close with the men, and woman, of Station 7, but the commander's reaction, a man he hadn't met until today, a man who'd literally saved his life, proved that no matter where they were stationed, volunteer or paid, firefighters were an honorable bunch.

"'Preciate it. Keep your eyes open for footprints or anything out of the ordinary. If she saw the fire or that asshole coming, she might've tried to hide." It was what he would've done. Conor took point this time since there was no fear of the fire coming back this way. There wasn't much fuel left for it.

The strange group—seven men, one woman, and one very grateful donkey—proceeded through the blackened countryside, their eyes peeled for any sign of Erin.

21

Erin lay still under her makeshift shelter. She couldn't feel the ants crawling on her arms, shoulders, and neck anymore, but that could've been because she was numb. Or maybe they'd been burned off. She had no idea. But she knew she was in trouble.

The sound of the hunter's horrified scream had been bad enough, but she'd barely heard it over the sounds of the fire consuming everything in its path above her. She couldn't help but try to wiggle her upper body even farther into the mud on the side of the stream, which made more ants swarm out of the nest she'd inadvertently disturbed.

But she didn't have time to worry about them, as the fire was suddenly there. She held her breath and eased back down into the water, ducking her head under for as long as possible. She had to come up a few times to gasp for much-needed air, but each time the temperature was almost too intense. She felt the heat on her upper back and shoulders and tried to sink farther back under the water.

After what seemed like hours, but was probably only minutes, the sound decreased and she moved her upper body out of the water. She stared up into the surprisingly blue sky and was actually shocked she was still alive, that she could breathe. Well, she could've if she hadn't been bitten by ants. Breathing was a problem. A big one.

Her skin felt tight where she'd been bitten and she could hear herself wheezing with every breath she tried to take. She could also feel her pulse hammering inside her body and she felt extremely dizzy.

Erin knew she had to move. She didn't want to pass out and slip back under the tree and water and drown herself, but she also needed to get away from the ants she'd disturbed. She took a deep breath and scooted back into the water. She let the current help push her body out from under the downed log. Once free of the dam, she turned over and crawled on her hands and knees to the side of the stream...checking to make sure she didn't land in the middle of another fire ant hill in the process. She collapsed on her belly in the mud, gasping for air and praying the hunter hadn't miraculously made it through the firestorm that had just raged over her. It would suck to have crawled out of her hidey-hole, only to be killed by an arrow through the heart.

She closed her eyes and tried to concentrate on slowing her pulse. Her body was in anaphylactic shock. She needed her epinephrine shot, but since she was wearing only boots, underwear, and a bra, she obviously didn't have it with her.

Erin knew she was dying. Dammit. It sucked. She'd escaped from the clutches of a cyborg madman hunter, and a wildfire, only to die from a fucking ant bite...or a couple hundred.

CONOR'S EYES widened as he and the firefighters made their way around a still smoldering group of trees and saw a stream gurgling happily along in front of them. It wasn't deep. He would've been really surprised if it had been with the lack of rain the area had received.

The donkey obviously saw the stream at the same time and quickly trotted past Penelope and lowered his snout into the cool water. After a moment, he waded in farther and simply plopped down. He rolled from side to side, the water obviously feeling good against his burnt skin.

Penelope chuckled at the sheer pleasure the animal was obviously feeling as it rolled around in the water. But Conor couldn't bring himself to even smile, not while he was so worried about Erin. He turned his back to the water and put his hands on his hips. Where could she be? Where could she have hidden?

He wondered if there were any caves in this part of the Natural Area. He hadn't explored this far out, so he had no idea. He was contemplating calling Juliette and having her ask the rangers, but before he could pull out his phone, he heard Penelope say, "No, Smokey, come back here."

Conor shook his head. Figured she'd name the

animal that. Although he had to admit, it fit.

Suddenly, the donkey began to bray.

Surprised—so far Conor hadn't heard more than a few funny little sounds from the animal—he spun.

"Conor, get over here!" Moose yelled urgently.

He'd already been on the move before Moose had said a word.

The donkey was nuzzling something half in and half out of the water. Conor hadn't noticed it before because it was covered in mud and blocked by some sticks and debris from the stream.

Erin.

He knew before he even got close, it was her.

She was naked, or nearly so. Moose had turned her over before Conor got to her—and Conor gasped at what he saw. Her face was so swollen, he could barely make out where her eyes were supposed to be. Her neck was bruised and she had scrapes all over her body.

Then he saw the bites. They looked like little white pimples, and there were dozens on her face, more on her arms and shoulders.

The fact that she was only in her bra and panties didn't even register. "She's allergic to fire ants!" he said in an urgent tone, but Pops was already digging into his pack.

He frantically sorted through a smaller bag and handed something to Moose. Without pausing, Moose uncapped the EpiPen and slammed the injector into Erin's thigh.

She didn't even flinch.

"Another," Moose ordered, and Pops put the pen into

his hand.

Conor kneeled by Erin's head as Moose injected her with a second round of Adrenalin.

Penelope put her fingers on Erin's carotid artery. "She's not breathing," Penelope said evenly.

Conor had no idea how she could be so calm. He was anything but.

He felt himself being pulled away from Erin as Tank took his place at her head. All he could do was watch with wide, horrified eyes as the firefighters worked on her.

Dirty-D kneeled on Erin's other side and injected something into her upper arm while Moose started chest compressions.

An oxygen mask appeared from somewhere and Penelope placed it over Erin's nose and mouth.

Conor watched as if from a great distance as the team did their best to save the woman he loved.

The more time went by, the more discouraged Conor felt. It was too long. He hadn't found her soon enough. He turned away from the scene and clenched his eyes shut. He couldn't lose her. He couldn't.

"I've got a pulse!" someone said.

Conor spun around and stared.

"It's weak, but it's there. Give her another dose of anti-histamine," Pops ordered.

Moose sat back on his heels and wiped a hand over his brow. He turned to Conor and smiled. "Fuck yeah. I knew she was too tough to give up."

Conor bowed his head and nodded. Yeah, that was his Erin. Stubborn with a core of steel. She was alive. It was all that mattered. She'd beaten the odds...more times than he could count. She was like a cat with nine lives. First, she'd survived her mother. Then she'd almost killed herself with food. Then she'd been kidnapped and hunted. Then the fire. And now fucking insects. Yeah, his woman was a tough motherfucker.

And he loved her just the way she was.

Conor maintained his distance as the EMTs did their thing. He kept his eyes on Erin's face. Her hair was matted and tangled. Her body was covered in scrapes, bruises, and hives. It was the first time he'd seen this much of her, but he couldn't take his eyes from her face.

The team made a makeshift litter and got Erin loaded onto it. Penelope was monitoring her breathing and Moose stood by her side, making sure her heart didn't stop. The other men alternated between carrying the litter and scoping out the fastest and easiest path to safety.

Conor marked the coordinates of where the dead body of the man remained, and called it in to Juliette. She informed him the fire was still blazing, but had been eighty percent contained. The fire service had brought in bulldozers to do the work their team had been doing and it'd been effective, cutting off the fuel to the fire. Their only concern now was wind, which was supposed to die down within the hour.

An ambulance was waiting for them about two miles to the north along a backcountry road. Conor told Juliette that he'd keep her informed of their location and hung up. He pushed his way next to the litter and put his hand on Erin's shoulder, making sure to stay out of the path of the other firefighters. He wasn't going to risk Erin's life by insisting he be the one to care for her. At the moment, he was simply a man who loved her. He'd leave the nursing to the amazing people around him who'd saved her life.

A LOUD SOUND irritated Erin enough to bring her back to herself. She tried to open her eyes, but for some reason, they wouldn't. She moaned and tried to bring her hand up to her face to see what was the matter, but it wouldn't move.

Panicking, thinking she was back in the clutches of the cyborg, she thrashed on the cot.

"Easy, bright eyes."

Conor.

Erin stilled and tried desperately to open her eyes. When she couldn't, and everything stayed black, she whimpered.

She felt a cool hand on her forehead and instinctively knew it was his.

"Shhhh. You're safe. I'm here."

"Conswfs." The word came out jumbled. It felt as if she had marbles in her mouth, and she frowned.

"Yeah, it's me, Conor. You're safe. Hear me? You're in an ambulance and we're on our way to the hospital."

Her brows furrowed.

"I know, the siren is loud, but it's getting the traffic out of the way. In a couple of minutes, we'll be meeting a helicopter, which will take you back to San Antonio to the hospital."

"Wha happ?" she managed to get out.

"You decided to bury yourself in a fire ant mound, bright eyes. Your eyes are swollen shut and you stopped breathing there for a while. But you were pumped full of all sorts of drugs and you're going to be okay."

Yeah, she remembered now. "Cybor?"

"What, baby?"

She frowned in frustration. She couldn't get her mouth to work right. "Man?"

"Was he wearing camouflage?"

Erin nodded.

"He's dead," Conor told her without beating around the bush.

"Shur?"

"Yeah, bright eyes. I'm sure. You did good in hiding under those trees in the stream...even with the fire ants. He wasn't so lucky to find a place to hide. He's most certainly dead."

Erin nodded and tried to relax. Her chest hurt for some reason, as did her head and arms, but she couldn't think anymore. She was safe and Conor was there.

She heard people talking above her but couldn't understand what they were saying.

"We're almost there, Erin," Conor told her, his lips right next to her ear. "They're going to take you to the hospital in San Antonio. I'll see you there later, okay?"

Erin nodded. She wanted him to go with her, but understood that he probably wouldn't fit in the helicopter. Besides, she was going to take a nap. By the time she woke up, he'd be there.

She felt pressure against her forehead, then nothing.

HOURS LATER, Erin woke up again. She still felt groggy, but she could at least open her eyes this time. She could feel an oxygen mask on her face.

She turned her head and saw Conor sitting next to her bedside. His chin was resting on his chest and he seemed to be asleep. Shifting on the bed, Erin winced when the sound startled him and his eyes popped open.

"Hey," she said softly.

"Hey back," he replied, then moved so his chair was right next to her bed. He picked up her hand and held it against his cheek. "How do you feel?"

"As if I took a nap in a fire ant nest?" she quipped.

His lips twitched, but he didn't smile. He brought his free hand to her face and brushed a lock of hair off her forehead. "Fuck, I was so scared," he told her.

"Me too."

"Can you tell me what happened?" he asked.

"I think that's my line," Erin said honestly.

"How about this: I call in Cruz's friend from the FBI and you tell us what you remember. Then I'll fill in the blanks."

Erin nodded. Conor leaned toward her and brushed his lips against her forehead. "I'll be right back," he said as he stood. Erin kept her eyes on him as he strode from the room. He was back within moments, with a man she'd never seen at his side.

Conor introduced him as being with the FBI.

Then she told them everything she'd been through. What the cyborg man had said, including how he'd bragged about perfecting his kidnapping and hunting techniques.

"His name was Wayne Everett Humphries. With the help of Conor's friend, Beth, we've been able to tie him to at least a dozen kidnappings. I'm sure with more time, we'll find more."

"Why do psychos always have three names?" Erin asked.

"What?"

"Huh?"

The men obviously weren't following her train of thought. "Think about it. Donald Henry Gaskins, Charles Edmund Cullen, John Wayne Gacy, and Tommy Lynn Sells. It's crazy."

"Bright eyes, most people have three names. For some reason the press just likes to use a killer's middle name when reporting on them."

"Well, it's creepy. They should stop it."

"And while we're discussing it...how do you know about those guys?" Conor asked.

"Who doesn't?" she asked. "Tommy Lynn Sells is the most dangerous Texan in history. He said he killed seventy people. He liked to stab them. He broke into people's bedrooms and killed them. Until one night he tried to kill a ten-year-old, but she survived and was able to describe him."

"Will you marry me?" the FBI agent drawled.

"Shut it," Conor griped, shoving the man with his shoulder. "She's taken."

Erin and the agent laughed. Then he got serious. "Anyway, I'm sorry we can't make him pay for his crimes."

"Oh, he paid," Conor said without a shred of doubt in his tone. "He suffered more than he would've if he'd been locked away for the rest of his life."

The agent nodded then turned back to Erin. "Thank you for talking to me. If I have further questions, can I contact you?"

She nodded. "Of course."

With that, the agent shook Conor's hand then turned and left the room.

"Can I take this off for a bit?" Erin asked, gesturing to the oxygen mask on her face. "I promise to tell you if I feel short of breath."

Conor helped her move the mask away from her mouth until it rested around her neck.

"What happened to him?" Erin asked.

"Why did you call him cyborg?" Conor asked back, not answering.

She sighed. "Because he was so cold and mechanical. He reminded me of some characters in a few books I've read."

Conor nodded. He sat down and gathered her hand back into his. He told her what he found when he'd arrived at the campsite to find her missing. He told her about calling Beth and the search and rescue teams. He even told her about Penelope's donkey, Smokey.

"Right before the commander threw the shelter over me, I looked up and saw Wayne standing there. The heat was so bad it was literally melting him. His scream was what drew me in your direction."

Conor leaned forward and put his cheek on her forearm. "It was actually the damn donkey that found you.

He brayed as if he was being slaughtered, and you have to keep in mind that the thing hadn't made one sound when his skin was literally burning from the heat. You weren't breathing, bright eyes," Conor whispered. "Your heart wasn't beating and it was the scariest thing I'd ever seen. Moose did CPR and you had two shots of Adrenalin and two of antihistamine before they were able to get your heart started again. It scared the shit out of me."

"I'm sorry."

"Don't. Don't be sorry. You did what you had to in order to survive both that maniac and the fire. *I'm* sorry I didn't find you earlier."

Erin bit her lip. "I didn't tell the agent earlier...but I started the fire, Conor."

"I figured as much."

"I didn't want to. But I knew I couldn't hide from the cyborg forever. He was going to find me. He really was a good hunter. It was the only thing I could think of to try to slow him down, distract him, and get people to where I was at the same time."

"It was smart," Conor told her.

"But Smokey and other animals suffered."

"Look at me," Conor ordered, standing up and leaning over her, putting his hands on either side of her neck and forcing her to look at him. "You're alive. *That's* all that matters."

Erin's eyes filled with tears and her lip quivered. "I didn't want to burn down your favorite place in the world."

"My favorite place in the world is right here. With you." Then he leaned down and kissed her forehead.

Erin couldn't hold back her tears anymore. She cried because of how scared she'd been and for what she'd had to do. She felt Conor sit back down next to her, keeping a hand on her as she lost it.

After her sobs had subsided, she wiped her eyes with her fingers and asked shakily, "What happened with Penelope and the donkey?"

Conor smiled. "She got in the bed of a pickup truck to be taken back to headquarters, and the thing ran down the road after the truck, braying as if his life was ending. Everyone just assumed he would go back to whatever farm he came from, but apparently, he had different ideas. Penelope made the driver stop, and she and Moose picked up the damn thing and put him in back of the truck bed with them. He followed her around the command post like a fucking dog. She couldn't leave him behind, so she left a report with the local shelter, in case someone comes looking for him, and she convinced Boone to keep him at his ranch."

"Hayden's boyfriend? The cowboy who runs Hatcher Farms?"

"One and the same."

"Wow."

"Yup. And now Penelope wants to find a house she can buy where she can keep him."

"She's that attached to him?"

"Apparently so."

"What does Moose think?" Erin asked, knowing how crazy the man was for the vulnerable firefighter.

"I don't think he's thrilled, but it's obvious how much Penelope loves that animal, even after such a short time.

He would never tell her she couldn't or shouldn't get attached. He's more than aware of her PTSD. Probably more than she is."

"True."

"And speaking of which...are you okay? He took your clothes."

Erin looked over at Conor. "I'm okay."

"Bright eyes, it's okay to be freaked. I mean, you love me, and you hadn't been able to take your shirt off in front of *me* before. To have to do it in front of a stranger, one who you were terrified of, had to be quite disturbing."

Erin carefully turned on her side so she could see Conor without putting a crick in her neck. "I'm fine. Seriously. He drugged me when he took me, so I wasn't awake when he took off my shirt and pants. And when I did wake up, I honestly had other things on my mind than what I was wearing. And you know what? When push came to shove, I realized how lucky I was to have this body. I never would've been able to outrun him if I didn't. I thought about it a lot when I was out there running for my life. Yeah, my boobs are a little saggy and I have some skin that isn't as tight as I'd like, but I was still able to keep ahead of that asshole. I decided that I really needed to give myself a break."

"As simple as that?" The doubt was easy to hear in Conor's tone.

"No. It'll never be as simple as that. I'll never be able to pick up a doughnut and eat it without thought. I'll never go to the beach and walk around in a bikini, but this body saved my life out there."

"God, you're amazing," Conor said.

Erin shook her head. "No, not really. There's more."

"What? Sock it to me."

Erin grinned. "I love you. So much. My body issues are getting in the way of what I want most in this world. You."

"Erin," Conor said in a low tone.

"No, seriously. You've told me time and time again that you love the way I look. That my body doesn't have anything to do with the person you fell in love with. And it's time I believed you. I'm doing our relationship a disservice by continuing to doubt you when it comes to that. Besides, if you can make me orgasm hard enough to almost pass out by touching me over my clothes, what can you do when we're both naked?"

"I do love the way you look. But I love who you are inside even more."

"I know. And that's why I decided to let it go. I want to see food the way you and your family do. I want to live my life loving every second of the time I spend with the ones I love, and that includes eating and drinking. So from here on out...that's what I'm going to do. I just need you to help me along the way."

"You know I will," Conor told her immediately.

"Besides, the more I weigh, the harder I am to kidnap."

Silence greeted her quip for a second, then Conor choked. Erin smiled and patted his hand as he tried to get control of himself.

She got serious again. "All I want, all I've ever wanted, was to be loved for who I am. And who I am is not a number on a scale. You've taught me that. And your family. Your dad loves your mom regardless of how much she weighs, that's obvious. It's the same with your sisters."

Conor nodded.

"Can I ask a favor?"

"Anything, bright eyes."

"I still want to go camping with you when I get out of here."

"Deal."

"But maybe not at the Natural Area. And maybe we can *both* set up camp this time."

Conor released a harsh breath. "I was an idiot for letting you go out there by yourself. My job got in the way of my common sense. I was the one who was lecturing you while we canoed about camping by yourself, and look what happened. I let you go off and do it even though I knew it wasn't safe."

"Don't blame yourself," Erin told him. "That asshole cyborg Wayne guy is who's to blame. Not you. Not me."

"You can think that, but I'll never put you in danger like that again."

They smiled at each other for a moment before the door behind them opened with a crash.

Conor stood and spun at the same time, ready to defend Erin.

"Mom!" he declared, exasperated. "You scared the shit out of me."

"Don't swear. And I came to make sure Erin was okay. Are you all right, sweetie?" she asked, peering around her son.

Erin wanted to laugh, but controlled herself. "Other

than being itchy and having little ant bites all over, I'm okay."

"Good." Pauline reached into her bag and pulled out something covered in aluminum foil. "I brought you some of those cookies Conor told me you loved so much."

Just then, Conor's dad came through the door. "Dang, woman, you could've waited for me to park the car!" he complained.

"You were being too slow. I wanted to come up and see for myself that Erin was all right."

Erin looked at Conor, who was staring down at her. She pulled on his hand until he was bending over her. "Food is love," she whispered. "And I love you. So much."

"The feeling is mutual," he said softly, and kissed her gently on the lips. Then carefully pulled her oxygen mask back up and over her nose and mouth.

"Enough of that!" his mom declared. "I want to know when the doctor said you could go home. I'm planning a week's worth of food to bring over to Conor's house, so you don't have to lift a finger and all you have to worry about is getting better. But don't worry...it's all healthy stuff. I've been researching, and I think you'll like what I've come up with."

Erin shared a secret smile with Conor before turning to his family. There was a time she would've freaked out at the idea of his mom knowing about her issues, and even about having that much food in her fridge, but with all she'd been through, the thought made her feel loved rather than panicky. It was a start.

22

A WEEK LATER, Erin smiled at her friends as she sat in the seat of honor at a table in The Sloppy Cow. It was one in the afternoon, and her boss had opened the bar a few hours early so everyone could celebrate the fact that Erin was alive and well.

She was taking the week off from classes at the university and Conor had taken it off as well. They'd spent just about every minute together since she'd woken up in the hospital, and Conor couldn't be happier. It was as if what Erin had been through had cleared her head and made her recognize how self-destructive she'd been her entire life. She'd been acting more confident in herself. In their relationship.

Conor sat next to her, with his arm over the back of the chair. He couldn't be prouder of her. Not only had she managed to make it through the horror of being kidnapped and hunted almost to the death, but the experience had actually been a breakthrough when it came to her attitude about food.

She still watched what she ate, but she didn't seem to be as stressed as she used to be when she *did* eat. He'd seen her eat an entire cookie and not panic about it afterwards. She still had her usual banana for breakfast, but she didn't seem to be as freaked out about food as she had been.

He knew she'd always eat differently than him, her modified body ensured that, but he was thrilled beyond belief that every bite of food that went into her mouth didn't send her into an anxiety attack.

He hadn't pushed her when it came to intimacy between them, although she made it clear she was more than ready. Before they'd left for the party, she'd informed him that if he didn't make love to her later that night, she'd have to take matters into her own hands.

He'd smirked at her and said he'd be glad for her to take *his* "matter" into her hands again. Instead of blushing, as she would've done a couple of weeks ago, she'd licked her lips and eyed him up and down as if she couldn't wait to undress him.

"How's Smokey doing?" Erin asked Penelope.

"He's great! That donkey is honestly like a big dog. I've been over to Boone's ranch every day, and every time he seems to know when I'm going to be there. He meets me at the fence, braying in the cutest way, and when I take him out to walk him around, he follows me like he can't stand to be away from me."

"Has anyone come forward to claim him?" Conor asked.

Penelope shook her head. "Nope. I can't believe someone doesn't miss him. He's the most amazing animal

I've ever met. When I'm sad, he seems to know it and nudges me with his snout. When I'm in a good mood, he's playful, bumping into me then leaping away when I reach for him."

"Any luck in getting out of your lease?" Sophie asked.

Penelope's shoulders slumped. "No. And I can't afford to buy a house and pay my apartment rent at the same time."

"He can stay at my place," Moose said into the silence that surrounded the table.

"What? Really?" Penelope asked, her eyes wide.

"Really. I've got a huge yard that backs up to a wilderness area. I can build a little barn for him there so he can get out of the heat in the summer and stay dry when it rains. I know Boone wouldn't mind keeping his eye on him for as long as needed, but he lives on the other side of the city. Since I live closer, if he was at my place, you could spend more time with him," Moose told her.

Penelope leaped out of her chair and threw herself into Moose's arms. He caught her and held her for a long moment, until Penelope realized what she'd done. She blushed and stood up. "Sorry, didn't mean to get so excited."

"No apology necessary," Moose said easily, steadying her with his hands on her hips.

"Thank you. Seriously."

As if it was just the two of them in the room, Moose didn't look away from her face as he said, "Anything for you, Pen."

Conor cleared his throat and the moment between

the two firefighters was broken. Penelope pulled away from Moose and sat back in her seat.

"I know everyone isn't here, but I wanted to make sure you all knew how appreciative I am that you came out to help when Erin disappeared."

When his friends all started to protest, saying there was no way they wouldn't have been there for him, Conor held up his hand to quiet them.

"I just...even though there wasn't a lot we could do, the fact that you dropped everything to come all the way out there to the Natural Area was amazing." He scanned the table, making sure to make eye contact with each of the firefighters who were there. Moose, Penelope, Sledge, Driftwood, and Taco. "The fact that you guys came out on your days off to help fight the fire...well...it's appreciated more than I can say," Conor said, barely able to finish his sentence.

All the firefighters weren't there, but Conor knew Moose would pass on his thanks to the guys who weren't able to make it to the bar that night.

"Hayden," Conor continued, "you were the voice of reason I needed when I was at my lowest. I don't know how to thank you."

Hayden blushed, but she reached over and grabbed his hand. "No thanks are necessary."

"My entire life, I've wanted this," Erin said softly. "But I never had it. No one wanted to be friends with someone who was as overweight as I was. Thank you, guys, for not giving up on me. Thank you for trying to find me, but most of all...thank you for being there for Conor." She turned to Cade. "Please tell Beth thank you for me. She's amazing. I can't believe she found out all that stuff on Wayne as fast as she did."

"She loves and hates mysteries at the same time," Cade told her. "She can't start to read a suspenseful book without turning to the end to find out who the bad guy is. She had a feeling there was something to be found, and literally couldn't do anything else until she discovered what it was."

"Well, she's amazing. I owe her."

Cade simply chuckled. "Right. Try telling her that."

"I will."

Conor grinned at the banter between Erin and his friend. He leaned forward and picked up his beer. "A toast."

Everyone grabbed their own drinks and held them up.

"To friends."

"To friends," everyone echoed.

Conor's arm shifted so it was resting on Erin's shoulders as she cuddled next to him. She leaned up and whispered in his ear, "How much longer do we need to stay?"

"Why, what's wrong?" Conor asked in alarm, looking her up and down, as if he could find the source of her wanting to leave already.

"Nothing's wrong," she soothed. Her hand went to the waistband of his jeans and she snaked a finger under the material at his belly.

Conor immediately went hard, and he grabbed her wrist to stop her from going any farther. "Erin?"

"I want you," she mouthed.

Conor turned to his friends. "And with that, me and Erin need to get going. She, uh...needs to take her meds."

His friends all chuckled knowingly.

Conor stood, making sure to keep Erin tucked into him, partly because he liked her touching him, and partly because he needed her to help hide his erection. Without apology, Conor waved goodbye to his friends and hustled Erin out the door. At his truck, he backed her against the passenger door and kissed her.

It was heated and frantic on both sides. They clutched at each other as if they couldn't get enough. Their noses bumped, teeth scraped, and their hands roamed. Conor finally pulled away abruptly. He held Erin by the shoulders and stared down at her.

"Are you sure?"

She didn't hesitate. "Yes. One hundred percent."

Conor reached for the door handle and opened it for her. He helped her in, then shut the door. He jogged around the back of the truck and climbed into the driver's seat without a word. The trip back to his house was silent, but he grabbed Erin's hand and held it the entire way.

Once at his house, Conor put the truck in gear and opened his door. He tugged Erin across the seat and she climbed out his side. He quickly walked them to the front door of his house and got them inside.

Then, still without a word, Conor took Erin's face in his hands and began to kiss her again. He didn't take his lips off her as he backed her down the hall toward his bedroom. He unbuttoned and unzipped his jeans as he moved them. She did the same.

Once in his room, by his bed, they broke apart long

enough to take their shirts off. As soon as the material was over their heads, they were kissing again. Their pants and underwear went flying and still they kissed.

Erin scooted up on the mattress and Conor followed, crawling over her on his hands and knees. He urged her to lie back and, when she did, Conor moved, latching onto one breast with his mouth and caressing the other with his hand.

Erin moaned. Her head went back and she arched up into his touch. Conor's other hand caressed down her body to between her legs. He sucked hard on her nipple at the same time he used his thumb, pressing in circles on her clit.

Within minutes, they were both moaning and his hand was soaked with her excitement.

"Now, Conor. I need you."

He didn't ask if she was sure. He simply let go of her nipple and grabbed one of her hands. He guided it to his cock.

She fisted it the way she knew he liked and pumped it a few times. When Conor groaned, she grinned up at him, then fit the head where she obviously needed him the most.

"I love you, bright eyes," Conor said.

"I love you."

"Watch me make you mine," Conor ordered, ducking his chin so he could see where they were connected.

Erin did the same, grabbing his hips as he slowly pressed inside her for the first time.

He didn't stop until he was inside her as far as he could go.

Looking away from where they were joined, he gazed into her eyes. "Okay? No pain?"

She shook her head. "No. It feels..." She paused and Conor felt her clench her inner muscles against him. "Amazing. So different than my vibrators."

Conor smiled. He pulled out a couple inches, then pressed back inside. "Yeah?"

"Yeah," she confirmed.

"Better?"

"Oh yeah."

On his next down stroke, Erin pressed her hips upward. And with that, Conor was done talking. He thrust in and out of the woman who meant the world to him with steady strokes. He ground his teeth together, trying to hold off on coming. She felt amazing. The sounds his cock made as he tunneled in and out of her hot wetness should've been embarrassing, but instead they only turned him on more.

Conor knew he wasn't going to last. He'd waited too long to get inside her and she felt too damn good. She was tight and so fucking hot. "Touch yourself," he ordered hoarsely.

As if they'd made love hundreds of times, she snaked her hand between them and began to flick her clit.

"Oh, Conor...yes....it feels so good. Harder... Please."

So he did. He increased his thrusts until he was pounding into her. He reached under her and grabbed one of her butt cheeks. He pulled on it, opening her to him, and at the same time pressing her hips upward.

She moaned and the finger on her clit moved faster.

"Yes, right there...I'm coming!" she announced.

She didn't need to tell him. Conor felt her clasping him in a grip so tight, he thought she was going to strangle his dick. Her thighs quivered, her belly tightened, and her hips thrust up toward him so hard he had to use both hands on the mattress by her hips to hold himself steady above her.

When she finished twitching, her eyes opened into slits and she stared up at him. "My God, Conor. That was…"

Her voice trailed off when she realized he was still rock hard inside her. A sly grin spread across her face. She tightened her muscles and it was Conor's turn to groan.

"Fuck me, Conor. Come inside me."

He couldn't hold back if his life depended on it. Holding her gaze with his, he did as she asked. He fucked his woman. Showing her with each thrust how beautiful he found her. How much he loved her. He felt his orgasm approaching way before he was ready. He wanted this first time with her to last forever.

One minute he was thinking about fucking her for eternity, and the next he was coming. He thrust inside her as deep as he could go and held himself there as he released. Each burst of come from his cock felt like heaven.

When his arms were shaking so badly he couldn't hold himself up, he eased down, putting his weight on his elbows and caging Erin in. He buried his nose into the space between her shoulder and the mattress and tried to get his breath back

Erin's fingertips lightly traced up and down his spine.

"I love you," she whispered, the air from her words puffing against his neck.

Conor lifted his head and said, "Marry me."

"What?"

"Marry me. I love you, Erin. So much. I thought I'd lost you and I regretted not making you mine."

"I...are you sure?" she asked in a small voice. Her fingernails dug into his back and he didn't think she even realized it.

"I'm sure. Although, I think I'm getting the better deal. I work too much. There will be times I'll be called away in the middle of the night. Vacations might get cut short if I have to get back for an investigation or if I have to testify in court. Hunting season is insane, you know that, I'm not around a lot. But I swear, I'll love you with everything I have for the rest of my life. I'll try to make up for the times when I'm not around—"

Erin put a finger over his lips to shut him up. "Yes."

"Yes?" Conor asked, pushing up to his hands over her. She smiled shyly. "Yes."

"When?"

"Whenever you want."

"Tomorrow," Conor declared.

Erin laughed and he felt it in his dick. He was still buried inside her, and feeling her movements against him made him start to get hard again.

Her eyes widened. "Is that normal?"

"Around you? Absolutely." As he hardened, Conor began to slide in and out of her, his way made easier by both his come and hers. "Are you protected?" he asked.

Her brows came down in confusion.

"Birth control, bright eyes. Are you on the pill?"

Her eyes widened a little. "A little late to ask now, don't you think?" she asked with a smirk, but let him off the hook when she continued. "I was, but with everything that happened and being in the hospital...I haven't even thought about them."

"Are you opposed to children?"

This time, her eyes filled with tears, and Conor froze above her. "Erin? Shit!" He started to pull out, but she grabbed his ass and held him to her.

"I've always wanted kids. I wanted to be the kind of mother I never had. I wanted to show them unconditional love." She chewed on her lip for a second, then blurted, "Are *you* opposed to kids?"

Conor smiled and renewed his slow thrusts. "I am definitely *not* opposed to having babies with you. Erin Dallas Gardner. Will you marry me? Let me give you children who will love you fiercely and unconditionally? A little girl we can share the joys of camping with and a little boy I can teach my love of the outdoors to?"

"Yes," she breathed.

Conor leaned down and kissed the side of each eye, absorbing her tears. Taking a chance, he pulled out and turned onto his back. "Make love to *me* this time, bright eyes."

When she hesitated, Conor worried he'd ruined the moment, but then she got a look of determination in her eyes and she swung one leg over his hips.

For the first time, Conor looked fully upon the naked body of the woman he loved. He'd been in too much of a hurry the first time to really see her.

She was beautiful. She wasn't perfect, he could see the scar across her belly where she'd had the tummy tuck to get rid of the excess skin there. She had them on her inner thighs and under her arms too. But to him, every inch was beautiful.

He took the time to run a finger over every scar he could see, whispering words of love and how beautiful he thought she was as he did. She'd stiffened when he first touched them, but with every word out of his mouth, she visibly relaxed.

"Put me inside you," he begged. He could see her inner thighs glistening with their combined releases as she lifted above him. She took his cock in her hand and fit it to her, then sank down with one fast move that made him groan in ecstasy.

"Oh!" she exclaimed. "You're so deep."

"Fuck me, bright eyes."

And she did. She bounced up and down on his cock, taking her pleasure, and Conor beamed throughout. Women were way too concerned about every little roll and wrinkle. In his eyes, his woman was perfect.

After she'd brought herself to orgasm, Conor took hold of her hips and held her still as he fucked his cock up and down inside her. Once again, he came way too fast, but same as last time, he came with a feeling so intense, it made stars swim in his eyes.

This time, she lay herself over him. "I'll go tomorrow and get the application so we can get married as soon as possible," he told her.

Without lifting off his chest, she said, "I want to do it at the campsite."

Conor stiffened, but she went on before he could protest.

"I don't want that place to haunt either one of us. What better way to do that than to change bad memories into good ones?"

Conor relaxed under her. She was right. "Okay, bright eyes, whatever you want."

She lifted her head then and smiled down at him. "I love you."

"And I love you back."

They slept then.

The contented sleep that only two people who know they're loved can.

EPILOGUE

THREE WEEKS LATER, Erin Gardner officially became Erin Paxton. They stood in the exact spot the picnic table had been when she'd been abducted. The bluebonnets had mostly died off in the field, but the birds were singing and there was a light breeze.

Erin looked around after the ceremony was over and marveled at how, for a girl who'd never really had any friends, she suddenly seemed to have more than her fair share.

There were dozens of people there. All Conor's law enforcement friends and their significant others. All of the firefighters and their girlfriends. Juliette Winston, the game warden who'd been such a help when she'd gone missing. Conor's parents and sisters. She'd even invited Alex, Chad, Matthew, and Jose, the young men who'd been on the canoe trip with them.

They hadn't planned on a wedding this large, but in the end, couldn't *not* invite anyone. There were tables set up in the small meadow nearby and they'd hired a company to make burgers and hotdogs. They wanted to keep it laid-back and casual, just like them.

Erin wore a white dress...and her hiking boots. Her lucky flint, still attached, having more meaning now and somehow it seemed appropriate to have the flint her dad had given her, and which had ultimately saved her life, on her feet.

She even managed to eat a couple bites of their wedding cake. All in all, the wedding and reception had been perfect.

"Hey, Mrs. Paxton."

Erin smiled as Conor's arms wrapped around her waist and settled on her belly. She relaxed against him. "Hey, Mr. Paxton."

"Happy?" he asked.

"Blissful. You?"

He turned her then, and put his finger under her chin. "You've made me the happiest man alive. Thank you."

"I think that's my line...well...except it's woman and not man. Thank you for humoring me and having our wedding here."

"You were right. This was the perfect place to do it. I love this area, but I'm not sure I would've ever come back."

Erin smiled up at him. "I know it's early...but I'm late."

"For what?"

She giggled. "My period. I'm late."

Conor went stock-still in her arms and stared down at her.

"It's possible it's just the stress of setting up the wedding, but I'm usually pretty regular."

"And...you're good with it?"

"Yeah, Conor. I'm ecstatic."

He breathed out a sigh of relief, then a huge smile crept across his face.

"But we can't say anything yet. Not until I'm sure and it's been at least three months. With my history, I want to make sure my body accepts the fetus."

"We'll go to the doctor as soon as we can," Conor reassured her. "You're going to have to work harder at making sure you get the right nutrition," he said hesitantly.

Erin grabbed his palm and rested her cheek on it. "I know. I'm not saying being pregnant will be easy for me. The last thing I want to do is gain weight, but you'll help me keep things in perspective."

"You know I will."

"I'm excited and scared at the same time," Erin admitted. "I want a baby, but I'm afraid what it'll do to me mentally."

"We'll find a good counselor you can talk to. One that specializes in people who have had a gastric bypass."

"Is there such a thing?" Erin asked, scrunching up her nose.

"I have no idea. But if there is, we'll find him or her."

She smiled at that. "Deal. I might have ups and downs, but I want this baby, Conor. I want children with you. If it's a boy...do you think we could name him Dallas...after my dad?"

"I think that's an amazing idea. And if we don't have a boy, we'll just have to keep trying until we do. I love you, bright eyes. You've made the best day of my life even better."

Erin smiled up at him. "Dance with me?"

"Gladly."

The newly married couple began to sway back and forth right where they were standing. There was no music, but neither needed it.

"I'M GOING TO HEAD OUT," TJ Rockwell told Quint and Corrie. They were standing off to the side talking about nothing in particular.

"Everything all right?" his friend asked.

"Yup. I'm on at seven in the morning, so I thought I'd head home and get some sleep before then."

"Drive safe," Corrie said softly.

TJ looked at his friend's woman and smiled. "Of course. It's what I do."

She smiled at him.

Quint shook his hand. "See you later this week at The Sloppy Cow?"

"Definitely. Let me know when," TJ told him.

They nodded at each other and TJ made his way through the crowd, stopping every couple of feet to say goodbye to his friends. When he'd left the Army, TJ never thought he'd be able to find a group of people he'd be as close with as he'd been with his Delta Force team, but he'd been wrong.

It was a different kind of friendship with his fellow

law enforcement and firefighter friends. More mellow, less intense. But that was okay.

But as each one of his friends found women to spend the rest of their lives with, TJ got more and more depressed. He'd seen bad marriages all the time in the Army. Women who couldn't handle being married to soldiers. Not able to deal with the stress of having them always gone and in danger.

But it was obvious he'd just been around the wrong kind of women. The ones who were with his friends were amazing. Tough, strong, and loyal down to their bones. He wanted that. Wanted to have someone to come home to after a long shift patrolling the roads of Texas. Wanted someone to lean on when he had a bad day. Wanted to be there for someone else when *she* had a bad day.

Unfortunately, he'd *had* that, but hadn't realized it at the time. He wasn't sure he'd ever find a woman like the one he'd left behind again.

He'd barely made it out of the Natural Area when his phone rang. TJ didn't recognize the number, except that it was from the Fort Hood area. Thinking it might be one of his Delta Force friends, he answered.

"Hello?"

"Is this TJ Rockwell?"

"Speaking. Who is this?"

"My name is Captain Chase Jackson. I'm Rayne Jackson's brother."

TJ knew who the man on the other end of the line was. He hadn't ever met him, but knew of him from Ghost. He'd heard the story about how his friend had met his girlfriend's brother, more than once. But he had no idea why the captain would be calling him.

"Is Rayne all right?" he asked quickly.

"Yes. Everyone is fine."

"What can I do for you, Captain?" TJ asked uneasily. If it didn't have to do with his friends, what *did* it have to do with?

"I'm currently looking into reports of a school down your way that may or may not be a front for some sort of cult."

"Looking into?" TJ asked.

"It's a long story."

TJ pulled over to the side of the road so he could concentrate on the conversation. "And you're calling me because…" He let his sentence trail off, hoping the Army captain would fill in the blanks. He heard the other man let out a big sigh before he spoke.

"I got a call from a man I know and respect. He works for McKay-Taggart."

"Isn't that a security company out of Dallas that specializes in undercover shit?" TJ asked. He'd heard of the notorious McKay-Taggart group. They were badass. If they were calling Captain Jackson, something big was up.

"Yeah, that's them. Anyway, one of their nieces, Sadie, went down to San Antonio to visit a friend. They got a call from her recently, and she has some suspicions about the school her friend's working at. She was worried enough to call her uncle, and he in turn called me after finding out the guy who runs the school is ex-Army. We've communicated in the past, and they thought the Army might be interested in looking into his operation. Unfortunately, without any hard evidence of any wrongdoing, my superiors won't get involved. You know...they don't want any bad press since the guy in charge is a former soldier. Anyway, after Emily's kidnapping when you stepped in to assist, and you being from San Antonio, I thought you might check in on Sadie and her friend Milena, see if there's anything to Sadie's concerns."

TJ hadn't been terribly alarmed at anything Chase was saying—until that name at the end of his explanation. His heart seemed to stop beating for a second before starting up at double its former rate.

It couldn't be.

"What's her last name?" he asked.

"Who, Sadie? Jennings," Chase said.

"No, the friend. Milena."

"Oh, uh...hang on..."

TJ heard papers shuffling, then Chase said, "Reinhardt. Milena Reinhardt. Twenty-seven years old. Blonde hair, blue eyes, five-five or so. Why?"

TJ ran his hand over his head. Milena Reinhardt. Holy shit.

He'd thought about her every day over the last three years. Ever since he'd made the worst decision of his life.

"No reason. I'll find out what I can. You have a file on the women and the school?"

"Yup. I'll send it over a secure link. I'm your contact on this, Rock," Chase said, using TJ's old Delta Force nickname for the first time. "Do not involve Ghost or the others on his team in this. Your job is recon only. Got it?"

"Yes, Sir." The title rolled off his tongue with ease, as

if he were back in the Army. Reporting to superior officers again.

"Thank you. I'll contact Sean Taggart, he's Sadie's uncle by marriage, and tell him to cool his jets and not to send his undercover army down to San Antonio just yet. I'll be in touch." Chase hung up.

TJ clicked off the phone and stared into space for a long moment. Milena Reinhardt. Fuck. He shook his head. He'd met her three years ago, right when he'd gotten out of the Army. He'd been a mess back then...and a complete ass. But she hadn't seemed to care. She'd somehow seen past the hurt he'd been feeling to the man he was underneath. She'd only been twenty-four, but she'd been so mature...even more than he'd been at twenty-eight.

He'd hurt her. Bad. Even when he'd done it, he knew he was making a mistake, but he didn't think he was good enough for her. She'd needed to live her life. Twenty-four had been too young to tie herself to an asshole like him.

He'd tried to put her out of his mind, but it was impossible. And now she was in trouble. Well, Chase hadn't come out and said it, but if he thought Sadie was down in San Antonio hanging out with her friend who was involved in a cult-like organization, it was implied.

"What have you gotten yourself into?" TJ whispered to himself as he put his car in gear and pulled back onto the road.

She might've been too young three years ago, but she wasn't any longer. And he was a different man. Better. His past would always be there, but he'd learned a lot over the last couple of years from watching his friends settle down.

The right woman could not only overlook the things he might've done in his past, she could make him an even better man.

His resolve strengthening, TJ made a vow. "I'll get you out of whatever you've gotten yourself into, Milena. Mark my words.

FIND out what Milena has gotten herself into in *Justice for Milena. Get it Now! Then, because you want to know about Milena's friend, Sadie, get Rescuing Sadie too!*

JOIN my Newsletter and find out about sales, free books, contests and new releases before anyone else!!
Click HERE

Want to know when my books go on sale? Follow me on Bookbub HERE!

Would you like Susan's Book Protecting Caroline for FREE?
Click HERE

Rescuing Aimee (novella)
Rescuing Emily
Rescuing Harley
Marrying Emily (novella)
Rescuing Kassie
Rescuing Bryn
Rescuing Casey
Rescuing Sadie (novella)
Rescuing Wendy
Rescuing Mary
Rescuing Macie (novella)

SEAL of Protection: Legacy Series
Securing Caite
Securing Brenae (novella)
Securing Sidney
Securing Piper
Securing Zoey
Securing Avery (May 2020)
Securing Kalee (Sept 2020)
Securing Jane (novella) (Feb 2021)

SEAL Team Hawaii Series
Finding Elodie (Apr 2021)
Finding Lexie (Aug 2021)
Finding Kenna (Oct 2021)
Finding Monica (TBA)
Finding Carly (TBA)
Finding Ashlyn (TBA)

Ace Security Series

Claiming Grace
Claiming Alexis
Claiming Bailey
Claiming Felicity
Claiming Sarah

Mountain Mercenaries Series

Defending Allye
Defending Chloe
Defending Morgan
Defending Harlow
Defending Everly
Defending Zara
Defending Raven (June 2020)

Silverstone Series

Trusting Skylar (Dec 2020)
Trusting Taylor (Mar 2021)
Trusting Molly (July 2021)
Trusting Cassidy (Dec 2021

SEAL of Protection Series

Protecting Caroline
Protecting Alabama
Protecting Fiona
Marrying Caroline (novella)
Protecting Summer
Protecting Cheyenne
Protecting Jessyka
Protecting Julie (novella)
Protecting Melody

Protecting the Future
Protecting Kiera (novella)
Protecting Alabama's Kids (novella)
Protecting Dakota

Stand Alone
The Guardian Mist
Nature's Rift
A Princess for Cale
A Moment in Time- A Collection of Short Stories
Lambert's Lady

Special Operations Fan Fiction
http://www.AcesPress.com

Beyond Reality Series
Outback Hearts
Flaming Hearts
Frozen Hearts

Writing as Annie George:
Stepbrother Virgin (erotic novella)

ABOUT THE AUTHOR

New York Times, *USA Today* and *Wall Street Journal* Bestselling Author Susan Stoker has a heart as big as the state of Texas where she lives, but this all American girl has also spent the last fourteen years living in Missouri, California, Colorado, and Indiana. She's married to a retired Army man who now gets to follow *her* around the country.

She debuted her first series in 2014 and quickly followed that up with the SEAL of Protection Series, which solidified her love of writing and creating stories readers can get lost in.

If you enjoyed this book, or any book, please consider leaving a review. It's appreciated by authors more than you'll know.

www.stokeraces.com
susan@stokeraces.com